CHRISTMAS CARD MURDER

CHRISTMAS CARD MURDER

Leslie Meier
Lee Hollis
Peggy Ehrhart

KENSINGTON BOOKS
www.kensingtonbooks.com

KENSINGTON BOOKS are published by

Kensington Publishing Corp.
119 West 40th Street
New York, NY 10018

All Kensington titles, imprints and distributed lines are available at special quantity discounts for bulk purchases for sales promotion, premiums, fundraising, educational or institutional use.

Special book excerpts or customized printings can also be created to fit specific needs. For details, write or phone the office of the Kensington Special Sales Manager: Kensington Publishing Corp., 119 West 40th Street, New York, NY, 10018. Attn. Special Sales Department. Phone: 1-800-221-2647.

Library of Congress Card Catalogue Number: 2020939641

Kensington and the K logo Reg. U.S. Pat. & TM Off.

ISBN-13: 978-1-4967-2822-7
ISBN-10: 1-4967-2822-X
First Kensington Hardcover Edition: November 2020

ISBN-13: 978-1-4967-2824-1 (ebook)
ISBN-10: 1-4967-2824-6 (ebook)

10 9 8 7 6 5 4 3 2 1

Printed in the United States of America

Contents

CHRISTMAS CARD MURDER

Leslie Meier

For Linda Randel and Helene Androski

Chapter One

People who made their beds every morning were 206 times more likely to be millionaires. That was the interesting factoid that Lucy Stone was mulling as she smoothed the sheets on the bed she shared with her husband, Bill, finding it somewhat hard to believe. She gave the blanket a yank and pulled up the comforter, noting that it was definitely beginning to fray along the top edge. She plumped up her pillow and set it in place, then added Bill's, thinking that she had been making her bed every morning since she was eight years old, and was still rather far from achieving millionaire status.

As she propped an accent pillow against the sleeping pillows, in its spot in the exact center of the bed, she considered various millionaires and billionaires, assessing their bed-making potential. Bill Gates, for example, probably made his bed as a kid, but now had people to do it for him; while she rather doubted that Mark Zuckerberg had ever made his bed. She couldn't quite picture Donald Trump making his bed, either. Even in military school he probably paid some kid to do it for him. Warren Buffett, on the other hand, probably still made his own bed, unless he had a wife to do it for him.

Come to think of it, weren't most millionaires and billionaires men? And wasn't bed making something that wives usually did? Or was she stuck in some sexist role model that no longer existed? Maybe Bill should make the bed, she thought, examining the worn blue-and-white French toile comforter she'd bought on sale years ago at Country Cousins, along with the coordinating linens and accent pillow. No, she decided, he'd make a mess of it; he probably didn't even know how to make hospital corners and would pretend it was a much-too-complicated task for him to learn.

Right, she thought, feeling the prickling of discontent. A man who made his living as a restoration carpenter, a man who could miter ogee moldings, couldn't make a hospital corner? She gave his pillow rather a hard smack and straightened up, banging her head right into the low, angled ceiling beside the dormer, which was a feature of their restored antique farmhouse in Tinker's Cove, Maine. A rather inconvenient feature, which required a certain amount of mindfulness when getting in or out of bed, or, in her case, when making the bed.

This wasn't the first time she'd banged her head on the ceiling, and she suspected it wouldn't be the last, but that didn't make it any less painful. If anything, it made her feel extremely stupid for letting her emotions get the better of her and causing her to forget the edge of the dormer. She sat down on the edge of the bed and rubbed her head, waiting for the pain to subside and hoping she wouldn't get a headache. Please, not today, she thought, she had too much to do.

Christmas was coming, as it did every year, and she had a long to-do list of holiday tasks that would have to be squeezed in between the demands of her job as a part-time reporter for the *Pennysaver*, as well as her responsibilities as a wife, mother, and grandmother. She was the one who made Christmas happen for her family, and she didn't want to disappoint them. That meant shopping and decorating and baking, and finding time to write those Christmas cards. They were a nuisance to send, but she loved getting them and hearing from old friends, especially the dear ones who sent long, newsy, handwritten letters and tucked them in their cards.

The pain was ebbing and she carefully stood up, crouching a bit until she got clear of the sloping ceiling. How long had she been doing this maneuver? Too long, she decided, wondering if she could rearrange the furniture so that the bed wasn't under the lowest part of the ceiling. Not possible, she realized, as the dresser was too tall to fit, as was her mirrored vanity table. The bed was where it was because it was the only piece of furniture that would fit in that cozy corner.

She hung her nightie on the hook in the closet and left the room, stepping into the hall, where she had a sudden insight. What if they broke through the wall into the next room? It would give them a generously-sized master bedroom, with plenty of headroom. There were four bedrooms on the second floor, but they didn't need them all. Not anymore. Toby had married and left years ago, and was now living in Alaska with his wife, Molly, and their son, Patrick. Elizabeth had also flown the nest, making her home and career in Paris, where she was a concierge at the tony Cavendish Hotel. Sara, next in line, had recently departed for an internship in Boston at the Museum of Science, hoping it would lead to a job, and was subletting a basement efficiency in Quincy from a friend of a friend who was an artist-in-residence at Vassar. Only Zoe remained at home, hopefully finishing up her bachelor's degree at nearby Winchester College. Even if they expanded into the next room, which happened to be the smallest of the four bedrooms, Zoe would keep her room and they would still have a guest room for visits from Bill's mom and the kids. They could even all visit at the same time, since there were twin beds in the guest room and Zoe's room and sleep sofas in the family room and living room, too.

There might be the possibility of adding a master bath and creating a genuine master suite, she realized, noting the location of the bathroom on the other side of her bedroom. Now that was an exciting thought, and lucky her, her husband happened to be finishing up his latest project and, as far as she knew, didn't have anything lined up until February.

Lucy spent the day in a happy fog, designing her longed-for master suite. The January sales were just around the corner, she could pick up some new curtains and linens quite cheaply. Maybe even add a sitting area, where she could retreat to read her favorite cozy mysteries. It was the possibility of that master bath that really excited her, however. She pictured an old-fashioned roll top tub, deep enough for a real soak, and there were such gorgeous faucets and vanities available. Should she go for a farmhouse look with distressed pine and aged bronze, or maybe a sort of Country French mood with a hand-painted vanity and porcelain faucet handles? She'd have to discuss her options with her best friend, Sue Finch, who knew all about these things.

However, when she broached the subject to Bill that evening, after his favorite dinner of meat loaf and mashed potatoes, he was less than enthusiastic. "It's a bigger project than you think, Lucy," he said, thoughtfully stroking his beard, now touched with gray. "And adding a bath, that might require some structural changes to support a tub."

"I think it sounds super," offered Zoe, helping herself to salad. "We really need two bathrooms in the morning, when everybody's trying to get ready at once."

"That's right," said Lucy. "Zoe could pop right into the shower without waiting for us—"

"You're forgetting about water pressure," said Bill, nodding sagely, "and we just got a new water heater. We'd have to replace it with a larger one, and, you know, they don't come cheap."

"But think how much it would add to the resale value of the house," said Lucy, in a last-ditch effort to save the project.

"We're not planning on selling anytime soon, are we?" countered Bill. "And these things age out. A bath we added now would look dated by the time we're ready to downsize."

"I suppose you're right," said Lucy, probing her scalp and feeling the tender spot where she'd hit her head. "I'll just have to get a helmet to wear when I'm in the bedroom."

"It's not that bad," insisted Bill. "You simply have to keep your wits about you and remember that dormer near the bed."

Lucy and Zoe shared a look, but neither one challenged Bill's attempt to imply that Lucy had hit her head because of her own carelessness. Instead, they discussed what to pack in the box of presents they were going to send to Toby and his family in Alaska, which they knew they had to mail soon if it was going to arrive before Christmas.

"It has to get there in time, because Santa can't be late," said Lucy.

"I wonder," mused Zoe, "whether Patrick still believes in Santa Claus?"

"Of course he does," insisted Bill, reaching for seconds.

Later that night, when Lucy was tucked in bed and preparing to sleep, Bill suddenly sat up and turned on the bedside lamp. "I forgot to shut the kitchen door," he said, turning back the covers.

"Oh, don't bother about it," said Lucy, sleepily.

"No. If I don't, the dog will wander into the family room and you know what happened last time."

Lucy knew. Libby, their aging black Lab, had recently made herself a nest on the sectional, shredding a couple of throw pillows in the process.

He sat on the side of the bed and stuck his feet into his slippers, then stood up carefully and made his way around the bed, keeping his head low. Lucy yawned, then turned on her side and shut her eyes. She heard him thump down the back stairs to the kitchen, heard the dog's clicking nails as Libby got up from her doggy bed to greet him, heard the click of the latch when he shut the family room door, and heard him thump back up the stairs. She heard his footsteps as he crossed the hallway and entered the bedroom, and she heard a *whump* and an "Owww" when he cracked his head on the ceiling.

"I guess you forgot to keep your wits about you," said Lucy, flipping onto her back.

Bill was sitting on the side of the bed, rubbing his forehead. "I guess I deserved that," he said.

"Do you want me to get some ice for you?"

"I'll be all right," he said. "Funny, I didn't see any stars when I looked out the window on my way downstairs."

"Well, at least you haven't lost your sense of humor." She paused. "Any chance you're reconsidering knocking through that wall?"

"Okay, I admit it. You're right. We're getting too old for all this crouching and remembering to duck." He slid back under the covers and she snuggled against him.

"With a master bath?" she asked.

"With a master bath," he said, sighing. "I'll start tomorrow," he promised, pulling her closer.

The next morning was Thursday, the day Lucy met her friends for breakfast at Jake's Donut Shack. The weekly breakfast had become a way for the four women to stay in touch when their kids grew up and they no longer ran into each other at sports practices, PTA meetings, and bake sales. She always enjoyed getting together with Rachel Goodman, Sue Finch, and Pam Stillings, and today she was excited and eager to tell them about the master suite project.

"That's a really good idea," said Rachel, approvingly. "Too often people get stuck in a rut and don't make the adaptations they need as they transition through the various stages of life. Your nest is emptying and it's time for you and Bill to focus on your needs." Rachel, who was married to a successful local lawyer, had majored in psychology in college and had never gotten over it.

"That's so true," offered Pam, who was married to Lucy's boss, Ted.

"Enough of this talk," declared Sue. "I want to know how you're planning to decorate this fabulous master suite."

"Well, I was going to ask you for advice," said Lucy.

Rachel and Pam both gave approving nods. They all knew that Sue was the most stylish member of the group, and her home was not only beautiful and comfortable, but always featured the newest trends. She was the first in Tinker's Cove to have granite countertops and an undermounted kitchen sink; she'd installed radiant heating and heated towel bars in her bathrooms; her latest improvement was a hands-free kitchen faucet.

"Well, get me a floor plan and I'll see what I can come

up with," she offered, taking a sip of coffee. "You know what I'm seeing a lot now? Antique dressers converted into vanities, they give a bath a lot of character."

"Never thought of that," Lucy admitted as Norine, the waitress, arrived with their orders: a sunshine muffin for Rachel, granola and yogurt for Pam, hash and eggs for Lucy, and more black coffee for Sue.

"Wouldn't kill you to eat something," she muttered, filling Sue's cup.

Sue tucked a lock of expensively-cut hair behind her ear with a perfectly-manicured hand and gave Norine a big smile. "Thanks, but not today," she said, revealing freshly-whitened teeth.

The others shared a look reflecting their suspicion that Sue survived on a diet of black coffee, white wine, and little else.

"What's the exposure there?" asked Sue, returning to her favorite subject. "Does it face south?"

"Uh, no," answered Lucy, biting into her toast. "North."

"We'll definitely have to warm it up then," Sue said as the wheels started to turn.

Returning home, Lucy was pleased to notice that Bill had installed a construction Dumpster in the driveway, and when she entered the house, she heard bangs and pounding that indicated demolition was already under way. She gave a yell, letting Bill know she was home and asking if it was safe to come up the stairs, and the banging stopped.

"Come on up," he invited.

She made her way up the dusty stairs, stepping over stray bits of plaster and chunks of splintered wood, which had spilled into the hall, and gazed through the open door at the work in progress. Bill had packed up the breakables in cartons, and had shoved the furniture in both rooms away from the shared wall and tarped it. He was making steady progress dismantling the wall, which Lucy saw was not constructed with plasterboard, but instead had old-fashioned wood lathing and real plaster. Big chunks of plaster were strewn on the floor, along with piles of ripped lathing strips, and everything was covered with a thick layer of filthy, century-old dust.

"It's one of the original walls," she said, taking in the mess and already having second thoughts. "It's kind of a shame to take down that plaster."

"It'll be worth it," said Bill, leaning on his sledgehammer. "It'll be a good-sized room, and I've already figured out most of the bath."

"I forgot about demo and how messy it is," admitted Lucy, glancing at the shrouded furniture, which was covered with bits and pieces of wood and plaster, along with plenty of dust. "Where are we going to sleep?"

Bill shrugged. "Guest room?"

"In twin beds?"

"Sleep sofa downstairs?"

"I guess so."

Bill picked up the sledgehammer and swung it at the wall, causing Lucy to flinch at the sound of impact. She watched as a large hunk of plaster fell away. Bill bent down to pick it up, then leaned closer, looking into a newly-exposed area behind the baseboard. "Hmm, there's something here," he said, reaching into the space.

"Buried treasure?" asked Lucy, smiling. Back when they first moved into the derelict old Maine farmhouse and began the long process of rehabbing it, they had often expressed the hope that they would uncover something valuable that would reward them for their efforts. Nothing had ever turned up, however, except for some old yellowed newspapers used in a feeble attempt at insulation.

"Sorry," said Bill, producing a bit of red-and-green cardboard. "It's just an old Christmas card."

"With a ten-dollar bill inside?" asked Lucy, watching as Bill opened the card.

"Not quite," said Bill, handing it to her. "Take a look."

Lucy smiled at the plump image of the vintage Santa with his rosy cheeks, smoking pipe, and plump tummy, then opened the card. The printed sentiment was a standard *Merry Christmas and Happy New Year,* but the handwritten note beneath it certainly was not. She gasped in shock when she read the neatly-printed message: *You lied and I hope you rot in hell.*

Chapter Two

Lucy's jaw dropped as she studied the message, noting that there was no signature, but the sender had scrawled the initials *G* and *B*.

"Whoever got this must have known the sender, whoever 'GB' was," said Lucy.

"It seems like 'GB' was pretty mad at someone." Bill was picking up broken bits of plaster and lath. "But why do you think the card was received? Maybe GB lived here and wrote the card in a fit of anger and then decided not to send it and hid it away."

"Like putting a spell on someone by sticking pins in a voodoo doll?"

"Yeah."

"I don't think so." Lucy studied the card. "The recipient isn't named for one thing. You'd need some sort of identification for a hex to work. I think this was received by someone who lived here in this very room."

"And hid the card," added Bill.

"Yeah." Lucy stared at the jolly, happy Santa. "I wonder why they didn't simply rip it up and get rid of it? That's what I would have done. Do you think it could have fallen there, slipped behind the baseboard?"

Bill shook his head. "No. The baseboard was quite tight against the wall. It would have taken some effort to wiggle it back there."

"Out of sight, out of mind." Lucy studied the style of the card. "It's not real old. Forties or fifties maybe?"

Bill shrugged. "Could be older, I guess. That wall hasn't been disturbed since the house was built in 1865. We had to rip out the exterior walls to put in insulation and new wiring, but we left the interior partitions in place."

"Yeah, but the paper's not fragile, like you'd expect if it were over a hundred years old. It's actually kind of thick and glossy, and the Santa has a fifties look, like those old Coca-Cola ads."

"It doesn't seem right to use jolly old St. Nick to deliver such a nasty message." Bill was reaching for the sledge-hammer, and Lucy figured she'd better get out of the way.

"I think there's a story behind this," she said, heading for the door.

"And you're gonna want to find out all about it," said Bill, giving a resigned sigh, before taking an especially forceful swing at the wall.

"You know it," said Lucy, stepping into the hallway. Whoever had received that card didn't simply want to forget about it, they wanted to hide it. But why? Why the secrecy? Most people would be angry to get such a hateful message, and would have shared their indignation with loved ones, looking for sympathy and support. But this person had hidden the card, perhaps ashamed because the sender was justified. Maybe the recipient had lied about something that caused trouble for the sender. But what? Lucy started down the stairs, wondering what sort of lie could be so terrible that it merited consignment to hell everlasting.

Her thoughts were interrupted by the ring tone of her cell phone, which she'd left on the kitchen table. She hurried down the steep back stairway and grabbed it, discovering the caller was Rachel.

"Hi, Lucy. I'm just wondering if you're free for lunch tomorrow. Miss T is a bit out of sorts and I think she'd like some company besides me for a change."

Lucy smiled. She knew that Rachel provided home care for Miss Julia Ward Howe Tilley, the town's oldest resident. No one except Miss Tilley's oldest and dearest friends dared to call her by her first name, and they were a sadly-diminished group as age took its relentless toll.

"Sure," she answered, checking her calendar and noting that apart from a Hat and Mitten Fund meeting, she had a free afternoon. "That would be lovely. Can I bring something?"

"Just yourself. See you at twelve?"

"With bells on," answered Lucy. She wasn't just saying that—the warm wool hat she wore during the Christmas season actually did have bells sewn on it and jingled merrily as she walked along.

The little bell on the door to the *Pennysaver* office also seemed to jingle merrily when Lucy arrived at the office the next morning. Phyllis, the receptionist, paused in her task of tying Christmas cards to a small fake tree and greeted her with a big smile. Phyllis, as always, was togged out for the holiday in a sweater that was liberally appliqued with reindeer and elves.

"All quiet on the Western front," said Lucy, noticing that Ted's desk was vacant.

"Ted's covering a story. Word just came that Philip Ratcliffe is up for parole and Ted's interviewing the DA."

"Already? It seems as if it was only yesterday when he was convicted." She set her big handbag down on her desk and unzipped her parka, hanging it on the coatrack, as the memories flooded in. Seating herself at her desk and powering up her computer, she remembered the dread she'd felt when she'd learned that Sally Holmes was missing from her lifeguard post at the town beach. As the days wore on and she wasn't found, anxiety grew as people concluded that a kidnapper was on the prowl and began to fear for their own teenage daughters. There had been a huge communal sigh of relief when Philip Ratcliffe was caught and sentenced to life. "Do you think he'll get out?"

"It's unlikely," said Phyllis, snapping the hole puncher that she was using on a Christmas card featuring a bright red cardinal. "It gives me chills to think of what the prosecution said he did to that poor girl," she added as she threaded a thin red ribbon through the hole and tied the card to a branch with a neat bow.

"Me too," said Lucy, shuddering and resolving to push the whole sad affair to the back of her mind and get to work. She began by checking her e-mails, discovering only a couple of announcements for upcoming holiday events, including a concert at the high school and a display of antique Christmas cards at the historical society. Lucy decided both deserved previews and made appointments for interviews, then settled down to write up the "Town Hall News" column. It was close to noon when she finished and headed over to Miss Tilley's.

The little gray-shingled Cape house was only a few blocks away, so Lucy walked, enjoying the sunny but brisk weather and the charming streetscape of the little coastal Maine town. She loved seeing the old houses, many built

by sea captains and dating from the eighteenth and nine-
teenth centuries, and the occasional peeks at the bay, which
was bright blue today. The sidewalk, made of granite slabs,
buckled and dipped thanks to tree roots and frost heaves,
so she watched her footing as she walked along, occasion-
ally pausing to admire the various holiday decorations.
Most of the stately homes were decked with tasteful garlands and wreaths, but a few free spirits indulged in dis-
plays of rooftop sleighs with reindeers, set inflatable Santas
on their lawns, and draped thousands of colorful, twinkling lights on their trees and bushes.

Miss Tilley went for none of that, of course. A single
bough of fragrant balsam pine, with a narrow plaid ribbon
tied in a modest bow that hung on the front door, was the
sum total of her holiday décor. But the welcome that greeted
Lucy when that door was opened was warm and friendly,
and a delicious fragrance filled the air.

"Come on in out of the cold," invited Rachel.

"What are you cooking?" asked Lucy, unzipping her
parka. "It smells fabulous."

"*Boeuf Bourguignon,* it's Julia Child's recipe," replied
Rachel, taking her coat and hanging it up on the hall tree.

"Sit here with me by the fire," invited Miss Tilley, who
was seated in the front room. A toasty fire was blazing
away in the fireplace, and Lucy eagerly went to join her
old friend. "Now I want to hear all the news, especially
the parts that are unfit to print," continued Miss T, giving
Lucy a big smile.

"Lunch will be ready in a few minutes, would you like a
small sherry to stimulate your appetite?" asked Rachel.

"I certainly would, and so would Lucy," asserted Miss
Tilley, who was especially fond of a nice amontillado.

"Lovely," said Lucy, "but make it small. We have that

Hat and Mitten Fund meeting later and I can't be falling asleep."

Rachel promptly appeared with two glasses on a tray, setting it on the antique cobbler's bench that served as a coffee table, then returned to the kitchen to finish preparing lunch.

"Cheers," said Miss Tilley, hoisting her glass and clinking it with Lucy's. "It's Christmas, after all."

"Not for three weeks," said Lucy, taking a small sip of the golden liquid and finding it delicious and warming.

"It will be here before you know it," said Miss Tilley, with a sigh. "I've got to buckle down and finish up my cards." She took a sip of wine. "Though I don't send too many these days."

"Speaking of Christmas cards, I do have a bit of a story for you. Bill's been ripping out an upstairs wall so we can enlarge our bedroom and we found an old card tucked behind the baseboard. As a matter of fact, I've got it with me."

Lucy pulled the card out of her bag and passed it to Miss Tilley, curious to see her reaction when she read the message inside.

"Oh, my," gasped the old woman after she unfolded the card. "That's not a very pleasant holiday message."

"What is it?" Rachel inquired from the kitchen.

"It says, 'You lied and I hope you rot in hell,'" quoted Lucy.

"Wow, that's not the sort of thing you expect on a Christmas card." Rachel appeared in the doorway, wooden spoon in hand, and peered over Miss Tilley's shoulder. "Did you say you found it behind the baseboard?"

"I think it was hidden there by a previous occupant of the house," said Lucy. "Maybe in the fifties, from the look of the card."

"Who lived there then?" asked Rachel.

"Oh, my goodness, let me think," said Miss Tilley, fingering the card. "The house was empty for quite a while before you and Bill bought it. I remember thinking it was a shame that nobody was living there. I thought it was a nice house and didn't deserve to be neglected."

"That sounds as if there was a bit of an atmosphere associated with the house," Rachel said as she returned to the kitchen.

"There was, Rachel's right about that," said Miss Tilley. "It was a sad sort of place, very stark up there on the hill. Very bare, no trees or flowers. Not unkempt, just unattractive, and then the husband died and the wife went away." She stared into her empty glass, then set it down on the tray.

"They didn't have any children?"

"They did, now that you mention it. A daughter. Poor thing, I don't think she got out much. They were pretty old when she was born, and they were quite religious. No drinking, no cards, no dancing." She looked up at the ceiling. "I can't quite remember their name . . . I suppose you could look it up on the deed."

"No. We bought the house from the bank."

Miss Tilley took a sip of sherry and closed her eyes. "I can see her, though, in my mind's eye—the daughter. She'd come into the library and grab a book, then scoot home, hardly saying a word. You would have thought she was doing something sinful, just borrowing a Nancy Drew book."

Miss Tilley had been the town librarian years ago.

"Didn't her parents encourage her to read?" mused Lucy, amazed. When Toby was in middle school and had shown little interest in reading, she'd subscribed to *Sports Illus-*

trated, leaving the magazines in the bathroom, where she noticed they were definitely read.

"I don't think they encouraged it," admitted Miss Tilley. "Or maybe they disapproved of me. I've always been a free thinker, and I don't hesitate to say exactly what I think. I certainly encouraged girls and young women to pursue higher education and careers."

Lucy smiled and nodded, acknowledging this truth. "Maybe they thought you would influence their daughter to think for herself."

"Dorcas! That was her name. Dorcas."

"That's an unusual name."

"Biblical. Dorcas made clothing and gave it to poor people," said Rachel, reappearing. "Lunch is ready."

Miss Tilley grabbed the arm of the sofa and used it to help her stand, brushing aside Lucy's attempt to help her. "A lot of churches had Dorcas societies for the ladies, they did good works."

"I think Rachel did some good work this morning, from the looks of our meal," said Lucy, holding a chair for Miss Tilley.

A steaming blue-and-white antique Canton china tureen full of *Boeuf Bourguignon* was placed in the center of the table, accompanied by crescent rolls and a crisp green salad.

"She's been cooking for days," said Miss Tilley, "teasing me with delicious fragrances."

Conversation stalled while they loaded their Canton plates and began eating. Lucy was savoring a delicious mushroom when Miss Tilley suddenly broke the silence. "I remember now. Dorcas came back as an adult when her father died, but she didn't want to be called Dorcas anymore. She insisted that everybody call her Doris." Miss

Tilley took a bite of her roll. "I guess she thought it was more modern or something."

"Tell me about the card, Lucy," invited Rachel.

"Right. Bill said it must have been hidden there on purpose. The board was quite tight against the plaster."

"That's interesting," she said, chewing thoughtfully. "Who do you think was the recipient? Dorcas or one of her parents?"

"Who do you think?" Lucy asked Miss Tilley. "You knew them all."

"My vote's for Dorcas," said Miss Tilley. "I didn't know them well, but the parents . . ." Her eyes brightened and her cheeks grew pink with excitement. "The Pritchetts!" she declared, stabbing the air with her pointer finger. "That was their name. The Pritchetts had the reputation of being very no-nonsense folks. They would have wanted to get to the bottom of things, grilled Dorcas unmercifully until she confessed whatever she'd been up to, and probably prayed that the Lord would smite whoever sent it."

"Reverse revenge," said Lucy, spearing a cherry tomato.

"I tend to agree," said Rachel. "It sounds like a fairly classic family dynamic. The parents were deeply committed to a particular set of values that came into conflict with their child's need for social acceptance and approval. Society was loosening up, women were smoking and drinking . . ."

"And listening to rock and roll, and dancing," added Lucy.

"Dating," offered Rachel.

Lucy smiled naughtily. "And that meant necking and making out . . . "

"Which the Pritchetts certainly would not have allowed," said Miss Tilley.

"And that's why Dorcas had to hide the card," said Lucy. "She couldn't afford to let her parents see it, or she would have been in big trouble. They would have demanded to know who 'GB' was, and what she lied about, and how she was involved with 'GB.'"

"Do you think 'GB' was a man?" asked Rachel.

"Might have been a girlfriend, suggested Miss Tilley. "Girls can be very emotional, very mean."

"They could even have been lesbians," suggested Rachel.

"But you knew Dorcas? Wouldn't you have remembered something like that?" Lucy asked Miss Tilley.

Things were different back then," she said, with a shrug. "I'm sure there was plenty of that going on, but it was all very much hidden, secret."

"That's true," agreed Rachel. "And even today there are hate crimes against anyone who's perceived as different."

"But we don't know that Dorcas was the victim," suggested Lucy. "From the message on the card, it seems she may have been the perpetrator."

"Or the accuser," added Miss Tilley.

Lucy sighed. "I'd love to be able to meet Dorcas and talk to her."

"I bet she has a story to tell," agreed Rachel, pushing away from the table and picking up Lucy's and Miss Tilley's plates. "But first, who'd like some dessert?"

"Dessert? How did you ever manage that?" marveled Lucy.

"Oh, easy. It's just brownies from a mix."

"I know I shouldn't, but I'd love a small one," admitted Lucy.

"With a scoop of ice cream," insisted Miss Tilley.

Lucy was pleasantly full when she left, having enjoyed both the meal and the company. But as she walked back to get her car, her mind was full of questions: Was Dorcas/ Doris really the recipient of the card? Was she still alive? Did she really hide the card because of her parents? And finally, what did she lie about? As she walked along, back to her car, Lucy was more determined than ever to find out.

Chapter Three

Once she was back in her car and on the way home, however, she decided that before she did any more investigating into the mysterious Dorcas Pritchett, she really had to find the Christmas cards she'd bought on sale last January and, she thought, tucked away with the Christmas decorations. They weren't in the plastic tubs of tree ornaments or with the lights; they weren't even with the holiday place mats and napkins in the sideboard. Frustrated at her own lack of memory, and wondering if this was the early onset of some dreaded dementia, she went upstairs to Bill's attic office to search in the storage area under the eaves. There, on her hands and knees, she didn't find the missing boxes of Christmas cards, but she did find a banker's box full of old papers among the retired furniture, trunks, and stacked artwork.

Curious to see if there was anything about the purchase of the house that might have mentioned the previous owners, she dragged the box out of the dark, dusty space into the brighter and cleaner office and began to flip through the old files. She'd never been terribly organized, so old bank statements and electric bills were mixed in with the kids' school papers and even artwork. She smiled to see Toby's kindergarten class photo, featuring an adorable group of kids and a dark-haired Lydia Volpe, who was now gray and retired from teaching. She touched a faded Mother's Day card made from construction paper and liberally sprinkled with glitter. It was signed by Zoe, spelled with a backward *e*. Lucy brushed the cascading glitter off her lap, remembering the days when glitter was everywhere, seeping out of the cracks, thanks to the three girls' art projects.

Working her way through the box, she saw how the kids progressed through school, growing taller in the class photos. The awkward writing became more controlled and the text more sophisticated. Sara's fifth-grade report on otters featured an accomplished crayon portrait of an otter family and well-organized information, and had earned her a big red A. Fingering the aging paper, Lucy remembered that Sara had fussed and fretted, breaking into tears as she struggled to make the report perfect. That was Sara, she thought, always a bit of a perfectionist, and she wondered how she was getting along at her internship in the geology department at Boston's Museum of Science.

While Toby, Sara, and Zoe had regularly and reliably received A's and B's on their report cards, Elizabeth's cards told a different story. She got A's on the subjects that interested her, like English and history, but her science and math grades were disappointing. *If only she'd try a little harder and put in a bit of effort,* Lucy remembered thinking at the time. She was certainly bright, but motivation was lacking. And glancing at the conduct grades, Lucy grimaced. Elizabeth didn't pay attention, failed to follow instructions, and was even suspended at one point in her junior year for smoking pot.

As Lucy stared at the notice the principal had mailed to the house informing them of this infraction, and the punishment, she felt all the shame and frustration she had felt when she opened the envelope and read it. That had been an especially difficult year when she and Bill hardly recognized their eldest daughter, who seemed to be constantly in trouble. Worst of all, she remembered, had been the discovery that Elizabeth had lied to them on several occasions. She'd told them she was staying over at a girlfriend's house, and they later discovered she'd been out with a boy, drinking beer in the conservation area. She'd denied using drugs then, but there was the pot incident when she was caught smoking the illegal substance in the high-school girls' room. The only thing that gave her desperate parents any hope at all was the surprising discovery that she'd gotten the highest SAT scores in her entire class, including the math portion of the test.

Growing up was hard, thought Lucy, wondering if Dorcas had been a bit of a rebel, like Elizabeth. A girl like that would have chafed at small-town life in the conservative fifties, when conformity was highly prized. Nowadays there was a sense of nostalgia for mid-twentieth-century furniture and decoration, which Lucy found awkward and unappealing. She preferred a sturdy antique wooden table or chest to a garish piece of kidney-shaped Formica with spindly black wire legs. Nevertheless, she couldn't help smiling at saucy greeting cards that mocked the stifling conventions of that period, when women were supposed to be thrilled to stay home and keep their homes sparkling clean thanks to the miracles of modern chemistry. Modern chemistry that also provided the tranquilizers that got them through those long, boring days with nothing better to do than get busy with Mr. Clean.

She wondered if Dorcas had done something that got her in trouble, something that she didn't want her strict parents to know about. Perhaps she'd been caught on an illicit date, or drank some liquor, or shoplifted. If she'd gotten caught doing something like that, she might have pinned the blame on somebody else. Somebody who didn't appreciate being ratted out, and then sent her the card.

It must have been a terrible shock to open that card, and Lucy felt a certain sympathy for young Dorcas. She knew that kids frequently didn't realize that their actions had consequences; this was something most people learned the hard way. Dorcas must have been both ashamed of herself, and fearful of being discovered, and her first impulse was to hide the card and try to forget all about "GB."

Lucy was about to replace the lid on the box when she noticed the file tab labeled *House,* which she'd overlooked. As she'd suspected, the file contained all the papers pertaining to the purchase of the house on Red Top Road, including the mortgage application. The price, which had once seemed so steep, now seemed laughable. Of course the mortgage had grown through the years as they refinanced several times, using the money to help pay for the kids' college educations and various home improvements.

As Lucy remembered, the purchase and sales agreement specified that the seller of the house was the Seamen's Savings Bank, but the accompanying title search indicated that Amos Pritchett had indeed been the previous owner. There was no further information, apart from the notation that the property had reverted to the bank.

Lucy was thoughtful as she replaced the lid on the box and shoved it back into the storage area. She wondered what would happen to their house if she and Bill suddenly died in an auto accident or a plane crash. It would go to the kids, but since it was still mortgaged, they would probably have to sell it, hopefully gaining a profit for themselves. Why didn't Dorcas, or her mother, inherit the house? Why didn't they make an effort to retain the property? Houses were usually a family's most valuable asset, and it seemed odd that the supposedly conservative and no-nonsense Pritchetts would have let it slip through their fingers.

She closed the door to the storage area, then stood and stretched. She really needed to think about dinner for Bill and Zoe, who always came home hungry. She smiled at the thought that maybe she wasn't so different from those mid-twentieth-century housewives she'd mocked! *What is that proverb?* she mused, heading back downstairs. *"The more things change, the more they stay the same."*

She made her way downstairs to the kitchen, where Libby greeted her with a halfhearted wag of the tail before settling herself back on her cushy dog bed. Lucy was shocked to see by her prized antique regulator clock on the wall that it was almost four o'clock, when she was ex-pected at the Hat and Mitten Fund meeting. Back when their kids were small, Lucy and her friends had been shocked to see that many of the local children didn't have adequate winter clothing, so they established the fund to remedy the situation. At first they collected used and outgrown winter gear, which they relied on the schoolteachers to distribute. As time went on and the fund's reputation grew, they began to hold regular fund-raisers that allowed them to buy new winter clothing for the kids, as well as backpacks and school supplies. The fund also sponsored an annual Halloween party, which was always highly anticipated, and collected toys at Christmas, which were distributed through the food pantry. Today's meeting was planned to sort and organize the toys, which would be wrapped and labeled according to type and age.

She quickly took a look in the freezer, where she found a container of beef stew she'd made a couple of weeks ago, and transferred it to the fridge. It wouldn't thaw entirely, but it would be easier to get out of the plastic container, and it would be a quick meal. Then she headed over to the Community Church, where she met Pam in the parking lot and greeted her with a hug.

"Looks like we might get a white Christmas," observed Pam, sniffing the air as they made their way up the path to the basement parish hall.

Lucy cast her eyes to the sky, where thick gray clouds were gathering, and found herself shivering despite her warm down parka. "It does feel like snow," she agreed, grabbing the door and holding it for Pam.

Rachel and Sue were already inside the large room, along with numerous boxes and piles of unwrapped toys and dozens of tricycles and bicycles.

"Wow," marveled Lucy, "this is amazing. Where did it all come from?"

"Ask Rachel," Sue said as she gave her a little bow and flourished her perfectly-manicured hand. She was dressed for the work session in skinny jeans and an oversized turtleneck, along with a cozy pair of fur-lined boots.

"It's really thanks to Bob," said Rachel, smiling as she named her attorney husband. "He handled the Toyland bankruptcy and got his bar association buddies to buy up all the toys at a huge discount to donate to the fund."

"That was back in June. How come you never mentioned it?" asked Lucy.

"She's a sly one," agreed Sue.

"Come to think of it, I wondered why there was no liquidation sale," said Pam.

"It was at the Toyland owners' request," reported Rachel, smiling sympathetically. "They were embarrassed and didn't want a lot of attention. They preferred a quiet, private resolution to their financial problems."

"Well, it's super for us, and the kids," said Sue. "I guess we'd better get to work. I suggest we start by sorting into

three piles—boys, girls, and unisex. Then we can sub-
divide the piles by age."

The women stripped off their coats and rolled up their
sleeves, unpacking the toys and stacking them in the appropriate groups. After about an hour of steady physical
work, fetching and carrying, Lucy plunked herself down
on a metal folding chair. "I don't know about the rest of
you, but I'm beat," she declared.

"We need nourishment," suggested Rachel. "I thought
this might happen, so I brought a thermos of tea and some
banana bread."

"Bring it on," declared Pam. She ducked into the adjacent kitchen and returned with borrowed mugs, a sugar
bowl, and a child-sized milk carton. "I don't think the Sunday school will miss one little milk." She set it down on a
table. "It was probably left over from last Sunday," she
added by way of rationalization.

"I'm sure we'll be forgiven," said Lucy, "considering all
our good work." The four dragged chairs over and gathered around; then Rachel poured the tea and Pam sliced
into the banana bread. Sue sipped at a mug of black tea
while the others munched on banana bread, which they all
agreed was delicious and just what they needed.

"My mom's recipe," said Rachel, looking around the
big room and the mountains of toys with a look of dismay.
"We're going to need more help. I don't know how we're
ever going to get through all this."

"I know," agreed Pam, nodding her head, which made
her ponytail bounce. "I don't know about you guys, but I
really don't have the time. I've got a ton of things to do,
and I'm beginning to feel frantic."

Lucy chewed her banana bread thoughtfully. "Me too.
I've got my job, and the family's Christmas, and I haven't

even found the cards I bought after Christmas last year for half price at the IGA, much less written them."

"Join the club," said Rachel, refilling her mug from the thermos and adding some sugar. "I have to confess, I really hate those bragging letters. I got one today from my college roommate whose son just got into Stanford business school, her daughter just had twin girls, the whole family loves getting together at the condo in Maui, and her husband was named one of the top society divorce attorneys in *Town and Country* magazine."

"I know just how you feel," agreed Pam. "Those bragging people are always the first ones to send out cards, too. It's like they can't wait to let you know how great their lives are and how pathetic yours is by comparison."

"It isn't even how successful they are, that's so bad," mused Lucy. "It's the fact that they're so organized, they've got Christmas under control."

"Oh, and those photos of the happy family in matching red sweaters," stated Pam, sighing. Her only child, Tim, was a confirmed bachelor living in London.

"Never mind," advised Sue, with a knowing expression. "If you ask me, those letters and photos are mostly wishful thinking. Next thing you know, the boy genius has moved into the basement, the daughter is having an affair with her obstetrician, the wife has joined a cult, and the divorce lawyer husband is filing for his own divorce."

"Talk about 'wishful thinking,'" Pam said as they all dissolved into laughter.

"If only," added Rachel, laughing so hard she had to wipe away a few tears.

"But I'm serious," protested Lucy, holding her stomach, which ached from laughing. "Where do you think I stashed those cards?"

"Check your pantry," advised Sue. "Since you bought them at the IGA, you probably put them away with the groceries."

"Good idea," said Lucy, standing up and brushing her hands. "I'll do that. Now what are we going to do with all these toys? It's an awful lot of extra work for the food pantry volunteers."

"I have an idea," began Pam. "You know how the Salvation Army sets up Christmas Castles and invites parents to pick out toys for their kids?"

"But we can't invite everybody," objected Rachel. "The bar association insisted that the toys go to needy families. We'd have to get financial statements from the parents and verify that they're qualified."

"The food pantry already has that information on file," suggested Lucy. "Brendan Coyle knows all those folks and could distribute tickets when they pick up their food, and then they could come here and choose the toys."

"Brilliant," said Sue, nodding sharply. "Is everyone agreed?"

They were. "And now we'll all have something to put in our bragging Christmas letters," said Pam. "We get to play Santa Claus for real." She grinned wickedly. "It's hard to beat that."

Chapter Four

A light snow was falling on Monday morning when Lucy drove her all-wheel-drive SUV to the Jacob Pratt House, which was the headquarters of the Tinker's Cove Historical Society, to view the exhibit of vintage Christmas cards. The snow wasn't deep, but was coming down steadily and settling on the electric wires, gathering on the branches of the balsam pines and outlining the bare limbs of trees. It covered up all sorts of eyesores like derelict cars and collapsing outbuildings, and for a day or two at least, the old Maine town would be as perfect as a Christmas card. Then, of course, the lingering snow would turn gray and ugly from the car exhaust and woodstove smoke, but that was in the future. For now, in this moment, Lucy was listening to carols on the car radio and enjoying the temporary beauty of the falling snow.

When she arrived at the Pratt House, a tiny little gray-shingled Cape-style antique that had been lovingly restored by the society, and stepped out of the car, she was struck by the peace and serenity. It seemed as if she was the only person in town who was out and about as she noticed there were no other cars in the parking area. She wondered briefly if she was too early for her appointment, or if perhaps the society president, Hetty Furness, might have decided to stay home and pamper her recently-replaced knee, when a little red MINI Cooper rolled up the drive and stopped beside her.

"Hi, Lucy, I hope you haven't been waiting long," said Hetty, who had rolled down the window.

"Nope. Just got here."

Hetty was rolling the window back up, and struggling a bit to open the door.

"Let me help," said Lucy, grabbing the door handle. When the door was open, she gave Hetty a hand to help her out of the car, but once she was on her booted feet with cane in hand, Hetty shook off Lucy's assistance.

"Thanks, but I'm fine, once I'm up," she insisted, taking off up the snow-covered brick walkway with Lucy hurrying to catch up. The stairs to the porch posed a bit of an obstacle to Hetty, but she grabbed the handrail and hauled herself up the three steps, taking them one at a time and leading with her good leg. Hetty then produced a huge ring of keys and unlocked the front door, which was decorated with a fragrant balsam wreath. The house was cool when they stepped into the hallway, but Hetty zoomed over to a modern thermostat on the wall. In a few minutes heated air began to flow through the vintage registers.

The hallway had been decorated for Christmas, and Lucy admired the garland that draped the bannister of the steep staircase and the red ribbons that festooned the chandelier. Greens had been tucked behind the spotty old hall mirror, and a lush arrangement of holly and red roses sat on the pine half-moon table beneath it. The house had that old-house scent, a mix of wood smoke and spice from all the meals that had been cooked there.

"Well, come along," said Hetty, leading the way into the dining room, where the cards were displayed. She plunked herself down on a curvaceous settee upholstered in green velvet, set the footed cane beside herself, and then began the process of removing her hat, gloves, and scarf. She unbuttoned her wool coat, but decided against taking it off.

Lucy did likewise as she wandered around the room, studying the various cards, which were arranged on the gate-leg dining table, the fireplace mantel, and the corner hutch. When she'd viewed all the cards, and snapped photos of several, she joined Hetty on the settee. By now, the room had warmed up and they both shrugged out of their coats.

"So tell me about this exhibit," began Lucy. "How did the society obtain it?"

"The cards were collected by one of our members, Sylvia Bradshaw, and she offered it to us for the holiday season."

"It's a very impressive collection," said Lucy. "I had no idea Christmas cards have been around for so long."

"The first ones were produced in England in 1843, and only a handful have survived. Sylvia doesn't have one of those cards, but she's seen it at the Charles Dickens Museum in London. She says she's keeping her eye out for one, but in the meantime the earliest card in this collection was made in 1877. It's the one with the holly and the ivy. That's when the idea of sending cards really caught on, and over four million were posted in Britain. We were a little slower and the earliest American card in this collection was printed in Boston in 1882. It shows a little puppy in a Christmas stocking."

"I got a picture of that one," said Lucy. "I assume it's okay to print photos of the cards in the paper?"

"Absolutely, that's why I hauled myself out of my comfy bed this morning to come and talk to you," snorted Hetty, thumping the floor with her cane for emphasis. "Play it up big. We want lots of people to come and see the exhibit. We're hoping it will be a big fund-raiser for the society."

She glanced around the lavishly-decorated room and sighed. "You have no idea how much it costs to maintain this old place."

"I can well imagine," admitted Lucy. "I live in a re-stored nineteenth-century farmhouse and there's always something that needs doing."

"Well, this old place was built in 1789 and it needs a new roof," said Hetty. "And don't forget to mention our open house on Sunday afternoon. There'll be cookies and punch, and Sylvia will be here to talk about the cards." She chuckled. "Admission is free, but donations will be encouraged." She looked pointedly at Lucy. "And we're always looking for new members."

"Well," said Lucy, who had learned early on in her ca-reer that she couldn't afford to support every worthy cause she wrote about, "you will be getting some free publicity."

Hetty sighed. "Can't blame me for trying."

"Not at all," said Lucy, reaching in her bag for her gloves and finding the card Bill had found in the wall. She pulled it out and showed it to Hetty, explaining how it had been discovered. "Can you tell me anything about this card?"

Hetty's eyes lit up as she studied the smiling Santa, with his rosy cheeks, sparkling eyes, and snow-white beard. "When I was first married, we sent out a card very like this one. I was so proud of it, being a married lady and all."

"And when was that?"

"Oh, I was married in 1966," she said, proudly adding, "Paul and I are coming up on our fifty-fifth anniversary."

"Congra—" Lucy had begun to speak, but then Hetty opened the card and gasped.

"What a terrible thing to send to someone!"

"I know," agreed Lucy. "Hardly a message of peace and

goodwill." She took the card back and folded it. "I think there's a story here and I'd love to discover it."

Hetty shook her head. "I don't think it's a happy story. If I were you, I think I'd leave it alone." She grabbed the cane and, leaning heavily on it, pulled herself upright. "Well, I don't know about you, but I don't have a day to waste. They're expecting me at the senior center for chair yoga."

They walked into the hall, where Hetty lowered the thermostat, and Lucy reached for the door.

"Not so fast," said Hetty. "I'd like to see that card again."

Lucy handed it over and Hetty peered at it sharply through her bifocals. "That's a man's handwriting," she said finally. "Definitely a man."

"I think so, too," said Lucy, taking the card back.

"And your house was owned back then by the Pritchetts, right?"

"Yes, it was. Do you remember them?"

Hetty shook her head and buttoned up her coat. "I didn't live here then. We only moved here about twenty years ago." She wrapped her muffler around her neck, slapped her hat on her head, and began pulling on her gloves. "I've done a lot of research on these old houses, that's how I know the Pritchetts owned your place, but that's all I know about them."

"I have a feeling the card was sent to their daughter, Dorcas," said Lucy, zipping up her parka. "I think she might have been the right age to get involved in some sort of trouble."

Hetty took hold of her cane, indicating she was ready to go. "Not a good girl, then, if that's the sort of Christmas card she got."

As a journalist, Lucy knew the danger of libeling or

slandering someone, but from what she'd been learning, she suspected that Hetty might be right about Dorcas. Nowadays slut-shaming was frowned upon, but that wasn't the case when Dorcas was in her teens, or even when Lucy was growing up. It didn't take much imagination to understand why young Dorcas might have felt she had to hide the card.

After she helped Hetty navigate the snowy parking lot and made sure she was safely installed in her tiny car and was on her way, Lucy headed over to the high school, where she had arranged to interview the music teacher about the upcoming holiday concert.

Lucy was a little early, and the lady in the school office told her Charlie Zeigler was still in class, so she paused in front of a trophy case in the hall outside the music room. She listened as the class rehearsed familiar holiday tunes, with frequent stops and starts. The case was set into the wall and contained a number of somewhat-tarnished trophies behind glass doors, as well as a number of aged black-and-white photographs. As she studied the various loving cups, she noticed that the earliest ones dated from the early 1900s, while others had been won by the school's teams in recent years.

It was the photographs, however, that really caught her interest. A yellowing typed notice identified Maisie Francis, who was dressed in an unflattering 1920s chemise, as the state tennis champion in 1928. Meanwhile, a somewhat-more-recent photo pictured miniskirted Frankie Goddard as the 1968 state tennis champion. The family resemblance was unmistakable and Lucy did a bit of quick math and deduced that Frankie was quite probably Maisie's granddaughter, or even a daughter.

She was smiling to herself, wondering if it was nature or nurture that produced tennis champions in one family, while another family's members might excel in science, when another photo caught her eye. The label informed her that this was a group photo of the 1961 field hockey team, which won the state championship that year. All the team members were identified in the typewritten caption, including Dorcas Pritchett, front and center, proudly holding the trophy.

Leaning forward, Lucy studied the somewhat fuzzy black-and-white image. Dorcas was of average height, and her hair was combed into a smooth pageboy. She was wearing a dark, pleated gym dress over a white blouse with a round collar, dark knee-high socks, and white sneakers. Her face was round, her eyes were shadowed, and she was smiling. She was the very picture of a model student-athlete, perhaps an outstanding player or even team captain, since she was given the honor of holding the trophy.

Lucy was staring at the photo, wondering what this apparently typical high-school girl had done to inspire the sender of the Christmas card to send such a vile message, when the bell clanged, making her jump. In moments the classroom doors flew open and students poured into the hallway, filling it with noise and confusion as they hurried on to their next class. She made her way against the flow of streaming students to the music room, where Charlie Zeigler was erasing the blackboard; she waited for him to finish. When he'd set the felt eraser down on the ledge and turned around, she greeted him with a big smile.

"Hi, Lucy," he said, indicating one of the student chairs with its big arm. "Take a seat."

He seated himself in an adjacent desk chair, waiting while Lucy fished her notebook out of her big handbag.

"From what I heard while I was out in the hallway, it sounds as if we're in for a real musical treat," she said, beginning the interview on a positive note.

"Thanks, Lucy. I think the kids are coming along nicely, and the program has something for everybody. It's a holiday concert, not just a Christmas concert, you know, so we've got a nice mix. It's not just vocals, there's some instrumental music, too. Some of it is familiar to everyone, but we've got some pieces that will be new to most people." He paused. "We're presenting the concert here at the school, of course, but we're also presenting programs at the senior center and the town hall."

Lucy listened with one ear, jotting down dates and times, and probed for an interesting anecdote or two; at the same time her mind kept returning to the photo of Dorcas. When she'd finally finished interviewing Charlie, including his confession that he was really quite excited about Billy Winslow's amazing skill with the pennywhistle, she'd decided to head upstairs to the school library to check out some old yearbooks. Especially ones from the early 1960s.

Lucy found Jackie Lawton tacking up some Xerox prints of book covers on the "New Books" bulletin board in the hallway outside the library; she noted with interest that most were graphic novels.

"Whatever happened to books with words?" she asked, smiling.

"These have words, just not very many," replied Jackie, shrugging. She was a tall black woman who was always eager to help with difficult research problems, and popular with both students and faculty. "I can't say I like them myself, but the kids devour them." She stuck in a thumbtack, then turned to Lucy. "What can I do for you?"

"I'm interested in looking at some old yearbooks."

"How old?"

"The sixties."

"No problem. Follow me."

Lucy followed her to a bookcase tucked beneath a large window, where she found yearbooks dating back to the late-nineteenth century. "I had no idea these things went back so far," she said, pulling out a faded paperbound volume.

"There are some nineteenth-century class annals, that's what they called them, from the Brooks Academy that don't have photographs, just short bios of the students. But once photography caught on, they started including head shots." Jackie flipped open one of the books, revealing row upon row of serious young men with slicked-down hair. "Only boys back then, of course. The high school was established in 1924, but even then, girls and boys had separate classes, even separate doors."

"Wow, how soon we forget," said Lucy. "We take education for women as a given, but it's not."

"Certainly not in parts of the Middle East and Africa," agreed Jackie, shaking her head. "But you said you're interested in the books from the 1960s." She indicated the lower shelf. Students were beginning to drift into the library and she made her excuse as the bell rang. "I've got a class now, so I'll leave you to your project."

Lucy piled up the heavy books from 1960 through 1963 and carried them to a nearby table, where she seated herself, piling her jacket and bag on a neighboring chair. Opening the first book, she felt as if she were traveling through time, to an era when girls wore plaid skirts and saddle shoes, and boys had crew cuts and always seemed to wear sweaters, pleated slacks, and loafers. Eyeglasses were thick and black, circle pins were all the rage, and only a few very fortunate kids had the benefit of braces to straighten their teeth.

Dorcas, however, had a perfect bite to go with that big smile, shining fair hair combed into a neat pageboy, and an enviable list of accomplishments that would have gotten her into a top-notch college. She was a member of the National Honor Society, class president, and president of the Key Club, in addition to her prowess on the field hockey team.

In addition to her head shot as a member of the junior class, Dorcas was included in numerous group photos and seemed to be quite the belle of the ball. Except she wasn't. She wasn't voted prom queen, and she didn't even appear in any of the pictures taken at the winter mixer or the junior prom. Was that because her parents didn't allow her to go? Hadn't Miss Tilley suggested that her parents were very strict and disapproved of dancing and dating? No hanging out at the soda shop for little Dorcas, who must have chafed at her parents' restrictions. Or maybe she'd made the best of things, putting her time and energy into extracurricular activities that they approved of, like performing good works with the Key Club and playing on the girls' field hockey team.

That didn't seem to be the case, however. If Lucy's suspicions were correct, Dorcas had managed to get out from under her parents' control and got herself entangled in some sort of relationship that hadn't ended well. Was "GB" one of the clean-cut fellows in the yearbook photos, members of the Key Club or the student council? She scanned the names beneath the photos, looking for a George or a Gary, a Geoff or a Gerald, but she only found Greg, who was two years younger than Dorcas and whose last name was Widdicombe. Nevertheless, she decided it was worth trying to track down the students who had known Dorcas, so she lugged the big books over to the photocopy machine. There she emptied her change purse as she made copies of the group photos in Dorcas's senior yearbook.

Her spirits were high when she replaced the books on the shelf and left the library, giving Jackie a smile and a wave. People who grew up in Tinker's Cove tended to stay in Tinker's Cove, some of their families had been around for centuries. She was pretty sure that she could find at least a few of Dorcas's former classmates, people who actually knew her and might be able to tell her why "GB" had been so angry with her.

Chapter Five

Lucy intended to google Dorcas, or Doris, when she got to the newspaper office, as well as the others named in the yearbook photos, but realized as soon as she stepped through the door that she would have to postpone that plan. Phyllis was actually pulling her hair out, at least it seemed that way, since much of it was standing straight up. She was talking on the phone through her headset, which Lucy knew she hated and only used when the call volume couldn't be managed any other way, and was frantically riffling through a stack of papers on her desk.

"No, Ted, I don't have it right here, and I've got five calls backed up!"

Lucy immediately went into action, plunking herself down at her desk and hitting the button for line 2 on her phone. Lines 3, 4, and 5 were also alight, indicating a number of callers were on hold. But why? What had prompted all this unusual interest from readers?

"Thanks for calling the *Pennysaver,* this is Lucy," she said, speaking into the receiver.

"About time," replied the caller, who sounded like a rather elderly woman. "I've been on hold for, well, forever."

"I'm sorry about that. How can I help you?"

"Well, it's about that letter. I guess it's a posting, it was in the online edition. Saying that awful, horrible, nasty Philip Ratcliffe should get out of jail. Why would you print something like that? He should've been executed, and if Maine had a death penalty, he certainly would have been. And that's all I have to say."

"I understand how you feel," said Lucy. "I'll make a note of your call for our editor and I'm sure he'll return your call. Just give me your name and number . . ."

The phone went dead.

Okay, thought Lucy, somewhat surprised at the caller's reaction, then hitting line 2. "Thanks for calling the *Penny-saver*, this is Lucy. How can I help you?"

"You can help me by printing the truth about that Philip Ratcliffe and what he did, that's how you can help me. He's coming up for parole and people should be writing to the parole board and making sure he never gets out of prison. You should start a letter campaign or something, make yourselves useful for once."

This time the caller was male, and loaded for bear. Lucy remembered the Ratcliffe case, it was one of the first stories she'd covered when she began working for Ted at the *Pennysaver*. The alarm was first raised by a young mother who had brought her kids for swim lessons at the pond and called the town recreation office to ask if the classes had been canceled for the day because Sally wasn't there. When Sally's mother confirmed that her daughter had indeed left for work as usual, searchers began scouring the nearby woods, but found no trace of her. The search continued for weeks, her family made desperate pleas for her return, but it wasn't until nearly a year later that bloody bits of her red swimsuit were found by hikers some miles away. DNA tests linked Philip Ratcliffe to her disappearance, and he was convicted of kidnapping and murder, but Sally's body was never found.

Lucy remembered interviewing Sally's parents, who were understandably desperate for their daughter's return; she recalled struggling to contain her emotions until she was out of their house and in her car. Then the floodgates opened and she sobbed, clutching the steering wheel, shaken to her core by the family's horrible situation. But she had to admit to feeling rather uneasy about the verdict when Philip Ratcliffe was convicted and sent to prison for life, because it seemed to her that the evidence was rather flimsy. A fisherman testified that he saw Ratcliffe's truck near the pond, but couldn't quite remember the date, and didn't see him with Sally. The only physical evidence was that tattered, bloody lifeguard swimsuit, but it had been exposed to the elements for months, and the DNA evidence linking it to Ratcliffe was "suggestive," but not "conclusive."

"I understand how you feel, and I'll be happy to pass your concerns along to our editor. If you'll give me your name . . ."

"Sure. Jack Borowitz," he declared, going on to give her his phone number. "I'd like to give that idiot Ted Stillings a piece of my mind."

Lucy smiled, since this was a sentiment she sometimes shared, and jotted down the information. "Thanks for your call."

The phone lines were still alight, but Lucy leaned back and sighed. Turning to Phyllis, she asked, "How long has this been going on?"

Phyllis removed the headset and rubbed her temples. "Ted posted the letter around ten this morning. It was from a retired prosecutor who's been researching old trials and said the Ratcliffe case deserved another look, and the calls started coming in right away, just a few. But as word spread, they started coming faster and faster."

"If we don't answer, what happens?"

"I guess they'll go to voice mail, after ten rings."

"That's what we have to do. We can't spend the entire day taking calls. I've got stories to write and deadlines to meet. What did Ted have to say?"

"He went over to the courthouse, he's digging up the transcript of the trial. He wants to do a reprise, he calls it." She rolled her eyes as the phones continued to ring. "I think he wants you to interview the prosecutor."

Lucy remembered how high emotions had been during the trial, how extra security had to be provided for Ratcliffe when anger seemed to overtake the county, simmering in the summer heat and threatening to boil over. "Well, that's his decision, but I don't think it's wise. The parole hearing is bad enough for Sally's family, I don't quite see why he has to rake this all up again." She stared at the phone, willing it to stop ringing. "It was bad enough the first time."

"Amen," said Phyllis, replacing the headset. "I'll take as many calls as I can, the rest will have to go to voice mail. Can you work with all this ringing?"

"I'll have to," said Lucy, realizing she would have to postpone her investigation of Dorcas Pritchett's circle of friends. The next few weeks were going to be very busy, what with the Ratcliffe parole hearing coming up, in addition to the usual increased workload covering holiday events and celebrations. She was going to have to wait to satisfy her curiosity about Dorcas and "GB," whoever he was.

At five o'clock precisely, Phyllis threw down the headset, powered off her PC, and stood up. "I'm done," she said, grabbing her green-and-red–plaid coat and jamming her Santa hat on her head. "See you tomorrow."

"Okay," said Lucy. The constant ringing had stopped, but calls kept coming in steadily, which Lucy ignored. "I'm almost done here," she said. "I'm just finishing up this story. I'll turn out the lights and lock up."

"I just hope some angry reader doesn't torch the place," said Phyllis, grabbing the door and setting the little bell to jangling.

When she was gone, leaving Lucy alone in the brightly-lit office, Lucy suddenly felt exposed and vulnerable, as she was clearly visible through the large plate glass windows. No point in inviting trouble, she thought, getting up and closing the old-fashioned wood venetian blinds. Then she sat back down, wrote a few sentences to finish the Christmas card story, and after a quick read to check for typos, she sent it to Ted's file. Then she shut down her computer, bundled herself up in her winter clothes, and paused by the doorway, making sure everything was in order. The coffeepot was off, the computer screens were dark, one of the phones was ringing. She ignored it, set the lock on the door, flicked out the lights, and made sure the door was closed tightly behind her.

As she walked down the street to her car, she checked her phone, noticing calls from Ted and Rachel. She figured Ted was going to assign her to interview that prosecutor, so she called Rachel first.

"What's up?" she said when Rachel answered.

"Meeting tomorrow to set up the toy giveaway. Ten o'clock at the church."

Lucy groaned. "I don't think I can make it. Things have exploded at the paper." She had a sudden inspiration. "Hey, do you think you and Miss T can do some research for me? I found photos of Dorcas Pritchett with other high-school students and I wanted to try and track them down and see if any of them remembered her."

"That sounds perfect for Miss T, she's just discovered Google. She began with her Christmas card list, looking for some addresses, and now she's addicted."

"I'll e-mail her the list tonight." Lucy seated herself in her SUV and started the engine. "I'll try to make the meeting, but no promises."

"I understand, Lucy. Take care."

She was driving down Main Street when her phone rang and she realized she'd have to face the music. "Hi, Ted."

"What have you been doing all day?"

"Uh, dealing with the firestorm caused by that posting about the Ratcliffe parole hearing. The calls came in faster than we could answer them. Your voice mail is going to be full and I predict there'll be a ton of angry letters, too."

"Fabulous!" crowed Ted. "It's about time we got readers excited about something."

"Don't you think playing this up is kind of mean to Sally's family? It's bad enough the Holmeses have to deal with the parole hearing, without all this to-do."

"We're in the truth business, Lucy," said Ted, defending his editorial decision. "Have you read the posting? It's from this retired prosecutor. He makes some interesting points."

"I didn't get a chance," confessed Lucy.

"Well, take a look at it and give him a call. He seems like an interesting guy and you can get a good interview from him."

"Righto," grumbled Lucy. "Nothing says 'Happy Holidays' like digging up horrible crimes and possible miscarriages of justice."

"That's the spirit, Lucy. Give 'em something to talk about at all those holiday parties."

* * *

Lucy ended the call as she began the climb up Red Top Road to home, and purposefully banished thoughts of Sally Holmes and Philip Ratcliffe and shifted her thoughts to the remodeling project. She was eager to see what progress Bill had made, and as soon as she had parked the car, she dashed into the house, gave the dog a perfunctory pat on the head, and continued up the kitchen stairs to the second floor.

Bill was in the bathroom, washing up, and she greeted him with a question. "How's it going?"

"Check it out," he said with a satisfied smile.

The door was closed, but when she opened it, she saw that the demo was complete. The wall between the two bedrooms was gone and the newly-created space seemed enormous.

"Wow!" she said. "This is going to be great."

Bill came and stood beside her, nodding his head. "I agree." He glanced around, assessing the space. "I've been thinking. Are you sure you don't want a walk-in closet? A really fancy one would be a lot easier and cheaper than the master bath."

Lucy was crushed. "Really?"

"Yeah. I think it would be a lot smarter to go with the closet. After all, the bathroom is just a few steps down the hall." He nodded. "And what do you think about paint colors? Any thoughts?"

"Uh, no. I don't know." She shook her head, confused. "It's been a crazy day. I haven't had time to think."

"Gee, Lucy, I've been slaving away here while you've been gallivanting around, too busy to even think about paint?" He gave her a look. "All you can think about is that Christmas card we found."

"That's not true at all," said Lucy, marching out the

door. "For your information, I haven't even had time to pee and that's what I'm going to do right now." She marched down the hall to the bathroom and slammed the door. What was the matter with the man? Why didn't he understand her need for a private, personal bathroom apart from the one used by the whole family? A retreat. A place where she could take a long, soaking bath without somebody knocking on the door, urging her to hurry up.

Lucy didn't even try to put on a happy face through dinner, but sulked and practically growled when Bill, obviously making an effort, complimented her on the pork chops. She left the table as soon as she finished eating, leaving the cleanup to Bill and Zoe. As she marched out of the dining room, she heard Zoe asking, "Is Mom sick or something?" She didn't wait to hear Bill's reply, but thumped upstairs to the guest room, where she closed the door and plunked herself on one of the twin beds and began thumbing through a tired *Better Homes & Gardens* magazine.

She dozed off while reading an article about new trends in paint color, only to wake up around midnight and finding the other bed empty. Bill had apparently bedded down in the family room. She got up to pee, changed into her nightgown, and went back to bed, where she didn't get back to sleep until the wee hours of the morning.

When she woke at nearly eight o'clock, the house was empty; Bill had probably decided to get his breakfast at Jake's Donut Shop, and she knew Zoe had an early class. Realizing she had the bathroom to herself, she indulged in a long shower and took her time drying her hair and even putting on a little bit of makeup. She dressed with special care, choosing a cashmere turtleneck and slacks instead of her usual jeans and sweatshirt. She looked great, she thought as she put on her pearl earrings, but she felt miserable. She hated fighting with Bill, and she suspected she had overreacted. Now she would have to make amends—and come up with a paint color.

It was a little past ten when she drove into town, passing the Community Church, so she decided to pop in and get some photos of the Hat and Mitten Fund volunteers preparing for the Christmas Free Store, which is what they decided to call the toy giveaway. Since she didn't have time to volunteer herself, at least she could get some free publicity for the event. Even Ted couldn't complain about that, since Pam was one of the volunteers.

There was quite a lot going on in the basement meeting room as numerous folks from the community pitched in to hang holiday decorations, trim a tree, and attractively arrange the toys on tables covered with red or green cloths. The bicycles and wheeled toys were gathered in one corner, along with a huge inflatable Santa on a motorcycle.

"Wow, this looks great," she exclaimed, catching Sue, who was carrying a box of ornaments over to the tree.

"So do you," replied Sue, giving her an odd look. "Is something wrong, which requires making a good impression? Do you have to testify in court or something? Apply to refinance your mortgage?"

"No." Lucy wasn't about to go into details. "I overslept and the house was empty, so I took some time for myself, that's all."

"You should do it more often," advised Sue. "But it is unsettling. You don't quite seem like yourself."

"It's really me. I'm here to take some pictures for the paper."

"Ah, trying to put off getting to work?" Pam laughed, joining them. "I heard it was a madhouse yesterday."

"It was pretty crazy, all because of the posting about the Ratcliffe parole hearing. Even after all these years, people are really upset."

"There was an awful lot of press coverage back then and emotions were running so high," said Rachel, stepping down from a ladder after suspending some crepe paper streamers from a light fixture. "Bob says they should have demanded a change of venue, but Ratcliffe only had a public defender straight out of law school. The guy did his best, but was way in over his head." She turned to Lucy. "Oh, by the way, Miss T found one of those kids in the pictures you sent. Well, Howard White's not a kid anymore. He's actually in assisted living at Heritage House, right here in town."

"That's great," said Lucy, her spirits lifting a bit as Rachel pulled a slip of paper with the information out of her pocket and gave it to her. "I'll give Miss T a call and thank her. But first, I need you all to stand over by the inflatable Santa for a group photo."

"Everybody! Attention!" called Sue, clapping her hands. "We're going to take a picture for the paper!"

The volunteers dropped what they were doing and gathered around the inflatable Santa, and after asking a few people to move here or there, Lucy got a terrific photo that she figured Ted would run on the front page.

"Thanks, everybody," she said, "and stay put for a minute or two so I can get your names."

When she'd finished and was ready to go, Sue walked with her to the door. "Out with it, tell me what's really going on," she demanded in a lowered voice.

"Oh, a spat with Bill. He wants to put in a walk-in closet instead of a master bath." She paused, thinking. "Do you think he was talking to Sid?" Sue's husband, Sid, had a thriving closet design business, which he claimed he had to do in order to keep up with Sue's penchant for buying new clothes.

"I don't think so, but I'll have a word with him."

"And he needs me to choose a paint color, which I haven't had a chance to do."

"That's easy. You want Hint of Pink."

"He'll never go for pink."

"Tough. If you're not getting your bath, you should definitely get your paint color." She smiled naughtily. "Besides, Hint of Pink is a very flattering color. It will make your skin positively glow."

"Thanks!" Lucy gave Sue a hug. "You are a great friend."

Sue gave a little bow. "As Superman used to say, 'Up, up, and away.' I must go where I am needed, and that doll table definitely needs me."

As she made her way to the car, Lucy unfolded the slip of paper and checked the name. Then she refolded it and put it in her purse, wondering when she'd find the time to talk to Dorcas's old classmate.

Chapter Six

The *Pennysaver* office was quiet when she opened the door, apart from the muted jangle of the little bell on the door. Phyllis was cool, calm, and collected this morning, dressed in a subdued blue sweater embroidered with sparkly-white snowflakes and matching snowflake earrings.

"So the firestorm is over?" asked Lucy, looking about cautiously in case the phones were suddenly going to start ringing, or perhaps an irate reader was going to jump out of the morgue.

"Yeah, things have definitely calmed down, but Ted's after you to interview that retired prosecutor."

Lucy sighed as she shrugged out of her winter puffy and hung it on the coatrack. "Maybe if I keep putting it off, he'll forget." She sighed. "If it means so much to him, why doesn't he do it himself?"

Phyllis propped her elbows on her desk and rested her chin on her hands. "What's the problem? Why are you so reluctant to talk to this guy?"

"I dunno." Lucy sat down at her desk and swiveled her chair to face Phyllis. "It seems mean to keep this thing going. Ratcliffe got a life sentence—that should be the end of it, but instead, every ten years they've got to go through the whole thing again."

"But what if he's innocent? That's what Wilf says."

Lucy shrugged. She knew Wilf was Phyllis's husband.

"Or maybe he's rehabilitated. That's what prison is supposed to do, isn't it? Maybe he's truly remorseful and sorry for what he did. Doesn't he deserve a second chance?"

"I hope you don't mean a second chance to abduct some other young girl," retorted Lucy.

"He must be getting pretty old, Lucy, and probably in poor health. There's really no chance that he'd do it again, and that assumes he did it in the first place, which I'm not one hundred percent convinced he did."

Lucy's jaw dropped. "You're not?"

Phyllis shook her head. "Not even when he was on trial. I remember thinking that if I were on the jury, I'd have a reasonable doubt. I think people were upset and wanted to punish someone, and he was in the wrong place at the wrong time."

"Well, then," said Lucy, sounding defensive, "maybe you should go interview this prosecutor."

"I wouldn't know where to begin," said Phyllis, giving Lucy a smile. "You're the ace reporter, and by the way, Ted also mentioned that the Girl Scouts are taking gifts over to Heritage House this afternoon and he'd like some photos."

"Now that's news that's fit to print," said Lucy, her spirits rising as she swiveled her chair around and powered up her PC. Not only fit to print, but a visit to Heritage House would give her a chance to talk to Dorcas's old classmate Howard White.

Lucy knew the girls wouldn't get out of school until three, so it was close to three-thirty when she shut down her computer and drove over to the assisted-living facility on the edge of town. Heritage House was a modern building in a desirable setting, perched on a hill overlooking the cove. She'd timed it right, she discovered, as the girls were just entering the luxury-appointed main entry with its brass chandelier, plush sofas, and colorful Oriental rug.

Felicity Corcoran, the activities director, greeted them and led the way to the dining room, where the residents were seated family-style at round tables enjoying tea and cookies. There was a vacant seat at each table, and these were quickly occupied by the Scouts, and soon the room was filled with lively chatter. When the greetings died down, Scout leader Betsy Wiggins signaled for the girls to gather at the front of the room, where they sang a few Christmas songs. When they reached the final verse of "Santa Claus Is Coming to Town," a costumed and fake-bearded Santa, obviously the largest member of the troop, appeared with a bulging sack and began distributing wrapped presents.

Lucy dutifully collected quotes and took photos, and when it was all over, she approached Felicity and asked if she could visit Howard White.

"You too?" she asked. "He's getting a lot of visitors lately."

"I just want to ask him about old times here in town," said Lucy.

"Great. He's sure enjoying all the attention. In fact," she said, scanning the residents who were filing out of the room, "that's him, over there. The tall man and his fan club." She grinned, pointing out a tall fellow accompanied by three or four white-haired ladies, all carrying their unwrapped presents, which were bars of fancy soap. "That's what I call them. Men are in short supply here and they do attract the ladies."

Lucy smiled. "Thanks," she said, and crossed the room to join the fan club.

"Well, well, it's Lucy Stone, if I'm not mistaken," said Howard. He was a good-looking, older man with a healthy crop of white hair, bushy white eyebrows, a hawk nose, and a square chin.

The fan club twittered and fussed a bit over Lucy.

"Aren't you the clever one."

"I love reading your stories in the *Pennysaver.*"

"What brings you here today?"

"Well," she began, "I want to ask Howard about an old classmate of his." She produced the photocopy of the group picture. "It's this girl, Dorcas Pritchett," she said, pointing her out.

"Oh, is that you, Howard? Wasn't he handsome?" enthused the liveliest member of the fan club, a tiny lady, with a tight perm, wearing bright red lipstick.

"Oh, my, always a heartbreaker," added another, a chubby lady in a bright pink tracksuit.

Howard stared at the photo, then returned it to Lucy with a "humpf."

"I gather you remember Dorcas, but not fondly," suggested Lucy.

"She got me in trouble. I saw her cheating on an exam, and I foolishly reported it to the teacher. Dorcas denied it and accused me of lying, and the teacher fell for it." He paused. "Looking back, I think pretty much everybody fell for Dorcas's stories—until they were the victim. I was scolded for dishonesty and I guess word got around in the faculty lounge because I couldn't breathe without some teacher giving me the evil eye."

Interesting, thought Lucy, with a rising sense of excitement. "So you didn't, by any chance, send her a Christmas card?"

"Are you kidding? I stayed as far away from her as I could. As it was, I was lucky to get into the state college. Thanks to Dorcas I had a real hard time getting recommendations." He paused. "She had no trouble, however, the little hypocrite. I couldn't believe it when she got accepted at some Bible college. I think it was in Boston." He rolled his eyes. "Butter wouldn't melt in her mouth."

"You poor thing," cooed the tallest member of the fan club, a rather stern-looking lady with a pixie haircut and eyeglasses with thick plastic pink frames. "So unfair."

"I did all right in the end," replied Howard, grinning broadly. "Funny to look back, though."

"Do you know anybody else in town who might have known Dorcas?" asked Lucy. "Are any of her other classmates still around?"

Howard scratched his chin, then nodded. "Franny Small. Franny wasn't in our class, she's a few years younger, but she was around then. She might remember Dorcas."

"Thanks for your help." Lucy smiled at the group. "And I'd like to wish you all a merry Christmas."

"Oh, it will be merry," cooed the tiny lady, her cheeks growing pink. "Christmas is always special with Howard."

Howard cleared his throat, then led the way down the hall, accompanied by his little clutch of admirers.

As she made her way back to the parking lot, Lucy thought about her conversation with Howard and came to the conclusion that she really hadn't learned much; he'd only confirmed what she suspected. Little Dorcas had figured out how to manipulate people and didn't hesitate to use that power for her own ends. Howard hadn't retaliated against her, like the sender of the Christmas card, but he hadn't forgotten the lies she told about him even after so many years. He had given her one bit of new information, however, which was his recollection that Dorcas had attended a Bible college in Boston. Lucy didn't know of any such institution, but that didn't mean it didn't exist. What with high-profile universities like MIT and Harvard in nearby Cambridge, and Northeastern, BC, and BU in Boston, it was easy to forget that there were plenty of other, lesser-known colleges in the area. The problem facing her, she decided as she climbed into her SUV, was finding time to do the research. Maybe Miss T and Rachel would help out once again.

Lucy spent the rest of the day finishing up her holiday stories and helping Phyllis with the events listings, which were much more numerous than usual thanks to the holidays. Meanwhile, she kept an eye on the clock for the four o'clock selectmen's meeting. For once, Lucy planned on being early in hopes of catching a word with Franny Small.

Selectmen's meetings were held in the basement meeting room at the town hall, but were sparsely attended, now that all the meetings were televised on the local CATV channel. Except for a few regulars, most people only bothered to go if they had a bone to pick with the town's governing body. Now, with the holidays approaching, Lucy found the meeting room quite empty, apart from three of the five members of the board. Joe Marzetti, chairman Roger Wilcox, and Franny were standing together, sharing a laugh.

Joe was the first to spot her and called out a welcome.

"Hi, Lucy. Better grab a chair while you can, before the crowd gets here."

"Thanks for the advice," replied Lucy, waving at the neat rows of chairs. "It's hard to choose."

"Too big a selection," agreed Roger. "It's like at the supermarket—too many cereals. It's overwhelming."

"Yeah," agreed Joe. "They seem to come out with a new one every week."

"Well, I always get my Raisin Bran," volunteered Franny. "But last week I got the wrong one. It had granola bits in it."

"New and improved," snorted Roger, checking the clock. "We don't have a quorum, maybe we ought to call Val Dennehy and Bill Shaw, see if they're coming."

"Good idea," said Joe, pulling out his cell phone and stepping away from the group to make the calls.

"Hey, Franny," began Lucy, "I've been wondering about the people who lived in my house before we bought it—"

"The Pritchetts," volunteered Franny. "I remember them quite well. I went to school with their daughter, Dorcas."

"She's the one I'm curious about. What can you tell me about her?"

Roger wasn't interested in Franny's trip down memory lane, so he wandered over to listen in on Joe's phone call. Franny took a seat in the front row of chairs and Lucy sat beside her.

"I heard she went to a Bible college in Boston," offered Lucy, getting her started.

"I think she did, she was a couple of years ahead of me. We all looked up to her, you know. She was a leader in the school, team captain and student council and all that sort of thing, always on the honor roll. I kind of idolized her, maybe it was one of those schoolgirl crushes, but I was in for a big disappointment."

Her curiosity piqued, Lucy asked, "In what way?"

"Well," began Franny, smoothing her wool plaid skirt, "you know how I started that little jewelry business using the nuts and bolts and things from the hardware store."

Lucy nodded, she didn't need to be told. Franny's "little business" had become a multimillion-dollar success.

"When I was starting out, I signed up for this women's entrepreneurship convention in Boston. It was expensive, but I was eager to learn about business and the fact that Dorcas—well, she called herself Doris by then—was one of the speakers, was pretty irresistible. So I coughed up the outrageous registration fee, I remember it was a real stretch for me, and off I went, hoping that Doris would give me some advice. Maybe even be a mentor to me."

"So she was very successful," said Lucy. "What did she do?"

Franny laughed. "I never did find out. I think she was really just an inspirational speaker. That was her gig, and she made a business of it, giving pep talks. She didn't miss a beat, that one, she also sold mugs and posters and things with inspiring phrases on them."

"So I'm guessing she wasn't terribly helpful to you?"

"Wouldn't give me the time of day, but she did give me a brochure about the pricey seminars she offered for Breaking the Glass Ceiling, or something like that." Franny looked up, noticing that the other board members had arrived and were taking their places on the dais. "I guess I've got to go, Lucy."

Franny took her seat with the others; Roger banged his gavel, opening the meeting; the town clerk came in and took a seat on the other side of the aisle from Lucy.

"First on the agenda," said Roger, "is a request from our town clerk, Sandy Greene." He smiled at her. "We know your time is valuable and you're eager to get back to your office."

"Right," said Sandy, a plump woman with dark hair. "This won't take long. I'm just asking for funds to digitize the town's real estate tax records so they can be accessed electronically. We get requests for information all the time and it ties up my assistants. There's a lot of information in those files and it would be great if people could access them by computer, rather than coming into the office and having my girls digging through a couple of centuries' worth of old records."

"And how much will this cost?" asked Joe.

"I have a couple of quotes," said Sandy, glancing uneasily at Lucy and distributing information packets to the board members.

From the expressions on the board members' faces as they studied the packets, Lucy was able to make two conclusions: Digitizing was going to be expensive, and the project didn't have a chance of getting the board's approval.

Lucy was a bit uneasy when she drove home from the meeting, since she hadn't seen or heard from Bill all day, and hadn't been on good terms with him the night before. Her mother had always advised her never to go to bed angry, and this evening she wished she and Bill had worked things through last night rather than letting their disagreement fester.

But when she turned into the driveway, she noticed a box containing a toilet sitting inside Bill's truck. She found this somewhat encouraging. However, she also knew that it might not be for the master bath she so desperately desired. It could be meant for one of his customers.

She wasn't quite sure how to handle this development, but resolved to do her best to restore peace and amity in the house. Bill was in the kitchen when she entered, sitting at the round oak table with a beer and a pad of paper. Libby was curled up on the floor beside him, but looked up and greeted Lucy with a thump of her tail.

"Hi," he said, greeting her with a smile.

"Hi, yourself," she said, hanging her coat up on one of the hooks by the door. She took a deep breath. "I'm sorry I was such a jerk last night."

"I think you were overtired," said Bill, smiling. "I peeked in on you around nine and you were sound asleep."

Lucy found this touching. "You did?"

"Yeah. I didn't want to disturb you so I camped out downstairs."

"That was awfully nice of you." Lucy went to the fridge and got a bottle of Chardonnay, poured herself a glass, and joined him at the table. "What are you working on?"

"The master bath. What do you think of this plan?"

Lucy couldn't believe her ears. "Really?"

"Yeah. I really thought you'd like one of those fancy closets. I didn't realize how much the bath meant to you, but Sid told me you'd been talking to Sue about it and were pretty upset." He slid the pad across the table. "I've already picked up a toilet. It was on sale, so I grabbed it. I figured you'd want to decide about the tub and vanity."

Lucy studied the neat drawing he'd made on graph paper and broke into tears. "It's the most beautiful thing I've ever seen," she said, laughing and wiping her eyes. "And even though Sue said we should paint the bedroom pink, we don't have to. You can pick the color."

Bill couldn't help laughing. "Well, I appreciate that," he finally said, taking her hand and leaning across the table to give her a great big sloppy kiss. "Zoe won't be home until nine or so," he added. "It's her seminar night."

Lucy smiled slyly. "Whatever do you mean, sir?"

"You know exactly what I mean," said Bill, pulling her to her feet.

Lucy did, and followed him up the stairs with light steps and an even lighter heart.

Chapter Seven

Waking very early on Saturday morning, Lucy decided it had definitely been a good idea to push the two twin beds in the guest room together, and wondered why she hadn't thought of it sooner. Bill was still asleep, snoring gently, so she tiptoed out of the room and downstairs, where she made a pot of coffee. While it dripped, she checked her messages and saw that Miss Tilley had texted her the name of Cromwell College, which was affiliated with the Congregational Church.

Lucy asked her phone for information about Cromwell College and the miraculous, automated voice that seemed to know absolutely everything told her in a crisp British accent that it was a small liberal arts college located in the Boston suburb of Waltham and offered pre-theological courses, as well as majors in sacred music, religious education, and church administration. Interesting, she thought as the scent of coffee filled the kitchen. She was planning on visiting Sara this weekend to do some Christmas shopping in Boston, maybe she could fit in a quick visit to Cromwell College. But if she was going to do all that, she decided as she filled her coffee mug, she had no time to waste.

Lucy made good time on the drive, enjoying the sunrise as she drove over the Piscataqua Bridge, and easily found Cromwell College—thanks again to the miraculous voice of her GPS. *How did we ever manage without our smartphones,* she mused as she parked outside the repurposed Greek Revival–style residence that now housed the college's combined admissions and alumni offices. Her very smart smartphone had already advised her that it was open on Saturday and offered campus tours to prospective students.

When she entered, she was greeted by a student receptionist, who asked if she wanted to join the handful of families waiting for the next tour. When she said she was looking for information about a graduate, she was quickly referred to the director of alumni services.

"Come on into my office," invited Susan Ellers, a recent grad, dressed conservatively in a turtleneck sweater and A-line skirt, along with stockings and low-heeled pumps. Her office featured color photographs of the campus, as well as black and whites of students dating from the 1940s and '50s.

When Lucy was seated in the visitor chair, Susan offered her coffee or tea. Lucy declined and got straight to the point of her mission. "I live in Tinker's Cove, Maine, in an old house and I'm curious about the people who lived there before us. I found an old Christmas card dating from the 1960s, you see, and it's caught my interest."

Susan was definitely intrigued. "And you think there's a link between those people and Cromwell?"

"It's just a hunch, but I know this family was very religious and it seems likely that they might have sent their daughter to a college that was affiliated with their church."

"The sixties, you say. Back then, Cromwell had a reputation of strict supervision of students. There were no long-haired hippies at Cromwell." She paused, smiling. "Things have changed quite a bit, but we're still quite traditional. Who was the student?"

"Her name was Dorcas Pritchett, though she later changed it to Doris."

"Let's see what comes up," suggested Susan, turning to her desktop computer. "I can't give you grades or personal information, but I can tell you if she was enrolled here." As she clicked away on the keyboard, she continued, "As you can imagine, we keep close tabs on our grads."

"For donations?" Lucy and Bill received frequent solicitations from their colleges, as well as the kids' schools.

"Oh, yes, but we also like to celebrate their successes. Ah, here's Dorcas. You were right, she was here for the 1963 through '64 school year."

"Just one year?"

"Yes. And there's been no contact since then. She's really dropped off our radar."

Lucy was disappointed. "No address changes, then."

Sally gave her a sympathetic smile and a shrug. "Sorry."

"Not even one donation?" asked Lucy, thinking that a check might give some information.

"That's personal information that I am not supposed to reveal"—Susan shrugged—"but like I said, no contact whatsoever."

Lucy stood up. "Well, thanks for your help. I really appreciate it."

"I'm happy to help. And I wonder, are you perhaps looking at colleges for your kids or your friends' children? Maybe you'd like to take a closer look at Cromwell?"

Lucy laughed. "I'm almost done. My youngest has dabbled in every possible major, but at long last is almost finished at Winchester."

"Congratulations. And keep us in mind, we really appreciate recommendations."

"I will," said Lucy, somewhat doubtful that the occasion would arise, but open to the possibility. "And thanks again for your time."

Weekend traffic was light on Route 128 and Lucy soon found herself looking for a parking spot near Sara's little borrowed apartment in Quincy. The narrow street was closely packed with three-deckers, and lined on both sides with parked cars, but a van pulled out a few doors down from Sara's place and Lucy popped into the vacancy. Sara welcomed her with a hug, and over a soup and sandwich lunch, they discussed their plans for the weekend.

"This is such a luxury, having a pied-à-terre in the city," enthused Lucy, biting into her grilled cheese sandwich. "And, of course, it's great to visit with you, too."

"I'm not exactly downtown," said Sara. "It's quite a long ride on the T, you know."

"It's a lot closer than Tinker's Cove, and it's great to be able to spend the night and not have to rush back home." Lucy paused to take a spoonful of soup. "And you've made the place so cute. You've added some nice little touches with things you brought from home, like the candles and throw pillows."

"I know, Mom. I wish I could do more, but it's not my place. And I've really been looking forward to your visit." Sara sighed and stirred her soup. "It's a little hard getting started in a new place. I like my job, but it gets a bit lonely on weekends, you know. It's hard to meet people."

"I remember," said Lucy, who tactfully didn't mention that this was one of the reasons she'd decided to make the trip. "It takes time, but it will all work out." She thought of her recent visit to Cromwell College. "You know, I bet Winchester could give you names of recent grads who are in the Boston area. They might even have a club here."

"That's brilliant," said Sara, perking up. "What made you think of it?"

"Oh, I've been doing some digging, trying to find out about this woman who lived in our house. You know your dad's remodeling our bedroom—"

"I didn't know." Sara furrowed her brow. "What about my room? Where will I stay when I come home?"

Lucy was quick to reassure her. "You can bunk with Zoe. Or in the guest room if you want more privacy."

"Well, I guess you and Dad are entitled to spread out," she said, somewhat begrudgingly.

"We just got tired of bumping our heads on the ceiling," insisted Lucy. "Anyway, to make a long story short, he found an old Christmas card." Lucy got up and dug in her purse, which she'd left on Sara's futon. "Here it is."

"Cute Santa." Sara opened the card and her eyes widened in shock as she read the message. "Oh, my! Not very nice."

"I think it was sent to a girl named Dorcas Pritchett and I'm really curious about what she did to make the sender so angry."

"Probably just some teenage spat. A rejected boyfriend, something like that. You know how emotional teenagers can be."

"So I do," agreed Lucy, thinking that even twentysome-things were prone to extreme emotional swings. She took back the card. "This seems like more than that to me. And the more I learn about Dorcas Pritchett, that's her name, the more I've come to think she was a rather unpleasant young lady."

"Wow, all from a Christmas card." Sara got up to clear the table, and Lucy went into the tiny bathroom to freshen up before heading into town, noting with approval the recent addition of some colorful towels and a matching bath mat.

The two exited from the Red Line at Downtown Crossing, but Washington Street was so crowded with holiday shoppers that they decided to walk through the Common and Public Garden to Newbury Street, where the prices in the boutiques were higher, which they figured would hopefully discourage some of the shoppers. After venturing into a few of the exclusive shops, Lucy decided that four-hundred-dollar belts and thousand-dollar raincoats were way beyond her means, too.

"Is there anything else around here that we could do?" she asked. "A museum or something?"

"The Boston Public Library is worth a peek, it's got murals by Sargent."

"Great," enthused Lucy. "I love libraries."

She found the murals rather a disappointment, since they were in muted colors and quite different from Sargent's usual lush and lively style, but the research department caught her attention. "Let's poke around in here," she suggested. "Maybe we'll find something about Dorcas."

Sara rolled her eyes. "You're out of your mind."

"I just have an inquiring mind," said Lucy, heading straight for one of the computer stations. "Come on, it'll be interesting."

Sara sighed heavily, but followed her mother and took a seat beside her, looking at the screen over her shoulder. Entries for *Dorcas Pritchett, Doris Pritchett*, as well as just plain *Pritchett*, came up empty, and *Red Top Road, Tinker's Cove, Maine*, only elicited a map. Forays into the sites of the Boston newspapers didn't produce information about Dorcas, but did give a lively picture of the social scene when Dorcas was a student at Cromwell College. Kennedy's assassination was the big story, but there were also reports about the birth control pill, the civil rights movement, and the nation's growing involvement in the Vietnam War.

"So all this was going on and Dorcas was stuck in that conservative Bible school?" asked Sara, amazed. "No wonder she left after a year." Sara was thoughtful. "I wonder if she went on a Freedom Bus to the South. That's what I would have done."

Lucy disagreed. "I don't think so. It's more likely she ran off with a man."

"What makes you think that?"

"I dunno." Lucy laughed. "I guess that's what I would have done."

"Well, it's probably more likely than becoming a Freedom Rider. And there's the fact that she must have returned home, because that's where you found the card."

Lucy thought a timeline was beginning to emerge. "So she went to college, got involved with someone that she made very mad for some reason, and then she ran home to her strict parents."

"Maybe she just went home for the holidays. Most people do."

Lucy sighed, logging off the computer. "You're probably right. So, what's next? Grab the Green Line to the MFA?"

Sara shook her head. "Nah. Let's go back down Boylston Street. There are some discount stores over there."

"Now you're talking." Lucy grabbed her purse and headed out, always eager to find a bargain.

Next morning Lucy made Sara's favorite blueberry pancakes for breakfast, having brought some frozen Maine berries, as well as a jug of local maple syrup. The two enjoyed the special treat, but Sara's face fell when Lucy announced she had to leave and started packing her overnight bag.

"I really miss home," Sara admitted, brushing away a tear. "Weekdays are okay, when I'm at work, but the weekends are *sooo* long."

"Well, if I were you, I'd head for the Laundromat. You might meet somebody there, and if not, you can check your phone for clubs and classes. You could even go to church. You could make an eleven o'clock service."

"I guess I'd rather stay here and wallow in self-pity while the laundry piles up."

Lucy smiled and gave her daughter a hug. "It's your choice. And remember, only a few more weeks and you'll be home for Christmas." Lucy paused. "And don't bring all your dirty laundry with you, like your brother used to do."

"I won't," promised Sara, adding, "And don't be disappointed, Mom, if I don't get any hateful Christmas cards from nonexistent spurned boyfriends."

"I won't be," promised Lucy, zipping her bag. When she was togged out in her winter coat and ready to leave, Lucy gave Sara a big hug. "See you soon."

"Drive safe, Mom." Sara opened the door and held it for Lucy, watching as she made her way down the walk and along the sidewalk to her car. She was still standing in the doorway, waving, when Lucy drove off.

Moving away from home and starting a career was a terribly stressful, lonely time, thought Lucy, wishing she could do more for Sara than offer advice. It was also a dangerous time, when young women out for a good time could get into trouble, going off with the wrong guy. As she drove, she reassured herself that Sara was a sensible girl, maybe even a bit too cautious. She chuckled to herself, thinking that Sara would probably require references and a credit check before agreeing to go out on a date.

She was zipping through the O'Neill Tunnel, empty on Sunday morning, when her thoughts turned once again to Dorcas. What had brought her back home? Was it simply the holiday break? Or had she returned to recover from some traumatic experience? A breakup? A pregnancy? Or something worse, like a crime of some sort? Was she the victim of a rape or a mugging? If not the victim, maybe a witness? Perhaps she'd been required to testify about someone, and that person hadn't appreciated it. Especially if she'd lied.

Lucy was on the Zakim Bridge, catching a glimpse of "Old Ironsides" and the Bunker Hill Monument, when she decided she was letting her imagination run away with her. This was all nothing but speculation without more information about Dorcas.

It was then that she remembered the town clerk's presentation at the selectmen's meeting and her assertion that there was a lot of information in the town's real estate records. That was the place to start, she decided. At the very least she'd get some names and dates, and maybe even the name of the law firm that handled the sale of the house. Somewhat encouraged, she decided to skip her plan to stop at L.L.Bean in Freeport and to head straight home instead. She could order whatever she wanted online and they'd send it right to the house. Besides, she was eager to see the progress on the master suite, and while she was Christmas shopping on the Web, she might as well take a few minutes to check out bathtubs and vanities.

Chapter Eight

When Lucy woke on Monday morning, it was snowing heavily. There was already a couple of inches on the ground but the forecasters expected the storm to move off shore by late morning.

Bill, however, was doubtful. "It looks to me like we could get at least a foot, maybe more," he said, standing at the kitchen window with his mug of coffee.

"Are the plows out yet?" asked Lucy, joining him at the window.

"One went by a few minutes ago, but the road is already covered again."

Lucy sipped her coffee. "Thank goodness for all-wheel drive."

Bill turned to face her. "You're not going to work, are you?"

"I've got to. I can't cover the storm from here. This is New England, after all. We're hardy folk, used to snow and hurricanes and whatever Mother Nature can throw at us."

"Lucy, you are not a native New Englander, you grew up in the Bronx."

"It was a very suburban sort of neighborhood, you

know. We had trees and lawns and all that." She sipped her coffee, remembering her father taking her sliding down a steep snow-covered road on his prized, six-foot-long Flexible Flyer sled early one morning before people began to stir. It was one of her earliest memories, so she must have been quite young, but she'd loved the sense of speed while safely enclosed in Daddy's arms. "And we had plenty of snow."

"I think you should wait until the snow stops and they've cleared the roads," insisted Bill.

Lucy watched as a big yellow school bus passed the house. "You're overreacting, Bill. The forecast calls for three to six inches and they haven't even closed the schools. This storm is news and I've got to cover it. Ted's going to be busy with that parole hearing, so it's up to me."

"Not much you can report if you're stuck in a snow-drift," argued Bill.

"My phone is charged, and I've got blankets and food, a shovel, and plenty of kitty litter, and the town plows will be out." She drained her mug and put it in the dishwasher. "There won't be much traffic, either. I'll probably be safer out there today than on a normal summer Saturday when the roads are filled with tourists."

"You're out of your mind," he said, putting his hands on her waist and pulling her close. She felt his beard on the back of her neck. "Be careful, okay?"

"Always," she said, turning around and wrapping her arms around his neck, raising her face for a kiss.

Bill obliged and she lingered in his arms for a moment or two before pulling away. "Time and tide wait for no one," she said, sighing.

"Make that time and Ted," he said with a wry smile.

"You can say that again." Lucy began the process of

putting on snow pants, boots, jacket, scarf, hat, and gloves. By the time she was ready to leave the house, she noticed another inch had accumulated, and she thought anxiously about the kids at school. If it kept snowing at this rate, they were going to have a tough time getting home, she decided, clomping through the snow to her SUV.

Thanks to the excellent work of the Tinker's Cove DPW, she found the roads were in pretty good shape and she made it to work without incident, except for a teeny bit of fishtailing when she braked for the stop sign at the bottom of Red Top Road. After that, she drove extra carefully, well below the posted speed limit.

Lucy was surprised to find Phyllis in place behind the reception desk at the *Pennysaver* office, togged out in her Irish fisherman's sweater and lined jeans.

"I'm glad to see you, I thought I'd be all alone here," said Lucy.

"I got a ride with my neighbor, he's got a new plow on his truck and wanted to try it out."

Lucy pulled off her gloves and began unwinding her scarf. "I'm beginning to think he may get to use it quite a bit. Bill thinks the weatherman got this one wrong. We've already got at least four or five inches and it doesn't look like it's stopping anytime soon."

"I think they should've canceled school," said Phyllis, watching the enormous flakes swirling down outside the window. "I can't imagine what that superintendent was thinking."

"Like everyone else in Maine, he was thinking that when you live in New England, you simply deal with the weather, you don't let it stop you."

Just then, the police scanner squawked, reporting an

overturned truck on Route 1. "Good thing I didn't get my coat off," laughed Lucy, rewinding her scarf. "Give Ted a call and tell him I'm on it, okay?"

"Will do. And be careful out there."

With a wave Lucy was out the door and back in her SUV, which today she was able to park right in front of the office. Driving down Main Street, she noticed that while some of the shops were closed, an equal number were open, including Jake's Donut Shack, the hardware store, the IGA, and all three banks.

She saw from the approach that traffic was already backed up on the northbound side of Route 1, so Lucy made her way cautiously along back roads until she was well past the accident and was able to approach it on the southbound lane. The tractor trailer was on its side, having apparently flipped over as the driver attempted to turn onto the exit ramp, and was partly blocking the northbound lane. Officer Barney Culpepper was directing traffic around the crash, bundled in his official navy blue police jumpsuit, with boots and gloves. The only parts of his body not covered were his eyes and his nose, which was very red.

"Hi, Lucy." He hailed her as she approached through the swirling snow. "First accident today, but it won't be the last."

"This turn always gets 'em," observed Lucy. "How's the driver?"

"He was lucky, not a scratch." He waved on a small pickup truck. "I wish folks would just stay home. What's so important that it can't wait a day?"

"Some folks don't have a choice, like that truck driver," said Lucy. "And you and me."

Barney's words stuck with her as she drove very slowly and very carefully back to town. There was no sign that the snow was diminishing, it was falling so fast and hard that the plows couldn't keep up with it and the pavement was quickly filling with snow. It was slippery but manageable now, but Lucy knew that if it kept up at this rate, the region's main road would soon be impassable. All-wheel drive could only do so much, and the snow would soon be too deep for anything but snowmobiles. It looked as though some drivers on the highway would be marooned in their vehicles before long, and if Route 1 was in bad shape, she could only imagine what the side roads would be like.

Maybe she was being too pessimistic, she thought, when she finally made it to Main Street and parked once again in front of the *Pennysaver* office. So far, so good, and the snowfall surely couldn't keep up at this rate indefinitely. When she got out of the car, she took a few moments to savor the view as snow blanketed the quaint seaside town, which was pretty enough to be the December photo on a calendar. Come to think of it, not only Main Street but the cove, with its colorful lobster boats and the lighthouse on rocky Quissett Point, did show up frequently on calendars, notecards, and in the travel sections of Sunday newspapers.

It was only a few steps from the car to the office, but in the few minutes she paused to admire the view, she had accumulated so much snow that she looked like a snowman, she realized, catching sight of her reflection in the plate glass windows. Enough of this woolgathering, she would no doubt have plenty of work as long as the power held. Oh, right, she sighed, yanking open the door. There was no way the lights would stay on in a storm like this, once the heavy snow began to break tree limbs and snap power lines.

"Thank goodness," said Phyllis, when Lucy stepped inside the warm office. "I was beginning to worry about you. They've changed the forecast. The storm has stalled or something, and now they're calling for a record snowfall."

"It's no picnic out there," said Lucy, stamping her feet and shaking off the snow before removing her winter gear, beginning at the top with her hat and working down to her boots. A large, heavy mat covered the floor between the door and the reception desk, so she didn't have to worry about the snow that fell from her clothes, but she did have to find a warm spot where they would dry. The office still had old-fashioned steam radiators, so she strewed her things atop them, where they soon sent up a woolly scent.

"Ah, winter," she cooed, holding her hands out to feel the heat.

"Looks like we're in for it," announced Phyllis, checking her phone for an update. "They're saying we could get as much as two feet. Everybody's supposed to shelter in place as the roads are expected to become impassable."

"That's not good," said Lucy, thinking of the drivers stranded on Route 1, the kids stuck in school, and herself, no doubt spending the night in the chilly, dark office. "I better get as much done as I can before we lose the power," she said, settling herself at her desk and powering up her PC.

As the day wore on, reports flooded in of road accidents and strandings, power outages, a house fire out on Bumps River Road, and even an emergency delivery of a baby. First responders were doing their best to keep up with it all, employing their heaviest equipment, but when even the powerful, extreme-brush Bulldog 4x4 fire truck got stuck, rescuers had to switch to using borrowed snow-mobiles.

Phyllis and Lucy had just finished lunch when she was able to get a few words from Fire Chief Buzz Bresnahan, who had just returned from Bumps River Road, and was upset that they couldn't save the burning house. "At least no one got hurt, the house was empty, but now a couple of old folks have lost their house." He sighed. "I guess the silver lining is that their daughter lives only a few doors down and they can stay with her, but I'm not convinced they even had insurance."

"I know everybody did the best they could," said Lucy, hoping to console him. "These are extreme conditions."

"Looks like one of those 'hundred-year storms' that we get every year now."

Lucy was about to agree with him when the lights went out, her computer screen went black, and her desk phone died.

"I guess we're going to be here for the duration," said Phyllis, peering out the window at the unplowed street. "If they don't get the plows out, I'm afraid we're not going to make it home tonight."

"Now I wish I hadn't eaten all my lunch. I should've saved something for dinner."

"I think we've got some of those peanut butter crack-ers," said Phyllis, rummaging through the shelf beneath the coffeepot. "Well, it'll be a light dinner. There's only two packs," she reported.

"Better than nothing."

"I suppose." Phyllis sighed and plunked herself down on a chair in the half-light coming through the windows.

"What are we going to do all day, with no computer or phone?"

"Maybe the cell phones still work," suggested Lucy. "Who should I call?"

"Who's on your phone?"

"Well, a lot of cops and firefighters, but I don't want to bother them. They've got enough on their hands. I was thinking of somebody in town hall, see what's going on over there."

"I've got Sandy Greene's number. We're neighbors and she waters my plants when I'm away."

"The town clerk? Perfect." Lucy added the number to her contacts for future reference, then dialed. Much to her amazement, Sandy answered.

"We're down to cell phones here at the paper, since we lost our power," she began, "and I was wondering how you guys are doing over there."

"About the same," said Sandy. "Anita got the cribbage board out, so that's about it for us."

"Any food?"

"There's stuff in the staff refrigerator, but I suspect some of it's been there for quite a while. Leftovers, you know. I'm hoping I won't have to eat somebody's expired yogurt."

"How many of you are over there?"

"Only four or so. Most people were smart enough to stay home."

Lucy got the names of the hardy workers who were now holed up in the town hall and was about to end the call when she had a brainwave. "Hey, since you've got time on your hands, maybe you could do a bit of research for me? From the old paper records?"

"Sure, Lucy. What do you need?"

"Well, I'm just curious about my house. Bill found an old Christmas card when he took down a wall. We're ex-

panding our bedroom, you see, and I'm curious about it.
There's no name, but I think it was sent to Dorcas Pritchett. She lived there before we bought the house. I'd like to
get in touch with her, but I can't find her. Maybe there's
some info in the town real estate records?"

"Doubtful," said Sandy. "All we've got is tax records.
The deed and all that go to the registrar. But," she added,
"it won't hurt to take a look."

"Great, I really appreciate it."

"No problem. Meanwhile, how are you guys doing over
there?"

"We're okay. I'm writing with a quill pen, Phyllis has
her knitting, and we're each having a packet of peanut
butter crackers for dinner."

Sandy laughed. "We complain a lot about technology,
but when we lose it . . ."

"Ain't that the truth," said Lucy.

She didn't have to use a quill pen, her Bic worked just
fine as she wrote up the bits of information she'd gotten
from Sandy and the fire chief. When she finished with
that, she got up and walked around, noting that the temperature in the office had dropped to sixty-two. She was
doing some yoga poses when her cell phone rang; it was
Sandy.

"Talk about luck of the Irish!"

"I'm not Irish."

"Well, you are lucky, because I found a copy of a tax lien.
The previous owners were way behind on their taxes."

"There was a foreclosure. We bought the house from
the bank."

"And there was a letter from a law firm asking for more
time for the owners to pay up, they were trying to do one
of those short sales to avoid foreclosure. They would certainly have information about the owners."

That answered one question, thought Lucy, who had wondered why the Pritchetts let the house go. They had tried to save what they could, going so far as to hire a law firm and attempting a short sale, but hadn't been successful.

"Great. Who is it? Somebody here in town?"

"No. In Florida," said Sandy, rattling off the name and letterhead information.

"Thanks. I'll give them a call," Lucy said as a blast of wind shook the building. "If I can't be in Florida, at least I can find out what the weather's like there."

"I can pretty much guarantee it's not snowing."

Lucy still had four bars on her cell phone, so she decided to throw caution to the wind and make the call to Florida. The receptionist who answered the phone wasn't terribly impressed with Lucy's story and doubted that the firm retained any information from such a distant time in the past, but she finally relented and transferred Lucy's call to an associate.

Poppy Porter sounded young and perky and seemed quite intrigued by Lucy's story. "All I do all day is redact documents," she said, whispering. "I'm the newest in the firm and they've got me in the dead file room until somebody dies and frees up an office."

"Any chance of that happening soon?" asked Lucy, amused.

"I don't think so. Some of them are really old, but I have this theory that the sun kind of wrinkles them up and preserves them, like raisins."

"Too bad. Up here it's the cold, people are frozen. Like peas in the freezer, they never go bad." She glanced out the window. "We're having a blizzard right now, in fact."

"I miss snow," volunteered Poppy. "And skiing. I love to ski."

"Well, come on up," urged Lucy.

"I wish." Poppy sighed. "So, what exactly are you looking for?"

"Any information you might have about the Pritchett family. Your firm handled the attempted sale of their house, way back when. And I'm especially interested in one member, Dorcas Pritchett, who was also called Doris."

"I will see what I can find and get back to you," promised Poppy.

"That would be fabulous. Thanks."

The day wore on with no further communication from Poppy, but Bill checked in with her from time to time, making sure she was all right. They finally heard from Ted in the late afternoon, calling from the nearby town of Gilead, and Lucy asked about the parole hearing.

"Did they have it? How did it go? Did he get parole?"

"No way. They turned him down flat. So it's back to jail for Ratcliffe. I got some good quotes from the Holmes family. As you'd expect they're mighty relieved."

"Not just the family. I don't think most people wanted him to go free."

"No chance of that. Last I saw, two burly guards were taking him up to the county jail for the night, and as soon as the roads are clear, it's straight back to the state pen for him." He paused. "So look, if you and Phyllis can't get home tonight, I think you should bunk down in the police department across the street. They've got generators and stuff, it's your best bet. Plus, you'll be on the spot if there's any breaking news."

"Okay. I think we'll go now." Lucy looked around the dimly lit office, where the temperature had fallen to fifty-four degrees and Phyllis was gently snoring at her desk, wrapped in her coat. "It's getting cold in here."

"Good idea. But first I want you to get over to the elementary school, where the students who made it to school this morning are sheltering in place. It's going to make a great photo essay," he told her. "Take lots of pics."

"And just exactly how am I going to get to the school?" inquired Lucy.

"I've arranged with Marcel Benn to give you a ride on one of his snowmobiles."

Lucy knew that Marcel owned the Ski-Doo dealership, and also sold motorcycles, ATVs, and Jet Skis, none of which interested her in the least. "Are you kidding? I'll freeze."

"It's just for a couple of blocks, Lucy. It'll be fun, trust me. Marcel will pick you up in five, and tell Phyllis to close up the office."

"Better make it fifteen. It'll take me at least that long to dress for the ride."

"Dress warm. Good idea," he said, ending the call.

Phyllis had wakened with a start, and Lucy passed along Ted's instructions while she got ready to leave. "I was thinking along those lines myself," she said. "I'd better call Wilf and tell him I'll be spending the night at the station. He's probably worrying about me," she said, reaching for her cell phone.

It took Marcel rather longer than five minutes to arrive, so Lucy was fully dressed and waiting by the door when he drove up on the snowmobile. The snow had piled up and was blocking the door, but Lucy gave a big push and got it open wide enough that she could wiggle through.

Marcel was dressed for the job in a snowmobile suit that covered him from helmet to boots, and he greeted her with a big smile. She thanked him for giving her the ride, and he told her he and other snowmobile owners had been out all day, rescuing stranded motorists. He handed her an extra helmet, and once that was in place, she climbed on the back of the machine and they were off, not exactly zooming, but gliding steadily through the deserted, snow-filled streets. The weak daylight was already fading on this brief December day and some of the houses and shops had a light or two from a generator, but most were dark, and the town was eerily quiet as the snow muffled sound, except for the snowmobile's engine.

The elementary school was partially lit, thanks to generators, and principal Jim Sykes greeted Lucy and Marcel at the front door and ushered them to the cafetorium, where the kids were gathered.

"We've got games and puzzles, and plenty of food," he assured them. "Parents can rest easy that their kids will be well taken care of. We've even got cots for the night, since this is an emergency shelter for the community."

"Are you expecting folks to come in for the night?" she asked.

"Not really. Most everybody is snowbound at home, and people around here are well equipped to handle power outages. If they don't have a generator, they've got candles and flashlights and fireplaces or woodstoves. Snow isn't exactly a novelty in this part of the country."

Lucy agreed, aware that Bill and Zoe were tucked up cozily in the house on Red Top Road, where Bill always joked they'd have to watch TV by candlelight. "Is it okay if I interview a few of the kids?" asked Lucy.

"Sure. Just check with me after, since some parents haven't given permission for their kids to be mentioned in media."

Marcel went in the kitchen, where some of the teachers were having coffee, and Lucy got to work snapping photos of the cozy scene. The kids seemed in high spirits, enjoying this change from the usual routine. "We've got hot chocolate," announced one little boy, "with marshmallows."

"And they're going to give us pizza for dinner," said another.

"And there's no homework, since we can't go home," volunteered a little girl with braids.

"But we'll be able to go home tomorrow," said one little boy, probably only in kindergarten or first grade and sounding a bit anxious.

"It can't snow forever," declared his friend, a solemn little girl with curly hair.

"That's right," agreed Lucy, who was beginning to think that the snow might, in fact, never stop until it reached the eaves of the houses, requiring people to tunnel from place to place.

But when she and Marcel left the school, they noticed that the snowfall was diminishing, and the huge flakes had given place to tiny little specks of glitter that danced in the snowmobile's headlights. "A good sign," said Marcel, pointing to the sky where a few stars had appeared and the moon was rising. "So, where to, madam? Do you want to go back to the office?"

"I guess I better make sure Phyllis closed up the office and remembered to unplug the computers in case there's a surge when the power comes back on," she told him. "Then I'm planning on going across the street to the police department for the night."

Marcel smiled. "I've heard the jail is pretty cozy."

"Better than the *Pennysaver* office, that's for sure. And I'll be right in the thick of things, it's a reporter's dream. If anything newsworthy happens, I'll be on the spot."

"Okay," said Marcel, starting the engine. Lucy hopped

on the back of the machine and they were off. This time the ride was a lot more enjoyable, since the wind had died down and the town looked magical, covered in a thick blanket of snow. Soon, she knew, the plows would be out, followed promptly by the electric company trucks, and life would go back to normal. But for the moment it was like going back in time. Except she wasn't riding in a horse-drawn sleigh, but on the back of a gasoline-guzzling, noisy machine.

Chapter Nine

Within a few minutes they arrived at the office, which was now completely dark. "Are you sure you want to go in?" asked Marcel. "I can have you over to the police department in two secs."

"Yeah. I'll feel better if I know things are secure, and I've got the flashlight on my phone."

"Well, I'll wait for you."

"There's no need. The storm's over and a little exercise will do me good."

"Okay," he said, giving her a wave and driving off.

Lucy tramped through the deep snow to the door, which was unlocked. Even so, she had a bit of a struggle opening it because the snow was piled up against it. No wonder Phyllis had decided not to lock it, she thought, figuring that nobody was out and about, and Lucy might need to retrieve something before heading over to the police station for the night.

No harm done, thought Lucy, when she'd scooped enough snow away with her gloved hands and finally got the door open enough so she could squeeze through. She'd just make sure everything was switched off, unplug the computers and printers, and then she'd make sure to lock the door when she left. No big deal. So she flicked on the flashlight app on her phone and stepped inside, carefully closing the door behind her. Then she cast the light around and was surprised to see Phyllis, who was still sitting at her desk.

"What are you doing here in the dark?" she asked, but at the same time realizing something was very wrong. Phyllis's eyes were huge, and she couldn't answer because her mouth was covered with shipping tape. The shiny tape was also wrapped around her shoulders and upper arms, fastening her to her desk chair.

Lucy whirled around and reached for the door, intending to run for help. Before she could even yell, she was caught from behind and a hand was clapped over her mouth. She kicked and squirmed, but was no match for whoever had grabbed her. She tried desperately to free herself, but couldn't catch her breath, since her assailant had covered both her mouth and nose with a gloved hand. She struggled frantically and tried to pull the hand away from her face, desperate for air, but felt herself weakening and soon all went dark.

When she came to, she was trussed up like Phyllis in cello packing tape. Her mouth was taped shut, her arms were fixed to a chair, and her ankles were bound. She was still dressed in her parka, though she'd lost her hat, so she wasn't cold, but she did have a terrible headache. Her heart was racing, she was dizzy and sweaty, and she knew she'd pass out again if she didn't calm down. Slow, steady breaths, she told herself, that was the ticket.

Her captor was holding her phone, which lit his face, and she realized he looked familiar. Like someone she'd known a long time ago, who had aged. It took a few minutes, but it finally came to her: Philip Ratcliffe. But how had he gotten out of jail? What was he doing in Tinker's Cove?

Then the pieces began to fall into place. She remembered that Ted went to the parole hearing, which was scheduled for today, at the courthouse in Gilead. The hearings usually took place in the state prison, but the Holmes family had requested the change because Sally's mother was too ill to travel. Not only had she lost her daughter, but she'd been diagnosed with ALS soon after. Her condition had recently deteriorated to the point that she was wheelchair-bound and required oxygen to breathe.

Somehow, she concluded, Ratcliffe had managed to escape. Perhaps a crash due to the snow? Perhaps a mistake? A moment's distraction and the convict had seized his chance. But what now? Why had he chosen the newspaper office to hunker down from the storm? And what was going to happen to her and Phyllis?

"I'm not gonna hurt you," he said. "All I want is a car. Have you got a car?"

Lucy nodded and tilted her head toward the street, where her SUV was parked.

"Keys?"

Again she motioned with her head toward the door, where she'd dropped her bag in her struggle with Ratcliffe. He used the light on her phone, flashing it around in the doorway, and when he spotted her purse, he grabbed it. The keys were in an outer pocket and he found them easily, then pressed the fob, and the lights on the car flashed outside the window. "Soon as they plow the street, I'm outta here. So relax and nobody gets hurt."

Lucy nodded her assent. She was still terrified, but she felt somewhat reassured that she and Phyllis had a good chance of getting out of this situation alive. Losing the car was a small price to pay, she decided, concentrating on those deep, regular breaths. She could see a bit more now, since her eyes had adjusted to the dark. The moon was out, too, and its dim light was reflected on the snow. She could make out Phyllis's shape, behind her desk, as well as Ratcliffe, who was standing by the window, peering out at the street. When he whirled about suddenly, she flinched.

"Is there any food? Anything to eat?"

Lucy thought it was worth trying to get the gag off her mouth, so she nodded and made a noise in her throat, trying to communicate the message that she'd tell him if he removed the tape.

"Don't yell, okay?"

She nodded again and he gave the tape a painful yank, which she figured meant she certainly wouldn't need to wax her upper lip anytime soon. "There are some crackers on the shelf under the coffeepot."

Once again he searched the office with the flashlight until he found the coffee station and the two packs of crackers. "Is this all?"

"Sorry." Lucy spoke softly, careful not to alarm her captor. "You can take the tape off Phyllis's mouth, too. She won't make a peep."

"That so?" he demanded, lighting Phyllis's face and getting a nod.

"Okay. But I'm warning you. This tape can go back real fast."

Phyllis nodded again and he ripped the tape off her mouth, causing her to yelp with pain. Panicked, she gave him a pleading look.

He responded by apologizing, "Uh, sorry."

"It's okay," she whispered, watching with huge eyes as he returned to the window and peered through the old-fashioned wood blinds. Then he ripped open one of the packs of crackers and began eating them.

"What the hell's keeping them from plowing?" he muttered, his mouth full. "The storm's over."

Lucy found herself agreeing with him. She couldn't imagine why the town's DPW crew was delaying; they were usually out with the plows the minute the snow stopped falling. She had an awful suspicion that the workers might be getting some rest, since they'd plowed earlier in the day, and would get back on the roads closer to morning. That meant she and Phyllis would be spending a very uncomfortable night. It also meant that Ratcliffe's escape would be much riskier, since he wouldn't have the cover of darkness and would have to make his way in daylight. He would know that state police, local police, sheriffs, everybody, would be looking for him; he was an escaped felon, a convicted killer, also a kidnapper, so he'd probably take her or Phyllis with him. He'd figure that a hostage would be his best ticket to freedom.

"So, how did you get away?" she asked, hoping to get him to talk with her. That's what they said you were supposed to do in the unlikely event that you were taken hostage and she figured it was worth a try. "You had the parole board hearing today, right? I heard it didn't go so well?"

He snorted and tossed the wrapper on the floor. "A joke. There's no way I'm ever going to get parole. So when I saw a chance, I took it."

"What happened?"

"They were taking me out of the building, the courthouse. There were two guards, one on either side of me. It was snowing real hard, you couldn't see too good, and the one guy slipped and went down. I punched the other guy—"

"Weren't you handcuffed?"

"Guess they forgot, or maybe they figured it was too much trouble to get 'em on over the gloves and everything. I don't know. It was a big mistake because I was gone before they knew what happened." He grinned. "Stupid cops even left the engine running on the van, warming it up."

"Lucky for you."

Ratcliffe shrugged and shook his head. " 'Course I don't know my way around here, I just followed the best roads, the ones with less snow, but after a while, the snow was too heavy for the van, so I had to hoof it. I saw a sign for this Tinker's Cove business district, I figured I'd find some shelter. When I got to this street here, I tried the doors and this one opened. I shoulda kept going, found a place with food, maybe a generator." He started to unwrap the second packet of crackers, then stopped. "Got any water?"

"There's a cooler over there."

He clomped across the office and Lucy heard the sound of running water as he filled one of the paper cups. "Say, you want some?" he asked.

"Sure," said Lucy, shocked to her core by this desperate escaped convict's thoughtfulness.

He brought a cup over to her and held it while she drank, then did the same for Phyllis.

"Are you sure you're a ruthless fugitive?" asked Phyllis.

"I'm innocent. I'm not a bad guy. I mean, I've done some stuff, but I never saw that girl they said I killed. I was framed. I know everybody says that, but in my case it's true. I don't deserve to spend the rest of my life in prison and I'm not going back." He went back to the window and peered out at the snow-filled street. "I'm not going back, no matter what."

"What time is it?" asked Phyllis.

"Around five-thirty," he said, still at the window.

"Any signs of life out there?" asked Lucy. It seemed possible to her that Ratcliffe had been tracked to the office and some sort of operation to capture him might be in the works. Maybe Marcel had noticed something amiss and had gone for help.

"Nuthin'. It's dead out there."

So much for that idea, she decided, discarding any thought of rescue. It would be nigh impossible for a SWAT team to get to Tinker's Cove, much less plan a stealth operation. She resigned herself to a long night in the chair, which was getting pretty uncomfortable. Her legs were beginning to ache and she longed to stretch them. "My legs are cramping," she said. "Any chance you could loosen them?"

"Uh, no. Sorry. Can't risk it."

"Really, you could. I'm not going to cause you any trouble. In fact," she added, hoping to convince Ratcliffe she wasn't a threat, "I'm kind of on your side."

"Right," he scoffed.

"Really. People get railroaded all the time. I'm a reporter and I've seen it happen too often. And I remember your trial. It wasn't fair. We even printed a letter from a retired prosecutor saying exactly that. There was a lot of anger and grief in the community and people wanted closure. They wanted to blame somebody for Sally Holmes's murder. The trial should've been moved to someplace where there hadn't been so much news coverage, where people didn't know the family."

Ratcliffe stepped back from the window and went over to Ted's desk, where he plunked himself down heavily into the swivel chair. "Somebody shoulda told that parole board," he said. "All they heard was a lot of crying from that girl's family, about how the father can't work because the mom is sick—she was in this fancy wheelchair—and the brother has PTSD." He sighed. "I've got PTSD every morning when I wake up and see that I'm still in that lousy, stinking cell."

A noise, the sound of an engine, was heard in the street and Ratcliffe dashed to the window, peeking out. As they listened, the sound grew louder, the scrape of a plow could be heard, and then flashing yellow lights lit up the office. "Finally," he said. "It's about time."

Lucy watched as the light of the plow moved along the window and disappeared down the street, leaving it lit only by the moon once again.

"That's my ticket," he exclaimed. "I'm outta here."

"What about us? You can't leave us tied up here all night."

He stared at Lucy. "Okay. This is what I'll do. I'll cut one hand loose, if you promise to wait till I'm gone. Then you can work yourself free. Deal?"

"I promise."

True to his word, Ratcliffe found the scissors in Lucy's pencil jug and quite carefully snipped some of the tape holding her right hand to the chair. She was still trussed up pretty tightly, but she knew she'd be able to eventually free herself and Phyllis. "Thanks," she said as he tossed the scissors onto her desk and headed for the door.

"Sayonara," he declared, opening the door. A sudden bang, a pop, was heard and he was propelled backward onto the floor, where he lay motionless.

A shocked cry escaped from Lucy's lips and Phyllis's too. "What the . . . ?" she said as the lights went on and a SWAT team swarmed into the office. Officer Sally Kirwan was right behind them and bounded across the office to Lucy, asking if she was okay. Then she got to work freeing Lucy from the tape. Her uncle, Police Chief Jim Kirwan, was doing the same for Phyllis. A SWAT team member was on his knees, checking Ratcliffe for signs of life. Finding none, he declared, "That was a clean shot. Got him right in the heart."

Lucy found she was suddenly trembling all over, and tears were filling her eyes. "It's okay, you're safe now," said Sally. "He got what he deserved."

Lucy wrapped her arms across her chest, hugging herself, and a silver blanket was wrapped around her. She was safe, it was true, but except for those first few minutes when she'd struggled with Ratcliffe and the panic she'd experienced when she found herself in captivity, she'd never really felt in danger. She didn't know if Ratcliffe was truly innocent or not, nobody could know that, but she didn't think he deserved to die.

"It's okay," repeated Officer Sally.

But Lucy knew it wasn't. It wasn't okay.

Chapter Ten

Officer Sally gave Lucy a lift home in the department's all-wheel-drive truck, chatting excitedly the whole way. "We had the office under observation right from the start," she said. "It's right across the street and you know how it is with a big snowstorm, you keep checking out the window to see if it's letting up or not. We'd gotten the APB about Ratcliffe escaping from the courthouse, and when Barney saw him staggering down the street and into the newspaper office, we knew where he was. But we knew Phyllis was there, and then you showed up, so we had to figure out what to do. The state cops were really great, they helicoptered the SWAT team in, they landed the copter in the parking lot by the cove, and we made sure there was nothing that would alarm Ratcliffe. We even kept the power off and didn't plow the street, so he was isolated. It was a brilliant plan, if you ask me. They figured he'd make a run for it as soon as the street was plowed, the tip-off was when he flashed the lights on your car. So the sniper was ready and everybody was in place when he decided to make a run for it."

"He wasn't armed," said Lucy. "They didn't have to shoot him."

"Procedure. That kill was completely justified. He was

a convicted felon, a murderer, and was considered armed and dangerous. That guard he knocked out has a concussion, and the other one broke his leg. We don't take chances with guys like that. Believe me, it's all for the best. Our top priority during the entire op was guaranteeing the safety of the hostages—you and Phyllis."

Lucy didn't like feeling that she bore some responsibility for Ratcliffe's death. Maybe it was the Stockholm syndrome? Maybe she'd begun to believe he might be innocent? Or maybe it was simply her deep conviction that he was a human being, a human being who'd made mistakes, maybe even did terrible things, but that didn't mean he deserved to be shot. The SWAT team could have easily overpowered him. She thought about it all that sleepless night, reliving the moment when he opened the door and was shot.

Lucy was up before dawn, clicking away on her laptop in search of that letter from the retired prosecutor that had caused such a flap. When she found it, she discovered with a shock that the author was none other than Howard White, the man she'd interviewed at Heritage House about his former classmate Dorcas Pritchett.

The sun was bright and the roads were nearly clear of snow when Bill gave her a ride into town so she could retrieve her SUV. They worked together to clear the snow from the car and then he left to pick up tile for the master bath at the home center. She returned to Heritage House to finally get the interview she'd been putting off for so long.

"You're back," Howard White said, welcoming her to his little efficiency apartment. "Come on in."

"I met Philip Ratcliffe," she said, seating herself on his couch.

"I heard, it's all over the local news," he said, taking his usual seat, a wing chair angled toward the TV, which was playing NECN. A table next to the chair was piled with newspapers and magazines. "What did you think about him?" he asked, picking up the remote and turning off the TV.

"I don't know. It's possible he killed Sally, it's also possible he was framed. I'm really confused. I can't believe they shot him dead, right in front of me." She sighed. "What do you think? You wrote that he didn't get a fair trial. What's the remedy? How can we ever have a justice system that's completely fair? How can we be certain if someone's innocent or guilty?"

"We can't," he replied. "All we can do is try, that's why the standard is *beyond a reasonable doubt*. I do believe that people act on their deepest beliefs and convictions, they do try to do the right thing, but we're all flawed. We all have emotions and prejudices and opinions, and sometimes those things get in the way of impartial, thoughtful judgment." He tented his fingers and smiled at her. "I never said Ratcliffe was innocent, I only said that he didn't get a fair trial." He paused. "I've studied it pretty closely and in the end I think he really was guilty."

"He didn't seem like a murderer last night," said Lucy.

Howard shrugged and rubbed his swollen, arthritic knuckles. "He's probably changed. It all happened over twenty years ago. He may even have repressed memories of the entire thing. He may have truly believed in his innocence. It's amazing what the human mind can justify, the ways we can rationalize terrible behavior."

"I know. You're right." She stood up to go. "But something's wrong when you're taken hostage, and the worst part, the most traumatic part, is getting rescued."

He chuckled. "I think that may be a more common reaction than you think." He took her hand. "It could have ended very differently. You were saved. Now go and live your best life."

"Thanks," she said, giving his hand a squeeze. "You've really helped me."

"Anytime," he said with a wave as she stepped through the door and walked down the long hall.

Lucy was thoughtful as she drove to the office, where she found that Phyllis was taking the day off. "Her husband says she's pretty shaken up," said Ted, who was sitting at the antique rolltop desk he inherited from his grandfather. He looked her over. "How are you doing?"

"Okay, I guess," admitted Lucy. "Still processing everything that happened."

"That's understandable." Ted nodded thoughtfully. "Best way to do that is probably to write about it. How about a first-person account? I can post it online."

Lucy couldn't believe what she was hearing. "You're kidding, right?"

Ted was absolutely serious. "No. I'll need it in an hour."

"I'll do what I can," said Lucy. "No promises."

When she settled herself at her desk, where the chair still bore torn strips of cello tape, Lucy had to fight the urge to flee. Instead, she carefully peeled off the tape and wadded it into a ball, then sat down carefully, feeling a bit fragile, as if she might break. *I don't know if I can do this,* she thought, fingering the small pile of papers on the desk pad and staring at her blank computer screen.

She bent her head, eyes closed, and concentrated on breathing in and out. She thought of her happy place, the glassy blue pond surrounded by lush green trees that she always pictured when they took her blood pressure. After a bit, imagining that it was 110 over 70, she opened her eyes and saw that Poppy had been true to her word and had faxed her Doris Pritchett's will.

It was only two pages long, and most of it was the usual legalese about settling debts and being in her right mind. Lucy scanned it quickly and got to the important part: the disposition of assets. There she was shocked to see that Doris had left all her worldly possessions to a man named Gilbert Brown. "GB"? The very person who had sent her the Christmas card? On a whim she googled Gilbert Brown and a news story featuring him popped right up.

According to this account, datelined Auburn, New York, he was one of the first persons wrongfully convicted of a crime to be exonerated by DNA evidence uncovered by the Innocence Project. The story said he had originally been misidentified by a witness, who wasn't named, but who Lucy suspected was Doris Pritchett. Sentenced to life, he served thirty-one years in prison, but was looking forward to starting a new life with his family in Geneva, New York.

Lucy immediately picked up her phone and dialed directory assistance, which provided Gilbert Brown's number and offered to dial it for her. She could hardly contain her excitement as she listened to the rings; she was finally going to talk to "GB" and get the story behind the Christmas card. However, she was in for a disappointment. In the end all she got was an answering machine's message. Sighing, she left her name and number, then stood up and got herself a drink of water.

"How's it going?" asked Ted, looking up from his desk.

"It's not," said Lucy, taking a swallow and remembering how Philip Ratcliffe had held the paper cup for her so she could drink. Then she drank the rest, tossed the cup into the trash, and put on her coat.

"What are you doing?" demanded Ted.

"I don't know, but I'm not doing this," she said, jamming her hat on her head and walking out the door, avoiding the freshly-scrubbed, but still-stained, place on the floor where Ratcliffe had fallen and bled the night before.

Once out of the office, and in her car, Lucy didn't know what she wanted to do or where she wanted to go. She finally started the engine and drove the block or two to Sue's house, not sure that she was even home. When she pulled up in front of the big old Captain's home, which was lavishly decorated with a huge wreath on the front door and smaller wreaths and electric candles in every window, she saw that Sue was just leaving. She honked the horn and Sue joined her in the car, leaning across the center console and giving her a hug.

"How are you? That was some day you had."

"I'm kind of a mess," confessed Lucy. "I can't concentrate."

"I think that's pretty normal." She squeezed Lucy's hand. "I was just going over to the Christmas Free Store, want to come along?"

Lucy felt her spirits lifting. "Yeah. I do."

In the remaining days leading up to Christmas, Ted called every morning to ask if she was coming in to work, and every morning she said she didn't think so. Then she went over to the free store to help distribute the toys, or worked alongside Bill on the master suite. She learned how to lay tile, she mastered the caulking gun, and she happily painted walls the palest of pale blues with crisp white trim. When Christmas Eve arrived, they finally moved into the master suite, temporarily making do with the old bedding and curtains. Lucy did splurge on new towels for the gorgeous master bath, but she had decided to wait until the January white sales to buy new linens for the bedroom. She was plumping up the pillows when Bill came into the room with some lightbulbs for the new fixtures.

"How do you like it?" he asked.

"It's great. It's the best Christmas present ever." She smiled at him. "No more bumped heads."

"I'm sure I lost quite a few IQ points over the years."

"Me too," said Lucy, wondering if she'd ever be ready to go back to her job at the newspaper.

"Sara's here!" yelled Zoe, so they hurried downstairs to greet her. Then they were off to church for the candlelight service, which Lucy always loved. There was something magical about the old church on Christmas Eve, with the piney scent from the evergreens arranged on the windowsills, the beloved carols, and the familiar story of the baby born in the stable. The best part was when the lights were turned out and the flame from a single candle was passed from person to person as the churchgoers sang "Silent Night." Then the sanctuary's darkness gradually gave way to the shared, flickering candlelight and everyone looked radiant and happy in that beautiful, magical moment.

When they returned home, Lucy got busy in the kitchen, setting out cookies and eggnog, while Bill went in the family room and started the fire. Zoe and Sara were with him, sorting the Christmas stockings and catching up with each other's news. Lucy had just returned the eggnog to the fridge when her phone rang and she grabbed it, thinking it was probably Toby, calling from Alaska, or Elizabeth, calling from Paris, but instead heard a strange male voice.

"I got your message. I'm Gilbert Brown."

Lucy sat down at the kitchen table. "Thanks for getting back to me. I called because I found a Christmas card that

I think you sent to Doris Pritchett. Do you remember that?"

"I sure do. She's the one who sent me to jail. She lied about me and I was very angry with her for a very long time." He paused. "You could've knocked me over with a feather when I got that check from the lawyers. Nearly half-a-million dollars. In the end Doris did right, and I gotta say, a half-million dollars buys a lot of forgiveness."

"So you've forgiven her?"

"Truth is, I forgave her before I got the money, long before. In prison you have a lot of time to think, you gain perspective, and I realized she was pressured to lie by her boyfriend at the time. He was the true killer. It was a bar fight, you know, and I was there, but I didn't kill anybody. I think she was terrified of him, he was real mean. She didn't get free of him until he died in a motorcycle accident. She was hurt, too, and spent months in the hospital. That's what she told me when she came to see me in jail and apologized. She was actually the one who got me involved with the Innocence Project."

"That's some story," said Lucy, who was itching to write it up for the paper. "Do you mind if I write this up and share it? I work for a little Maine newspaper."

"I don't have a problem with that. I'm free and easy these days. Fine and dandy. I wake up every morning with a song in my heart. I feed the birds, breathe the good clean air. Every day is Christmas."

"Do you want that card? As a reminder?"

"No, ma'am. You can just tear that thing up. Will you do that for me?"

"I sure will," promised Lucy.

"Merry Christmas to you," he said.

"And a happy New Year, new life to you."

Lucy already had the lead sentence of the story in her mind when she plucked the card from her purse and carried it into the family room, along with the tray of cookies and eggnog. Bill was poking at a log in the fireplace, where he had a nice blaze going, and the girls were relaxing on the sectional, where four big red plush stockings were arranged in a neat pile.

"I have to do something before we hang up the stockings," she said, setting the tray down on the coffee table. Then she joined Bill at the fireplace and tossed the Christmas card with its hateful message into the fire. She stood and watched as it curled and blackened, finally bursting into flame and sending fear and hate and anger right up the chimney. When it was gone, she smiled and announced, "Now let's get those stockings up! Now it's really Christmas!"

DEATH OF A
CHRISTMAS CAROL

Lee Hollis

Chapter One

Hayley could never have imagined in her wildest dreams that one simple Christmas card would alter the lives of so many people forever.

But it did.

And in dramatic fashion.

It all started on a blisteringly cold, gusty winter night in mid-December at the *Island Times* newspaper office on lower Main Street. The sky was already dark by four fifteen in the afternoon. The office holiday party was not scheduled to begin until six thirty, so Hayley still had time to get everything ready before the staff showed up to celebrate the end of another year of local news reporting.

It had become somewhat of a tradition for Hayley to take charge and plan the annual Christmas gathering. Luckily, she had some help this year. One of her besties, Mona, had generously donated enough lobster and crabmeat from her seafood business for some of the tasty appetizers Hayley had been tirelessly preparing for the last two days. These included a Spicy Tuna Dip, Blue Cheese–Stuffed Shrimp, and a Crab–Brie Cheese Ball. Hayley had sent Mona over to her house to pick up all the food she had prepared earlier. Mona was now setting them out on the serving table, but leaving them wrapped in tinfoil to keep the food warm until the guests arrived.

Meanwhile, Hayley was busy arranging her homemade Christmas cookies on a platter and keeping a watchful eye on Mona. She wanted to make sure Mona didn't scarf down half of her holiday cheesecake before anyone else had the chance to try it, like she had done last year when she unexpectedly crashed the party.

At least this year, Mona had been officially invited. Editor in chief Sal Moretti's one rule was that the holiday party was for employees of the paper only. However, everyone was welcome to bring one guest. Since Hayley and Bruce both worked at the *Island Times,* this year Hayley had made Mona her plus one. How could she not? Mona had given her hundreds of dollars of free seafood!

Her second helper assisting with party preparations, Sal's wife of twenty-six years, Rosana Moretti, was at the moment standing on top of a small ladder, up on her tippy toes. Her arms were stretched as far as they could be as she tried pinning mistletoe on the top of the door frame leading to the back bull pen. She was a tiny thing, barely cracking five feet tall. She had a mop of grayish hair and thick black glasses that made her look like an aged version of the bookish Velma character from all those *Scooby-Doo* episodes and movies Hayley watched as a kid.

Hayley suddenly noticed the ladder teetering from side to side as Rosana, a piece of Scotch tape attached to her right index finger, her tongue protruding out of her mouth as she concentrated, tried in vain to tape the string tied to the piece of mistletoe to the door frame. She suddenly lost her balance and started to topple over.

"Rosana!" Hayley squealed.

"I got her!" Mona cried. She was much closer to the ladder and managed to dash over in time to catch Rosana in her thick arms. Mona effortlessly set the woman down as if she weighed no more than a rag doll.

"Rosana, I told you to let Mona do that!" Hayley scolded. "She's taller than you."

"I know, I just didn't want to bother her," Rosana said meekly. "I'm sorry to cause such a fuss."

"It's fine. Don't worry about it. Just be careful," Hayley admonished.

Hayley adored Rosana. Unlike her blustery, loudmouthed, hot-tempered husband, Sal's wife was soft-spoken, sweet, never without a kind word, and was always concerned with keeping the peace.

The saying was true.

Opposites did indeed attract.

That old cliché probably explained Hayley and Bruce's surprising marriage as well.

Mona gently pushed Rosana out of the way, climbed up the ladder, and, without breaking a sweat, easily taped the mistletoe so it hung down from the top of the door frame perfectly. When Mona stepped back down, she turned to Hayley and barked, "When can we have some cheese-cake?"

"When the guests arrive, Mona, and not a moment before. Got it?" Hayley warned.

"That's two hours from now. I'm never going to make it," Mona groaned. "By the way, Dennis is coming. He's Bruce's plus one."

This unexpected news blindsided Hayley—not that Bruce had invited Mona's husband, Dennis, to be his guest, but that Dennis had actually agreed to get off the couch for once and appear in public. And at a Christmas party of all things! Dennis hated mingling and talking to people. He rarely talked to Mona. In fact, the only recent time Hayley had heard him speak was when she was over at their house earlier in the fall. Dennis was yelling at some Red Sox player on TV for striking out at the top of the ninth inning.

"I know, I know, I was as shocked as you. I don't know what's gotten into him lately. Suddenly he's acting like he's a real person in this world. Maybe he's dying and just hasn't gotten around to telling me yet," Mona said.

"Mona, don't say such things!" Rosana gasped, mortified.

"Trust me, Rosana, he's not going anywhere. The man eats and drinks too much, never exercises, has a negative attitude most of the time, but he's as healthy as a horse. I know God will kill me off first and let him live to be a hundred just to be funny!" Mona barked.

"It's Christmas! Let's talk about something more pleasant! Did you see the sweater I knitted for Sal? He wore it to the office today," Rosana chirped.

"Oh, yes, the one with the gingerbread man on it that says, 'Let's Get Baked'?"

"Isn't it adorable? I saw one like it on Pinterest, so I just had to make one for him myself."

Mona raised an eyebrow. " 'Let's Get Baked'? Do you know what that *really* means?"

Rosana nodded. "Yes. Sal loves eating my gingerbread cookies. I bake them every Christmas."

She clearly did not know the real meaning of the phrase.

Before Mona had a chance to explain to the naive Rosana that her homemade sweater was promoting the use of marijuana, Hayley quickly interjected, "You've done a wonderful job decorating the office, Rosana."

"Thank you, Hayley," Rosana beamed, glancing around and inspecting her work: the hanging Christmas ball tapestry, the flower tree, the blinking colored lights strung around the room.

Hayley spied Mona, who was about to covertly cut herself a piece of the cheesecake, when suddenly they heard a screeching voice coming from the back bull pen. "I saw you with my own eyes! You embarrassed me, yourself, and that poor woman you were accosting! Yes, you were, Leonard! There is no other word for it! You were *accosting* her!"

Hayley instantly recognized the voice. It was Andrea Cho, the *Island Times*'s new sports reporter who had moved down to Bar Harbor from Hampden in October with her husband, Leonard, to start working at the paper. Hayley believed Sal had hired her because she was his kindred spirit, outspoken and short-tempered. She was nice enough to Hayley, they got along just fine, but when it came to her henpecked, browbeaten husband, well, Hayley felt sorry for him. The few times she had seen them together, Andrea was always berating and belittling Leonard. In fact, she almost seemed to enjoy tormenting him.

"I wonder what he's done now?" Hayley asked absently, taking the last of her cookies out of the Tupperware container and arranging them on the platter.

"Oh, this has been going on all day," Rosana said. "I was here decorating during the lunch hour, and from what I could understand, apparently Andrea was out at the high school last night covering the boys' basketball game, where Leonard volunteers as assistant coach . . ."

"Yeah, I hear he's a real sports nut," Mona said.

Rosana lowered her voice, flicking her eyes around to make sure no one was around to hear. "Apparently, sports isn't the only thing he loves. He's also a big fan of the ladies. Andrea showed up and one of the varsity cheerleaders couldn't wait to tell her that Leonard had been shamelessly flirting with a woman who was watching the game in the stands."

"Who was the woman?" Hayley excitedly asked.

"She never mentioned a name. But Andrea's been calling him all day, yelling at him about it," Rosana said.

Suddenly, without warning, Andrea stormed out from the bull pen into the front office. Rosana, panicking, snatched one of Hayley's cookies and stuffed it in her mouth. "Oh, Hayley, these are delicious," she said, bits of cookie tumbling out of the sides of her mouth.

Hayley, Mona, and Rosana all struck awkward poses, desperately pretending they had not been eavesdropping on Andrea's intense phone conversation.

Andrea was an attractive, petite Asian woman. Her dark hair was pulled back in a ponytail, and she was wearing jeans and a bulky sweater. She marched over to the table with the big punch bowl of eggnog and stared at the one small bottle of Bacardi rum next to it.

"That isn't going to be nearly enough rum for the eggnog," she announced.

"Maybe Leonard could pick some up on his way over," Rosana chirped before her eyes bugged out as she realized she had just brought up his name.

Andrea rolled her eyes and snapped, "Leonard's not coming tonight."

"Oh, that's too bad. Is he sick?" Hayley asked, not at all convincing as she tried acting clueless.

"He's fine. He's just not invited," Andrea said, scowling. "We definitely need more rum. In fact, we're going to need lots of it, if I'm ever going to make it through this party tonight."

"Mona's got her truck outside. Maybe she can swing by the Shop 'n Save and pick some up," Hayley suggested.

"Forget it. I'll go get it. I need the fresh air. It's way too hot in here," Andrea said before brusquely pushing past them and out the door.

"She didn't even put on a jacket. It's like twenty degrees outside," Rosana said, shivering.

The door had not yet closed when they heard a man's voice outside say, "Merry Christmas, Andrea."

She didn't bother to answer him.

After a few moments, a young man in his midtwenties— tall, good-looking, wavy blond hair, bundled up in an L.L.Bean parka—ambled in with a bright smile on his face. "Good evening, ladies."

"Hi, David," Hayley and Rosana both said.

Mona just grunted.

Like Andrea Cho, David Pine was also a relatively new hire at the *Island Times*. He was a Maine native, his family from Bangor, and he had studied journalism at the University of Maine at Orono before interning at his hometown paper, the *Bangor Daily News*. He took an interest in crime reporting, and when the regular reporter was on vacation, he had written a few articles, which had impressed Sal.

Always scouting new talent, Sal had hired him to come down to the island and work at the paper. David was an avid kayaker and loved the idea of living near the ocean, so he had jumped at the chance. Bruce had quickly taken him under his wing and the two worked closely together on a few stories over the ensuing months. Bruce was equally dazzled by David's writing talent and considered him a protégé.

At first, Hayley worried the ambitious young cub reporter might be out for her husband's job, but Bruce didn't seem too worried. Not to mention the fact that Bruce had been making some noises lately about leaving the paper and trying his hand at writing true crime books. So things just might work out fine in the end anyway.

"Is something wrong with Andrea?" David asked.

They all looked at each other warily and said in unison, "No."

David cocked an eyebrow. "Is that a firm 'no,' or do you just not want to tell me?"

"It's more of an 'Ask *her* if you really want to know,'" Hayley answered firmly.

"Gotcha," David said, shaking off his parka to reveal a blue Oxford dress shirt with the sleeves rolled up and the collar open just enough to show off his smooth, muscled chest, which definitely got the attention of all three ladies in the room.

He then wandered over to the food table and perused all the delectable sweets. "Wow, this looks awesome."

"I get the first piece of cheesecake, so don't even *think* about it!" Mona barked.

David raised his hands in the air. "I would never want to get on your bad side, Mona."

Hayley smiled. "Help yourself to a cookie. We've got plenty."

David picked up a sugar cookie in the shape of a Christmas tree and took a bite. Once he swallowed, he said, "Oh, before I forget . . ." He reached into the pocket of his jacket, extracted a red envelope, and handed it to Hayley.

"Is this from you?" Hayley asked, brightening.

David shook his head. "No. Carol asked me to give it to you. To all of you."

"All *three* of us?" Rosana asked, confused.

David nodded. "I was over at her house earlier. She knew you would all be here setting up for the party. It's a Christmas card from her."

There was a pause.

Hayley's mind raced.

The rumors she had heard were true after all.

Carol Waterman, a local woman in her late forties, had

been spotted around town on the arm of David Pine, a man nearly half her age. No one was particularly surprised. Carol had a reputation for chasing after men young enough to be her son. There had been the twenty-year-old mechanic. The twenty-two-year-old house painter. The barely nineteen-year-old stock boy at the Shop 'n Save. Bruce had once joked that the Mount Desert Island High School yearbook was Carol Waterman's very own Tinder app.

"That's odd," Hayley heard herself saying. "Why would Carol give one Christmas card to the three of us?"

"Maybe she's just cheap," Mona said, shrugging.

Hayley turned to David, a perplexed look on her face. "And why would she have you hand deliver it?"

David shrugged. "I don't know. I just do what she tells me."

"I bet you do," Mona said, smirking.

"I thought Carol was coming tonight. She RSVP'd two days ago. Since she doesn't work here at the paper, I assumed she was attending as someone's guest. She could have just given it to us herself when she arrived."

"Who cares? I don't want to spend the whole night talking about Carol. You forgot napkins, Hayley. People are going to have to lick their fingers after eating your tuna dip. David, would you mind running to the store?" Mona asked.

"Not at all. Text me if you need anything else," David said, winking at them and then disappearing out the door.

There was another pause as they all stared at the red envelope in Hayley's hand.

"He seems like such a good kid," Mona remarked, shaking her head. "What in blazes does he see in that awful, stupid, shallow Carol Waterman?"

"Don't hold back, Mona. Tell us what you really think of her," Hayley said with a sarcastic edge.

"I just don't like the way she prances around town pretending she's as young and pretty as Meghan Markle," Mona snorted. "It's not becoming for a woman her age."

"Come on, Carol is a very attractive woman. I can see why all those boys would be taken with her," Hayley said.

"Well, I am never one to eavesdrop," Rosana whispered, completely ignoring the fact that she had been eavesdropping on Andrea Cho's phone calls with her husband all day. "But I overheard her talking to a girlfriend about how she was over dating boys and wanted to find a *real man,* someone 'more mature, with some miles on his odometer.' Those were her words, not mine."

"Good luck with that. All the older men in town are married or otherwise shacked up with someone. But I'm sure that won't stop Carol." Mona chortled.

"You talk about Carol as if she should have a scarlet *A* sewn onto her blouse, Mona. She's just trying to find a little happiness," Hayley said, feeling bad that they were mercilessly trashing her.

"Excuse me, Hayley, do you *not* remember what happened at the Way Back Ball last fall? You and Bruce had barely been married a few months and Carol was all over him, pawing him and stroking his face?"

"She came to the ball dressed as a 1920s flapper. She was just playing the part," Hayley said defensively.

Mona shot her a skeptical look.

"Aren't you going to open the card? I'm dying to know what she wrote," Rosana said, tapping her foot expectantly.

Hayley ripped open the red envelope and pulled out the card. The cover was a beautiful wreath, and in the center, *Season's Greetings* was printed.

Hayley opened the card and began reading the handwritten message.

Her mouth dropped open in shock.

"Well, go on, don't keep us in suspense. What does it say?"

Hayley looked up at them, her bottom lip quivering, a sick feeling in the pit of her stomach, and then she began reading out loud.

" 'To my Dear Friends, Hayley, Mona, and Rosana, Blessings, love, and peace to you all this holiday season. May the magic of Christmas fill every corner of your homes and hearts. If you haven't heard, I am moving away from Bar Harbor. I have so much to be grateful for this year, especially since one of you has given me the most wonderful gift that I will be taking with me as I embark on this exciting new journey: your husband!' "

Chapter Two

"This has to be some kind of joke," Hayley said, staring at the card.

Rosana snatched the card out of Hayley's hand and read the inscription for herself, her lips moving along as her eyes scanned the words. She finally looked up nervously. "It sounds real to me."

"Oh, Rosana, it can't be. David will be back soon from the store. We'll ask him. Maybe he's in on it," Hayley said, trying to reassure her and keep Rosana from devolving into full-on panic mode.

"I'm with Rosana. It sure doesn't sound like a joke to me," Mona said matter-of-factly, unconcerned.

"How do you know?" Hayley asked.

"Because Carol Waterman has no sense of humor," Mona huffed.

Rosana could not tear her eyes off the card. She just kept reading it over and over again. "Whose husband do you think she's talking about?"

"Carol is not running away with *anybody's* husband!" Hayley declared.

"But what if she *is* serious? I don't know what I would do if Sal left me for another woman!" Rosana cried, slapping a hand over her heart, as if she was suddenly suffering from palpitations.

"Well, I sure know what I would do if it was Dennis," Mona said.

"What?" Rosana gasped.

"Praise Jesus!" Mona shouted, getting down on her knees and clasping her hands together in prayer.

"Mona, you don't mean that!" Rosana howled.

"If Carol Waterman actually managed to get Dennis's fat butt off the couch, I'd hail her as some kind of miracle worker and I would be the first one in line to thank her!" Mona said, her eyes falling upon the still-untouched cheesecake on the dessert table as she slowly inched toward it.

"Mona, step away from the cheesecake," Hayley snapped before walking over to Rosana and putting an arm around her and giving her a slight squeeze. "Rosana, even if the card was true, it's definitely *not* Sal. I've worked for the man for over a decade. I know him pretty well. He's just not the cheating type."

Rosana, still visibly shaken, stared up into Hayley's eyes, desperately wanting to believe her. "I wish I could be as confident as you are."

"Has Sal ever given you one moment of doubt as to his fidelity in all the years you've been married?" Hayley asked.

Rosana broke away from Hayley and wandered over to the window, staring at the dark, deserted street outside. "Yes."

"Really?" Mona asked, suddenly interested.

Rosana nodded solemnly. "Once."

"*Rosana* . . ." Hayley was shocked.

Rosana slowly turned back around, clasped her hands together, and rested her fingers underneath her chin as she spoke. "About five years ago. We were hosting a Christmas party at our house. I believe you were there, Hayley. I remember you spent the whole evening bickering with Bruce."

"That makes perfect sense. We hated each other back then. He was the last person I ever thought I'd wind up marrying," Hayley said, laughing. "But I don't remember anything out of the ordinary happening that night . . ."

"Carol Waterman showed up," Rosana said quietly. "I don't remember inviting her. I assumed Sal had. I didn't think much of it at the time. I was so busy putting the food out and making sure everyone had a drink."

Mona flicked her eyes toward Hayley, intrigued to find out where this was going.

Rosana folded her arms, shivering at the memory. "She showed up with a present. The card was made out to both of us, but it was clearly meant to be a gift just for Sal."

"What was it?" Mona asked, filled with curiosity.

"A bottle of Johnnie Walker Scotch. The expensive kind. The blue label. I remember looking it up online and finding out it cost something like a hundred fifty dollars."

Mona whistled, impressed.

"In the box with the bottle were two glasses that were clearly labeled. From the Lucerne Inn."

The Lucerne Inn was a quaint two-hundred-year-old hotel tucked in the scenic hills between Bar Harbor and Bangor. Known for its eighteenth-century ambiance, the inn captured the spirit of the Maine Coast with its charm, spirit, and feel of romance. Many dignitaries, celebrities, and politicians frequented the hotel, and a host of weddings was held on its expansive grounds overlooking Phillips Lake and Bald Mountain.

"I don't understand the significance of the Lucerne Inn," Hayley said.

"Neither did I. But Sal sure did," Rosana lamented. "When he took one of the glasses out and looked at it, he and Carol exchanged these knowing glances and started laughing, as if they were sharing some kind of private joke."

Hayley balked at the suggestion. "Rosana, you don't think—"

"Think about it, Hayley. Sal drives up there all the time to interview state politicians holding fund-raisers in one of the ballrooms, or when he is writing pieces on celebrities or newsmakers who are staying at the Lucerne while passing through. He's been up there countless times. And you know how Sal can get. Once he's done with the interview, he heads straight to the bar to down a few Scotches. More often than not, he gets so drunk, he decides to check into a room for the night and sleep it off before driving home early the next morning. What if that was just the story he told me? What if Sal was really rendezvousing with Carol Waterman all those times?"

"It sounds like my mother's favorite old movie she made me watch with her on VHS when I was a little kid about a man and woman who were both married to other people, but they got together every so often to have sex. What was the name of it, *Same Time, Next Month?*" Mona asked.

"I think it was called *Same Time, Next Year,*" Hayley corrected her.

"If Sal was getting busy with Carol, I'd say he was doing it a lot more than just once a year," Mona said bluntly.

Hayley shot Mona a look, trying to alert her to the fact that she was hardly helping the situation.

"This makes absolutely no sense whatsoever," Hayley insisted. "Carol has always had a thing for strapping young studs half her age. Sal is many things, but he's *not* young!"

"And certainly no stud!" Mona added. "Or strapping, for that matter. What's his belt size, fifty-two?"

"Mona!" Hayley cried.

"What? I'm just trying to help."

Hayley rolled her eyes and spun back to Rosana, who was still processing what she had just heard.

"Maybe you're right," Rosana muttered.

"On the other hand, Carol could have been dating all those younger men only because the older guys in town were already married and unavailable. But maybe she finally decided she didn't like her limited options and just said, 'Screw it! I'll pursue men who are taken and see how far I get?'"

Hayley gave Mona a withering look. "Thank you, Mona."

Rosana was so upset that she had to sit down behind Hayley's desk. She planted her elbows on the desk and covered her face with her hands. "I can't get the image of him at that Christmas party out of my head. He was drunk on the spiked punch and he was acting like a smitten teenager around Carol, even before he saw those glasses from the Lucerne. How could I have been so stupid not to see it until just now?"

"Rosana, you're just speculating. You have not one shred of proof that Sal has been unfaithful," Hayley insisted. "You need to stay calm until David gets back and we can ask him about that silly card. Right, Mona?" Hayley turned to Mona and forcefully mouthed the words *Help me here.*

Mona finally spoke up. "Uh, yeah, sure. Sal's a stand-up guy. He would never do anything like that."

But it was obvious from Mona's expression that she, in

fact, had serious doubts and didn't necessarily believe a word she was saying.

And Hayley breathed deeply, willfully ignoring her own memory of an incident just last week that did not make her feel any better about this Christmas card from Carol Waterman.

Chapter Three

Rosana paced back and forth, her mind racing. "I just realized, Carol is re-creating the plot from that old film they show on Turner Classic Movies all the time. *A Letter to Three Wives!*"

"Never heard of it," Mona barked.

"Really? It's so good. It starred Ann Sothern, Linda Darnell, Jeanne Crain, and a very young Kirk Douglas," Hayley said.

"Is it in black and white?" Mona asked.

"Yes," Hayley answered.

"That's why I've never seen it," Mona said.

"Mona, do you know how many incredible films you've deprived yourself of just because you refuse to watch anything that wasn't filmed in color?"

"No, and I don't care. Who's got time to waste watching people running around who have been dead for years?" Mona scoffed.

Rosana continued pacing. "In the movie, a local woman nobody really likes writes three women a letter claiming she's going to run off with one of their husbands. That's exactly what's happening here!"

"All the more reason to believe Carol is just playing some kind of joke," Hayley insisted.

"No, my gut is telling me she's completely serious, and I know it's Sal, I just know it!" Rosana squealed, her eyes brimming with tears.

Mona raced over to the table and grabbed a knife. "Rosana, you need to calm the hell down. Here, have some cheesecake! It'll make you feel better. It'll make all of us feel better!"

"Mona! I know what you're doing!" Hayley cried. "You just want to eat my cheesecake!"

"No, Mona's right," Rosana muttered. "Sweets always bring me back to my happy place."

Mona held the knife inches from the cheesecake, staring at Hayley, waiting for the go-ahead. Hayley finally sighed and nodded, and Mona eagerly started carving out three big pieces. "So, how does the movie end?"

"It was true. The woman *was* planning to run away with one of the husbands, it definitely was not a prank, but I can't remember which one, and what ultimately happens!" Rosana moaned.

Hayley tried recalling the movie plot in her own mind. "I can't remember, either."

"Well, like I said, I've never seen it, so I can't help you," Mona declared.

Mona handed out the pieces of cheesecake on paper plates, and then with relish dove into her own piece with a plastic fork, but she stopped suddenly just before shoveling a large hunk into her mouth. "Oh no . . ."

Hayley stepped forward, concerned. "Mona, what is it?"

"I just remembered something," Mona mumbled.

"What? What?" Hayley cried.

Mona set the plate down on the table. "I didn't think much of it at the time. In fact, I forgot about the whole thing until just now."

"Is it about Carol?" Rosana urgently whispered.

Mona nodded. "It happened last fall, right after Labor Day. I came home from the shop and I found this wrapped gift on the front porch. It was addressed to Dennis. At first, I panicked, thinking I had forgotten his birthday, but then I remembered Dennis was born in March and a Pisces, which is probably why the man can never make up his mind about a damn thing! Anyway, I took the gift inside and gave it to Dennis, who was, big surprise, on the couch watching TV. He didn't want to open it in front of me, but I was curious, so I told him to open the friggin' gift already, and so he did."

"What was it?" Rosana gasped.

"A DVD boxed set of that old *Knight Rider* series about the talking car that starred David Hasselhoff. It was the complete collection, all the episodes. Dennis lit up like a friggin' Christmas tree! It was his all-time favorite show when he was a kid!" Mona recalled. "I asked who gave it to him, and, at first, he was real cagey, tried changing the subject. But you know me, once I'm curious about something, I'm like a terrier with a steak bone and won't let it go."

"Did he finally tell you?" Hayley said quietly.

Mona nodded, staring into space. "I got him to talk by threatening not to make him dinner. He'd make a terrible spy. He'd give up the nation's secrets for a box of Hamburger Helper."

"Let me guess," Hayley said. "Carol Waterman."

Mona folded her arms, a little disconcerted as she flashed back to the conversation. "I said to him, 'Dennis, why on earth would Carol Waterman be giving anything to *you*? And how would she know your favorite show was *Knight*

Rider?' Well, he hemmed and hawed a bit, but I kept pressing him, and he finally explained that Carol had just wanted to show her appreciation."

Rosana's eyes widened. "For *what?*"

"Dennis has a part-time landscaping business in the summer. Trust me, I'm the breadwinner in the family by far, but when it's sunny outside during July and August, it's our best chance to get Dennis's butt off the couch. He used to mow lawns and clip hedges back when he was a kid, so the last few years, he started making a few extra bucks for his six-packs of beer by taking on a few clients around town," Mona said.

"Carol Waterman being one of them," Hayley said as a distant memory involving Carol and Dennis began gnawing its way into her brain.

"I guess Dennis must have mentioned he liked *Knight Rider,* so she ordered the set from Amazon or something, gift-wrapped it, and left it on the doorstep for him." Mona shrugged. "I have to admit, it was the perfect present for someone who is the literal definition of a couch potato."

"If Dennis was only working in Carol's yard once a week, how would she know such a personal detail like his favorite TV show when he was growing up?" Rosana asked, suspicious.

"I don't know, Rosana! She just did!" Mona snapped, suddenly discombobulated, disturbed by the recollection of events. "I'm sure there's nothing to it, right, Hayley?"

Hayley nodded, but her mind was elsewhere.

Mona instantly noticed. "What, Hayley? What are you thinking about?"

"Nothing . . . I . . . It's nothing," Hayley said, waving away the memory.

"No, you're obviously thinking about *something*! Come on, tell us!" Mona yelled.

Hayley took a deep breath, not sure if she should proceed, but it was too late now. Both Mona and Rosana were on pins and needles. "I honestly don't want to add to the hysteria, because I really don't think this means anything—"

"Hayley!" Mona bellowed.

"I put it out of my mind at the time, since I didn't think Dennis would ever be capable of anything like that . . ."

Mona was now seething. "What did that lousy dog do?"

Hayley raised her hands. "Nothing. What I saw was probably one hundred percent innocent, but I remember last August I was driving to the bank to get some money from the ATM and I passed by Carol Waterman's house on the way. I was surprised to see Dennis sitting on her front porch with her and they were having some lemonade and they were laughing about something."

"Dennis laughed? I've been married to the man for over twenty years and I've never heard him laugh," Mona said.

Hayley took another sharp intake of breath. "Um, he was also—"

"Stop dragging it out, Hayley, tell us," Rosana begged.

"He was also shirtless."

There was a pause.

Hayley quickly followed up. "But it was superhot that day and I'm sure he was just taking a break from his yard work."

"So, was Carol rubbing Dennis's fat beer gut like Aladdin's lamp or what?"

"No, of course not!" Hayley said.

"Then I'm not worried. Is that all you've got?" Mona asked.

"Well, no," Hayley continued, sighing. "The sight of the two of them struck me as odd, and I kept staring. I didn't see where I was going, and the next thing I knew, I plowed my car right into Carol's mailbox at the end of her driveway."

Rosana tittered, unable to control herself.

"Needless to say, I was mortified, and I apologized profusely to Carol. Dennis was kind enough to fix it, and Carol offered me a glass of lemonade, which I declined. I remember choking on the strong scent of Carol's perfume. She said it was White Diamonds by Elizabeth Taylor. Her favorite. I heard Dennis say—"

Mona stepped forward and growled, "What did he say, Hayley?"

"He said . . . 'I wish Mona would wear perfume sometimes.' "

"He did not!" Rosana shrieked.

"Well, that's just stupid! What am I, competing to be a stupid Miss America? I don't need to smell nice! I haul lobster traps for a living!" Mona huffed.

"I know, it was just an offhanded comment he said under his breath. It totally meant nothing!" Hayley said.

"How did Carol react to that?" Mona asked quietly.

"She didn't say anything. She just had this proud look on her face, and this big knowing smile. It was almost as if . . ." Hayley considered her thought before cautiously proceeding. "It was almost as if she was enjoying the fact that I had seen the two of them on the porch."

There was yet another pause.

Hayley felt awful for bringing any of this up, but given the circumstances, she felt compelled. And as she eyed her best friend, who was usually so unruffled about most things, she could sense Mona was suddenly rattled by this revelation.

And Hayley knew Mona well enough to know that she was right now thinking, *Does Dennis actually have it in him to have an affair with another woman?*

Chapter Four

Hayley stared into the blinking colored lights of the cheap desktop plastic Christmas tree that Rosana had picked up at the Christmas Spirit Shop on Main Street. She could hear herself breathing, in and out, slowly, as if trapped inside her own head. Rosana was next to her saying something, but the words didn't make any sense. Her mind couldn't grasp anything at the moment; she found herself in some kind of momentary paralysis, or shock.

It had crept up on her so suddenly when she realized she had her own Carol Waterman story to share, an incident she had totally forgotten about, something she had brushed aside, unconcerned, as if it had meant nothing. But now, with the power of hindsight, and the two disturbing stories Rosana and Mona had both shared, it finally had found its way back into her mind and could no longer be suppressed. As she recounted the details, she knew in her gut that this was not a story to be summarily dismissed as innocent or inconsequential.

"Hayley, are you all right?" Rosana asked, presumably again, since she hadn't heard her the first time.

Hayley robotically turned to Rosana, who had a distinct look of worry on her face, fearing Hayley was ill or about to faint. "Yes, sorry."

"What is it? You look as if you've just seen a ghost," Rosana gasped.

"I . . . I remembered something that happened . . . just last week," Hayley said in a monotone voice.

Rosana and Mona exchanged inquisitive looks.

Hayley paused, making sure she recalled the events correctly, before proceeding. "I came home from work, and when I walked into the kitchen, I saw Bruce coming up from the basement. He was carrying one of those old turntables, the kind you play old vinyl records on."

Rosana and Mona were both nodding, eager to hear more.

"He dusted it off with an old dishrag and took it into the living room. I didn't even ask him what he was doing. I just went about making dinner. I was filling a pot with water to boil on the stove—I remember I was making spaghetti—and all of a sudden, I heard music blasting in the other room. I recognized the voice. Stevie Nicks. It was an old song from the 1970s.

"After putting the pot on the burner and turning on the stove, I went into the living room and found Bruce sitting on the couch, reading the back of an old record album. It was that classic Fleetwood Mac album *Rumours*. I think the song was 'Gold Dust Woman.' He was beaming. He looked so happy. I asked him if he had been thumbing through his old record collection that day, and he shook his head and said, 'No, it was a Christmas present from Carol Waterman.' "

Rosana gasped, throwing a hand to her heart.

"I know, I know, I just didn't think much about it at the time," Hayley said, sounding a little defensive.

"What do you mean you didn't think much about it?" Mona scoffed.

"I didn't have any reason to. Not then. But now—"

"What did you say to him?" Rosana asked, tapping her foot impatiently.

"Nothing at first. He said his father was a huge Fleetwood Mac fan and turned him onto them, and *Rumours* became his favorite album. He had lost his old vinyl copy one summer after packing for college and never replaced it. I just remember thinking at the time, 'How on earth does Carol Waterman know Bruce's favorite band is Fleetwood Mac, and I don't?'"

"So, did you *ask* him?" Mona bellowed.

Hayley nodded her head. "Yes, eventually. I didn't want to be the nagging, jealous type, so I waited until we were sitting at the dining table eating our spaghetti. I just casually threw it out there that I was surprised Carol knew he was such a big Fleetwood Mac fan when he was younger. He explained to me that they had run into each other at a used-record store in Ellsworth. She had been looking at a copy and he casually mentioned in conversation how much he loved the album. So she bought it for him, gift-wrapped it, and dropped it off at the house."

"It is *not* appropriate for a single woman to buy a Christmas present for a married man and *not* include his wife!" Rosana cried.

"I know . . . I didn't want to make a big deal out of it. Of course, I—I trust Bruce," Hayley stammered.

"Well, that's your first mistake!" Mona huffed. "No man should be trusted!"

"I need a drink!" Rosana wailed as she made a beeline for the spiked-eggnog bowl and poured herself a plastic cup full with the ladle.

"I remember asking him if I should be jealous and he just laughed, as if it was the most ridiculous thought in the world. He assured me they were just friends . . ." Hayley's voice trailed off as her mind wandered.

"I feel as if you're leaving something out," Mona said, eyes narrowing.

Hayley took a deep breath. "Bruce told me something. I didn't give it any serious thought at the time. I just found the idea so utterly ridiculous."

"What did he tell you?" Rosana demanded to know, tightening her grip on the plastic cup of spiked eggnog.

Hayley took a deep breath. "He told me . . ."

Hayley could see both Rosana and Mona leaning forward, their entire bodies full of anticipation.

"He told me—"

"For the love of God, Hayley, *what?*" Mona wailed.

"That a few years back, when Bruce was still a single man about town, long before we ever got involved, mind you—"

"He dated Carol Waterman!" Rosana screamed, dropping her now-empty plastic cup to the floor.

"Just a couple of times, but he insisted nothing ever came of it, and they had remained friendly."

Mona shook her head. "Unbelievable. And he dropped this bombshell just *last week?*"

"Yes, I found the idea of Bruce and Carol as a couple so ludicrous. Plus, his account of what happened at the record store, and casually telling Carol his favorite band was Fleetwood Mac, seemed logical, so I didn't question it. I let the whole thing slip from my mind . . . until we got Carol's Christmas card."

"I'll tell you what I think!" Mona howled. "I think that Carol Waterman's favorite band is Supertramp, because that's exactly what she is, and she's probably running off with *all* of our husbands!"

Rosana covered her mouth with both hands, and her eyes were so big and bulging, Hayley thought they might just pop right off her face.

"No, I still think this card is some kind of joke. It's not real," Hayley said, trying to reassure them, and, more to the point, herself.

But as she re-read the message inside the card one more time, she had more than a slight pang in the pit of her stomach. For a brief moment, she wondered if Bruce, a man she had grown to trust implicitly, had actually been telling her the truth about his innocent run-in with Carol at the record store.

Or was he the one secretly planning to run off with Carol Waterman?

Chapter Five

The door to the *Island Times* office swung open, and David Pine blew in, his cheeks rosy from the frightfully chilly air outside. He was carrying a brown paper bag under his arm. He stopped short at the sight of Hayley, Mona, and Rosana. The trio stood in the middle of the reception area, among the plethora of Christmas decorations and party foods, staring numbly at him, as if they were seeing him for the first time.

He offered them a bright smile. "What'd I miss?"

At first, none of the women could find their voice to respond, but within a few seconds, Mona was the first to manage it. "Where the hell have you been?"

David chuckled, confused, and handed Mona the paper bag. "You sent me to pick up napkins, remember?"

Mona snatched the bag and peered inside. "You got the elegant ones. This isn't a state dinner for the queen. It's a friggin' office Christmas party."

"Don't worry. They were on sale. And it's my treat," David said, eyeing the bright yellow spiked eggnog in the bowl. "Would you mind if I help myself to a cup?"

Without waiting for an answer, he glided over to the

table and picked up a red cup and ladled some eggnog into it.

"You've been gone a while. What took so long?" Hayley asked casually as she continued exchanging curious looks with Rosana and Mona.

David took a generous sip of the eggnog. "Oh, that's good. I had to stop by my house and change, because when I was at the grocery store, I opened a can of soda while I was buying the napkins and these rug rats were running up and down the aisle, chasing each other. They slammed into my back, and I spilled Dr Pepper all down the front of my shirt. Does this look okay for the party? It was the only thing I had that wasn't in the laundry basket."

Hayley thought David had looked much better in the smart, tailored blue Oxford shirt, but even in a more modest black lightweight cashmere turtleneck sweater, the man still cut a mighty fine figure.

David finally seemed to notice the strained expressions on the faces of all three women.

"Are you three okay? You all look a little shell-shocked," he observed.

"No, we're fine," Hayley said quickly, instinctively hiding the red Christmas card from Carol behind her back.

"By the way, while I was home changing, I got a text from Carol. She had to cancel our date tonight."

"*What?*" Hayley gasped.

David stared at her, not sure why she hadn't heard him. "She's not coming."

"But . . . but . . . but why?" Hayley stammered.

David studied her, not sure what was bothering her, but then chose to ignore whatever it might be. "She's not feeling well. She thinks she may be coming down with something. I hear the flu's going around town."

Rosana's whole body shook as she croaked, "She's not coming to the Christmas party?"

David downed the rest of his eggnog as his eyes bounced around to all three women. "Uh, yeah, isn't that what I just said? What is going on with you three?"

"Nothing!" Mona snapped. "Mind your own business!"

David raised his arms in surrender and then turned his back to them to pour himself another cup of eggnog.

"And save some of that eggnog for the other guests!" Mona yelled.

"Relax, Mona, I saw Andrea at the supermarket. She was picking up some more rum. We'll have plenty," David said.

Luckily, he couldn't hear the alarm bells going off in all their heads. Hayley rushed over to her desk and plunged her hand deep inside her bag in search of her phone. As she plucked it out to speed-dial Bruce, she noticed Mona and Rosana scrambling for their own phones as well.

"Hi, this is Bruce. I'm somewhere stomping out crime, so leave a message and I'll get back to you."

Beep.

Dead air.

"Uh, Bruce, it's me. Call me when you get this. Please. It's not urgent, but . . . just call me."

Hayley ended the call and dropped her hand clutching the phone as she watched Rosana, her lip quivering, say into her own phone, "Sal, honey, I need you to call me back just as soon as you can." And then she lifted a shaky hand to her mouth.

Hayley glanced over at Mona, who was scratching her head, exasperated. "Dennis, where the hell are you? Why aren't you on the couch with your phone lying next to you on the coffee table, like every other day of the week? Call me back, you imbecile!"

Why weren't any of their husbands picking up?

All three calls had gone straight to voice mail.

It was so strange.

And more than a little disturbing.

Island Food & Spirits

By Hayley Powell

I have been in the Christmas spirit since before Black Friday, so I have been in my kitchen baking a lot of holiday goodies!

Last weekend, I thought it might be fun to prepare and send a Christmas care package filled with delicious cookies, pies, cakes, and candy to my daughter, Gemma, and her boyfriend, Conner, in New York, since they would not be flying to Maine to join us this year. Of course, I would make sure to include Gemma's absolute favorite . . . my Candy Cane Christmas Bark!

When my BFFs, Liddy and Mona, got wind of my plans, they invited themselves over for the day to help out, which I knew actually meant they wanted me to make them their own holiday favorite . . . my Candy Cane Cocktails!

When the girls arrived in the afternoon on Saturday, we put on some Christmas music while sipping our cocktails and got to work chopping candy canes and measuring and melting the chocolate, according to my grandmother's prized recipe. After finally popping the pans into the refrigerator to let our bark harden, before breaking it into pieces, we decided to reward ourselves with one more Christmas cocktail.

That was just about the time Bruce arrived home from the office. He had spent his Saturday morning covering a break-in of an ice-fishing shed out on Eagle Lake and breezed into the back door to the kitchen, loudly announcing, "I'm starving!" He sniffed the beef stew I had bubbling on the stovetop, but whined that he was in the mood for something sweet, so he snatched up one of the leftover candy canes we had on the counter and bit off a big piece. A few moments later, Bruce ambled over to the kitchen table, where Mona, Liddy, and I were deeply immersed in a gossip session. He said, only slightly concerned, "Honey, I think I chipped my tooth a little bit." He smiled wide to show us.

The three of us stared at Bruce, slack-jawed. One of his front teeth was completely gone!

Mona was the first to speak. "Good Lord, Bruce, you look just like the jack-o'-lantern one of my kids carved this past Halloween!"

"What?" Bruce cried, quickly slapping his hand over his mouth. He then turned and pounded out of the room to inspect his toothless smile in the mirror that hung on the wall in the hallway.

That's when all hell broke loose.

Bruce flew back into the kitchen, arms waving in the air, screaming, "Nobody move! You might step on my tooth!"

We sat frozen at the kitchen table.

Bruce blinked at us, then began yelling again. "Don't just sit there! Somebody call 911!"

Liddy, Mona, and I looked at each other. I then said softly to Bruce, "Honey, you told us not to move."

Bruce sighed, annoyed, then grabbed his phone to make the call himself.

I gently said, "Bruce, dear, please don't call 911. I don't think we'll be needing an ambulance. I can get you wherever we need to go without the assistance of any first responders."

Bruce then dropped to his knees and began frantically searching the linoleum floor with his hands. Finally he scooped something up. "Found it!"

He held it up for all of us to see.

We all had to squint to see the tooth wedged between his thumb and index finger. "Hayley, get a glass of milk! We need to keep the tooth moist! Mona, warm up the truck! You're driving me to the emergency room!"

Nobody argued with him, but none of us were at all surprised when we were told by the emergency room admitting nurse, in no uncertain terms, that this was *not* a medical emergency, this was a dental emergency.

As Bruce grumbled about the obvious lack of concern over what was happening to him, I got on the phone and tried to track down a dentist who would see us on a Saturday during the Christmas season. Well, none of the four dentists on the island were available, but we did find someone in Bangor who could see us later that afternoon, so we all hopped back into Mona's truck and sped off toward the Trenton Bridge.

Bruce held the glass of milk soaking his tooth out in front of him as Mona's hairpin turns caused him to splash himself a couple of times during the seemingly endless one-hour drive.

Unfortunately, Mona tried calming everyone down by making light of the situation. "Hey, Bruce, knock, knock."

"Who's there?" Bruce replied.

"Dishes."

"Dishes, who?"

"Dishes how I talk since I lost my teeth!" Mona roared.

Liddy and I both tried desperately to keep a straight face, but failed miserably. Bruce could plainly see our hysterical reactions, since we were all squeezed into the front of Mona's truck—me practically sitting on Bruce's lap, trying not to get milk spilled all over me. Suffice it to say, he was not amused.

Thankfully, everything worked out in Bangor. The dentist was able to bond Bruce's tooth and it was as good as new, but he sent Bruce off with a warning that he had had enough candy canes for one holiday season. Bruce agreed, especially after getting a look at the whopping bill we would have to pay after the receptionist handed it to us and chirped, "Merry Christmas!"

Finally we all climbed back into Mona's truck and headed home to the island, tired after a long day of drama.

That was when Mona decided to try and lighten the mood one more time.

"Hey, Bruce."

"What?" Bruce barked.

"What did the judge say to the dentist?"

Bruce sighed. "I don't know, what?"

"Do you swear to tell the tooth, the whole tooth, and nothing but the tooth?" Mona shrieked, tears streaming down her cheeks from laughing so hard.

Bruce just shook his head and pretended to be asleep the rest of the way home.

Candy Cane Cocktail

Candy Cane Vodka Ingredients:
3 cups vodka
20 miniature candy canes

Pour the vodka in an airtight jar, add the candy canes, and close the jar. Let it sit 10 to 12 hours, shaking every so often to mix.

Ingredients:
4 ounces candy cane vodka
2 ounces peppermint schnapps
Chocolate-flavored syrup
Crushed candy canes

Pour some chocolate syrup on one plate and place crushed candy canes on another. Dip rim of a cocktail glass in chocolate, then the crushed candy canes, and set aside.

In a shaker filled with ice, add your candy cane vodka and peppermint schnapps and shake to mix well. Strain into the decorated cocktail glass. Add a miniature candy cane if you desire! A yummy holiday treat with a big kick!

Candy Cane Bark

Ingredients:
8 ounces white chocolate, chopped
2 teaspoons vegetable oil, divided
½ teaspoon peppermint extract
8 ounces semisweet chocolate, chopped
¼ cup crushed candy cane pieces
1 baking sheet with parchment paper

Add the white-chocolate chips and 1 teaspoon oil to a saucepan and heat on medium-low heat, stirring until melted. Stir in the peppermint extract, then spread into a thin rectangle on the parchment paper.

In another saucepan, add the semisweet chocolate and melt on medium-low heat, stirring until completely melted.

Pour over the white chocolate and use an offset spatula to spread evenly and to cover the white chocolate. Immediately sprinkle the candy cane pieces over the chocolate and place into the refrigerator until completely hardened.

Then break into the size pieces you want and store in an airtight container or bag up as a cute Christmas treat for your friends!

Chapter Six

A good time was had by all at the *Island Times* annual Christmas soiree, with three noticeable exceptions. Although they kept happy smiles plastered on their faces, and made a valiant effort to engage in small talk with the entire staff and their guests in attendance, it was obvious to any clear-eyed observer that Hayley Powell, Mona Barnes, and Rosana Moretti were not enjoying the festivities. In fact, at one point, Mona had to pluck the red plastic cup of spiked eggnog out of Rosana's hands because she had guzzled down so much and could barely stand on her feet.

Her eyes were squinting and her words were slurring as she tried focusing on a random conversation with one of the reporters. Apparently, the reporter had just gotten engaged to her boyfriend of four years. Upon hearing this wonderful news, Rosana had burst into tears, sobbing so hard she could barely breathe. Mona had decided at that point that Rosana needed to be cut off from the eggnog.

As the host and organizer, Hayley worked hard to pretend nothing was wrong, trying to ignore the fact that all three of their husbands—Bruce, Dennis, and Sal—had yet to show up to the party.

Where were they?

What were they doing?

Had all three of them run off with Carol Waterman?

Hayley needed to keep her mind focused on the task at hand.

Make sure everyone kept having a nice time.

She circled the room, checking on all the guests, making sure they had sampled the hors d'oeuvres and their red plastic cups were filled with the spiked eggnog. She tried putting Bruce out of her mind. He would show up eventually. She could feel it in her gut. Or was that just indigestion from grazing on too many appetizers before the party?

Hayley spotted Mona, with her arm around Rosana, leading her over to a chair in the corner. Rosana was stumbling drunk, and could barely walk, the room obviously spinning fast. Mona gently lowered her down in the seat, and Rosana gave her a grateful smile. Hayley flew over to join them.

"I can't believe none of them are here yet. People are going to start leaving soon," Hayley said, gazing at the merry crowd, the volume of their chatter rising with each cup of eggnog.

"I really thought I was going to grow old with Sal . . ." Rosana was slurring, her tongue half hanging out of her mouth as her glassy eyes stared ahead, the tears on her cheeks finally having dried up.

"Don't talk like that," Hayley said, pointing a finger at Rosana. "We don't know why they're so late. There has to be a totally innocent and logical explanation."

"Then why are we all so upset?" Mona barked. "I'm ready to send out a search party for Dennis. This is the first time he's left the couch since the Clinton administration."

"Look, we need to stop obsessing about this," Hayley said, more to calm herself than her two friends. "We have no clue what's really going on with Bruce, Sal, and Dennis. Why worry until there is actually something to worry about? Right? Now let's get another cup of eggnog..." She stopped herself, glancing down at Rosana, who was swaying side to side. "Mona, let's get another cup of eggnog and maybe a bottled water for Rosana, join the party, mingle, and catch up with everybody."

"Sounds like a plan," Mona said, nodding.

Rosana tried nodding her head, but instead it just drooped forward as she slumped in the chair, seconds from completely passing out.

Mona reached down and pulled her back so she was sitting upright again. "Rosana, there's a couch in Sal's office. Let's take you there so you can sleep it off."

"No, I want to be right here when Sal arrives," Rosana insisted.

"How about this? The minute Sal walks through the door, we'll come and wake you up. Does that sound good?" Hayley suggested.

Rosana smiled, her eyes now at half-mast. "Okay..."

"Now, no more talking about our husbands," Hayley said emphatically.

As Hayley and Mona hauled Rosana to her feet to escort her to the back bull pen, where all the offices were located, Liddy breezed over to them. "How come all your husbands blew off the Christmas party this year?"

Rosana's body sagged again, making it harder for Hayley and Mona to drag her to Sal's office.

"We're not talking about our husbands," Hayley snapped to Liddy.

"I don't blame you. I've been trying to forget all about mine," Liddy said wearily.

"You don't have a husband," Mona growled.

"Well, I would have, if he hadn't ditched me at the

altar," Liddy said, sighing. "All men are scum. Am I right, ladies?"

"Yes," Rosana slurred, perking up for a brief moment, before slouching back down in Hayley's and Mona's arms.

"Liddy, excuse us. We need to get Rosana to Sal's office, where she can lie down," Hayley said.

Liddy didn't seem to hear her. "Men. You just can't trust them. It's as simple as that."

Hayley and Mona exchanged a cursory glance before continuing to haul Rosana away from the party. They had barely managed to move a few feet when Andrea Cho, armed with her own red plastic cup of spiked eggnog, appeared at their side, tipsy and eager to join the conversation.

"Liddy's right. If you meet a guy you think you can fall in love with, then get a dog," Andrea said, raising her glass. "Here's to a happy future with Fido."

Hayley sighed, straining under the weight of Rosana, whose eyes were now fully closed. "Andrea, can we continue this conversation a little later? We really need to get Rosana—"

Like Liddy, Andrea seemed to be tuning out Hayley and was in her own little world at the moment. "I say we form a group, like the First Wives Club, and make a pact never to allow men to screw up our lives ever again. Now that I think of it, we might not be able to call it the First Wives Club, since Leonard is my second husband."

"So is Bruce," Hayley wheezed, struggling with Mona to make a little progress on their long journey to carry Rosana to Sal's office.

"You're right. I'll come up with a better name," Andrea said. "Just as soon as I dump that good-for-nothing Leonard."

"Where is he tonight?" Liddy asked.

"I left him at home. I'm too mad at him to even look at him right now," Andrea hissed.

"What did he do this time?" Liddy asked, leaning in, delightfully curious.

"The usual. He was all over another woman in the stands at the high-school basketball game last night. I swear that man thinks he's as sexy and charming as Bradley Cooper. But we all know he's not!"

"Hardly," Mona grunted, pushing past Andrea with Rosana, perched on the threshold of the back bull pen.

"The worst part was, I had to hear about it from a cheerleader! A cheerleader, can you believe it?" Andrea cried before pausing to reconsider. "Actually, no, the worst part was who he was flirting with. Carol Waterman."

Hayley and Mona stopped suddenly, slowly turning back around with Rosana, who was now snoring.

"*What?*" Hayley gasped.

"I know! Of all people! Don't get me wrong! I blame Leonard one hundred percent for acting the way he did! But truth be told, I can't stand the sight of Carol Waterman, with her plunging necklines and come-hither smile, always cozying up to every unavailable man on the island! I know this sounds awful, but I am so furious, if I could have just one Christmas present this year, I'd want Carol Waterman to keel over and die!"

At that, Hayley and Mona let go of Rosana, who collapsed to the floor in a heap, still snoring.

Chapter Seven

When Police Chief Sergio Alvares, who also happened to be Hayley's brother-in-law, showed up in uniform at the *Island Times* office Christmas party, Hayley feared someone had called the police station with a noise complaint. Over the last hour, the festivities had become noticeably rowdier as people generously and enthusiastically ladled out more and more servings of the delicious rum-spiked eggnog. Someone had also cranked up the Christmas music and the high-pitched laughter from some of the tipsy revelers was at its earsplitting peak.

Having successfully delivered Rosana to the couch in Sal's office, where they covered her with a blanket, Hayley and Mona had rejoined the party just in time to see Sergio arrive.

Hayley raced over to him with a worried look. "I'm sorry, is the music too loud?"

Sergio gave her a quizzical look. "No, I just got off from work and thought I'd stop by. I am invited, aren't I?"

Hayley wasn't about to tell the chief of police that the party was for employees and their significant others only, so she just broke out into a wide smile. "Of course! The more the merrier!"

Sergio wandered over to the food table to grab himself a

Christmas cookie. Hayley glanced over at Mona, standing next to Liddy, who was prattling on about something. Hayley could tell Mona wasn't listening to a word Liddy was saying. Her mind was clearly elsewhere, undoubtedly on the whereabouts of her missing husband. A similar thought was raging through Hayley's mind at the moment, too. She wasn't going to panic. She was just grateful that Rosana, the most high-strung of them all, was sleeping peacefully, at least until she woke up and would most likely be suffering from a massive hangover.

Hayley heard a few partygoers greeting some new arrivals near the front door and turned around. She gasped. There, in the doorway, laughing and shaking hands with a few reporters, were Bruce and Sal. Hayley marched over and barked, "Why are you so late? Where were you?"

"Merry Christmas to you, too," Bruce said with a sly smile.

"I'm serious! We've been worried sick!" Hayley howled.

"Are we *that* late?" Sal asked, checking his watch.

"Yes, you are!" Hayley snapped.

Sal looked around. "Where's Rosana?"

"She had a little too much of the spiked eggnog and is in your office sleeping it off."

"Really? She rarely touches the hard stuff," Sal remarked. "She's more of a Pinot Grigio kind of gal."

"It's your fault, Sal. She had no idea where you were, and she got upset, and just started guzzling down the eggnog out of nervousness," Hayley explained before turning back to Bruce. "So, are you going to tell me what you've been up to?"

Bruce and Sal exchanged sheepish looks.

"Well?" Hayley asked impatiently.

"We skipped work to go ice fishing," Bruce said. "I know, we probably should've stuck around here to help set up for the party, but we got talking this morning. Sal mentioned how he hadn't had any free time to do much fishing this season, so on a whim we just decided to head out to his tent."

"They were biting today, too. You should see the haul we got," Sal said, beaming.

"Ice fishing?" Hayley asked, incredulous.

Bruce nodded. "We're going to have some nice trout dinners for the rest of the week."

"Why didn't you at least call or text to tell me where you were?" Hayley asked, folding her arms.

"We were camped out in the middle of Eagle Lake. You know how spotty the cell service is all the way out there," Bruce explained.

Hayley wasn't sure she believed them. That is, until her nose crinkled up at the fishy aroma emanating from Sal's clothes. Bruce, however, had no scent whatsoever.

"Why don't you stink like Sal?" Hayley asked pointedly.

Sal grunted, obviously insulted while smelling himself.

"We swung by the house first, and while Sal unloaded some of the catch, I ran upstairs to take a quick shower," Bruce explained, almost too quickly.

Hayley turned to Sal, recoiling. "And what about you?"

"We were late getting back. We didn't have time to stop at my house, too. Who cares if I smell? I'm the boss. Who's going to fire me?"

Bruce hugged Hayley, who stiffened. "You're mad at me for playing hooky today while you worked to get everything ready for the party, aren't you?"

He was right.

She was mad.

But her anger was slowly starting to melt as she accepted the explanation that Bruce and Sal had gone fishing, and that neither of them had been secretly plotting to run away with Carol Waterman.

"Come on, Sal, I'll buy you a drink," Bruce said.

"Yeah, real generous of you, but it's an open bar, and I'm paying for it!" Sal groused as Bruce led him away.

Mona suddenly appeared next to Hayley. "You buying their story?"

"Yes, I suppose so," Hayley said.

Mona shook her head. "Well, go figure, it's Dennis. Dennis is the one sneaking around with Carol Waterman."

"Mona, you don't know that!" Hayley cried.

"He's the only one still not here. He's obviously left town with Carol," Mona said. "I can't believe it."

"We still don't know if Carol was being serious!"

Mona checked her phone again.

Still, no word from Dennis.

Mona retreated from the party, slinking away to a corner to sit in a chair and stare glumly at the floor.

Hayley tried cheering her up, but to no avail.

But then, not five minutes later, the front door opened, and Dennis finally appeared. He looked calm and detached, almost as if he had just hauled himself up from the couch and driven over to pick up his wife.

Mona didn't notice him at first, but Hayley intercepted him as he made a beeline toward the spiked eggnog. "You need to go talk to your wife right now!"

Dennis looked at Hayley, surprised. "What's she done now?"

"It's not what she's done! It's what *you've* done!" Hayley said, squeezing his arm and steering him over to the corner.

Mona finally spotted them when they were right in front of her.

"Dennis, where the hell have you been?"

"Ellsworth," he mumbled. "Why?"

"What were you doing up there?"

"I decided to drive up and do a little Christmas shopping. What's the big deal? You've been yelling at me all month to get off my butt and help out buying stuff for the kids."

"So you chose today of all days to do it?" Mona asked.

"Yeah, why not? What's so special about today?"

"Why didn't you call me back when I called you?"

"You called me?"

"Yes, Dennis, don't you dare lie to me!" Mona fumed.

Dennis reached into the pocket of his jeans and pulled out his phone. He tried turning it on. "I guess my phone died. I told you my charger's not working."

Mona eyed him suspiciously, not sure if she should believe him or not. Dennis sighed, annoyed, tired of getting the third degree. "Can I go get some eggnog now?"

"Yes, Dennis, help yourself," Hayley said.

Dennis trotted off, smiling at a few people he recognized, and poured himself some eggnog.

Mona turned to Hayley. "Normally, I can tell if he's lying. But this time, I can't be sure. What do you think?"

"I think we have completely overreacted to that ludicrous Christmas card from Carol Waterman. It was obviously a joke," Hayley said. "And not a very funny one."

Chapter Eight

Hayley, flanked by Mona and Rosana, rapped on the front door to Carol Waterman's house.

Rosana cringed and closed her eyes tight. "Please, Hayley, not so loud."

Hayley shot her a grin, knowing the poor woman was suffering mightily on this bright and sunny, yet chilly, mid-December Saturday morning, the day after the office party. "Sorry, Rosana."

Rosana rubbed her eyes and nodded, but didn't have the strength to respond.

Mona sighed. "How long is this going to take? I got traps to haul today."

"We won't stay long, I promise. I just thought it would be a nice gesture if we stopped in for a quick visit to see if Carol is feeling better."

Mona rolled her eyes. "That's not why we're here, and you know it. You want to find out what's behind that crazy Christmas card Carol sent us."

Hayley turned to Mona and put a finger to her lips. "Shhhh, Carol doesn't need to hear that." She glanced at Rosana. "Cover your ears."

Rosana obliged and Hayley knocked on the door several more times, but there was still no answer.

"She's not home. Let's go get some blueberry pancakes at Jordan's. I'm starving."

They were about to turn and leave when Hayley stopped. "Do you hear that?"

Mona perked up her ears. "Hear what?"

Hayley listened for a few more seconds. "That."

"I don't hear anything, do you, Rosana?" Mona asked.

Rosana grabbed her temples, moaning softly. "Just the pounding inside my head."

Hayley distinctly heard the sound of faint singing, and as she pressed her ear against Carol's front door, she knew it was coming from inside the house. " 'Deck the Halls.' Carol is playing Christmas music. She probably can't hear us." Hayley hammered on the door again with her fist.

"Hayley!" Rosana cried, eyes squinting, near tears.

"Sorry, Rosana," Hayley mumbled before turning back and screaming through the door, "Hello, Carol! It's Hayley Powell! I'm here with Mona Barnes and Rosana Moretti! Can we come in?"

Still, no answer.

"What's she doing in there?" Mona scoffed.

Hayley could hear "Deck the Halls" finally wrapping up and then the first few bars of "Rudolph, the Red-Nosed Reindeer" start playing.

Hayley reached down and gripped the doorknob, turning it to the right. The door effortlessly opened. "It's unlocked. Should we go in?"

"No, that's breaking and entering!" Rosana cried, turning to flee before Mona grabbed her by the sweater.

"We're not breaking in, the door's unlocked. And we're only entering because we think she's home," Mona barked.

Hayley gingerly stepped inside the house, stopping in the small foyer to see one of those Amazon Alexa devices perched on top of a side table near a coatrack. The Christmas music was blasting out of it.

Hayley walked over to it. "Alexa, lower volume."

The music dropped in volume.

"Looks like she's planning to leave on a trip out of town," Mona said from behind Hayley. Hayley turned to see Mona pointing to a large suitcase sitting at the bottom of the staircase to their left.

Hayley marched over and lifted it up. It was heavy, indicating it was packed full of clothes. "Carol, are you home?"

"I have awful dry mouth," Rosana murmured. "Do you think Carol would mind if I helped myself to a glass of water?"

"I'm sure she would be fine with it," Hayley assured her. Rosana shuffled off toward the kitchen.

Hayley tried calling one more time. "Carol?"

"She has to be home. I can smell that rancid perfume she wears," Mona huffed.

"White Diamonds by Elizabeth Taylor, and I think it's a lovely scent," Hayley whispered.

"Well, I'm choking on it right now!" Mona barked.

Hayley shook her head and then wandered into the living room, where she suddenly stopped in her tracks, screaming at the top of her lungs.

She heard Rosana drop a glass in the kitchen and it shattered all over the floor. Mona bounded into the living room in a panic and came up behind Hayley, gasping loudly in Hayley's ear.

They both stared in shock at the sight of Carol Waterman lying on the floor underneath her Christmas tree, with all the colored lights still blinking. A decorative garland that had been yanked off the tree was wrapped tightly around Carol's neck and her head was turned to the side, where they could see her swollen, purplish tongue jetting out of her mouth as her glassy, dead eyes stared up at them.

Somebody had strangled her to death.

Chapter Nine

Police Chief Sergio Alvares was barreling through the front door of Carol Waterman's house less than three minutes after Hayley had called 911 on her phone. Arriving not far behind him, a county forensics team began expertly combing the premises for evidence as Sergio's officers, Donnie and Earl, escorted Hayley, Mona, and Rosana outside to wait on the street. They were placed alongside a number of rubberneckers drawn by the flashing blue police lights on top of the two squad cars parked out in front of the house.

Rosana gripped Hayley's arm, a bit woozy, her mind still cloudy from the consumption of too much alcohol from the previous evening. "They're going to find broken pieces of glass all over the kitchen floor. Should I tell them that was me and not the killer stopping for a glass of water before leaving the scene of the crime?"

Hayley gently patted Rosana's shoulder. "I'm sure you'll have the chance to explain all of that when they question us."

"So, do you honestly think she was murdered?" Mona whispered, low enough so the curious onlookers crowding around them couldn't overhear their conversation.

Hayley nodded as she leaned in closer to Mona and said in a hushed tone, "Definitely. The discoloration of her tongue indicated strangulation, so I'm pretty sure she didn't wrap that garland around her neck herself."

"Oh, boy," Mona sighed.

" 'Oh, boy' is right," Hayley said, her mind racing with a number of disturbing scenarios of what might have happened to poor Carol Waterman.

Rosana, who was two steps behind Hayley and Mona, suddenly gasped. "You don't think the killer could have been one of our—"

"Shhhh," Mona warned, clapping a hand over Rosana's mouth. "Not here."

The three women decided to move away from the crowd and over to a fir tree located on the far end of Carol's property. Officer Earl, whose job was to corral all the locals who were quickly gathering at the scene and growing in number, spotted them and called out, loud enough for everyone to hear, "Don't go too far, ladies! Chief Alvares is going to want to talk to you!"

"We know, Earl! You don't have to treat us like suspects!" Rosana wailed before whipping her head back around toward Hayley and Mona. "He thinks we had something to do with this! Which is crazy, right? The idea of us strangling poor Carol Waterman is just preposterous!"

"It's not us I'm worried about," Hayley said somberly. "That packed suitcase by the stairs is what makes me nervous."

Mona folded her arms, concerned. "Yeah, I know. If Carol was planning on leaving town, then maybe what she wrote in that Christmas card was actually true."

"Oh, dear," Rosana croaked.

"If she was telling the truth, and Carol was going to run off with one of our husbands, and something went seriously wrong with the plan—"

"Oh, dear!" Rosana cried, panicked. "One of our husbands is the *killer*!"

Mona covered Rosana's mouth again with her chubby, callused hand as Hayley glanced around to see if anybody had heard Rosana's hysterical declaration. Luckily, everyone's attention was still directed toward the house and what was happening inside.

"Rosana, please keep your voice down!" Hayley pleaded.

Rosana nodded her head and Mona released her.

They stood by the tree, agitated, their minds swirling with a number of unpleasant thoughts for a few more minutes until Sergio finally emerged from the house. A few reporters from both the *Island Times* and the *Bar Harbor Herald* raced forward like sharks toward floating chum and shouted a barrage of questions at him. The chief, however, ignored them and marched straight toward Hayley, Mona, and Rosana.

"He's coming this way! What are we going to say?" Rosana cried.

"Stay calm," Hayley said under her breath. "We just have to be honest about what we know."

Sergio offered them all a sincere, rueful smile. "I'm sorry you had to be the ones to stumble upon the crime scene. Can I ask what brought you over to Carol Waterman's in the first place?"

"She sent her date a text last night that she wasn't feeling well and wouldn't be attending the *Island Times* office Christmas party, so the three of us decided to come over here and check on her this morning," Hayley explained evenly.

"That's not the reason—" Rosana said before stopping midsentence.

Mona sighed loudly as Sergio eyed her suspiciously.

Rosana turned to Hayley. "You said to be honest!"

Hayley reached into her back pocket and pulled out a red envelope with Carol's Christmas card inside and handed it to Sergio. "We also wanted to ask her about this."

Sergio opened the card and read the inscription, his lips moving along and his eyes widening when he reached the end. He then closed the card, almost dismissively, before looking back up at Hayley, Mona, and Rosana. "This can not be serious. It's some kind of joke, right?"

Hayley shrugged. "We assumed so at first . . . but given what's happened, we thought it might be evidence, which is why we're handing it over to you."

Sergio stared glumly at the card, which he slid back into the red envelope. He thought for a moment, and then shook his head. "I find it impossible to believe that Bruce or Sal or Dennis had anything to do with—"

"So do we, but you always say, 'it's important to follow all leads, no matter how uncomfortable,' " Hayley reminded him.

"I did say that, didn't I?" Sergio muttered. He sighed and then said with more forcefulness, "All right, then. I will talk to all three of them, and see what they have to say."

Sergio excused the women and told them they were finally free to go home. Hayley hugged Mona and Rosana tightly. They had all been through a traumatic ordeal together and felt a tight bond. Even Mona didn't wrestle herself free from Hayley's hug, she needed a little comfort at this moment, too.

When Hayley arrived home, she received a text from

Bruce that he was heading to the police station because Sergio wanted to talk to him. Hayley drew a breath, worried how her husband might react when he learned he was a suspect because of her. But in her heart, she knew he was innocent, and it wouldn't matter in the end anyway. Hayley tried busying herself by baking some gingerbread and was in the middle of sifting together the flour, baking soda, salt, cinnamon, ginger, and cloves when her phone buzzed.

It was a text from Bruce: **Just finished chatting with Sergio. Going to swing by the office and do a little work on Monday's column.** He said nothing about his conversation with the police chief. She couldn't possibly wait until he got home to press him for details. But she did not want to disrupt his Saturday-morning writing session at the office, either, so she called Sergio instead. After waiting on hold a few minutes, Sergio finally picked up.

"How can I help you, Hayley?"

She didn't waste any time on small talk. "What happened with Bruce?"

"Nothing. I talked to all three of them. Bruce and Sal were ice fishing together out on Eagle Lake, and Dennis was Christmas shopping in Ellsworth. They all seemed pretty believable, so as far as I'm concerned, they're in the clear for now . . . until we find further evidence."

"Did you ask them about Carol's Christmas card?"

"Yes, none of them knew anything about it. They all think it was probably Carol just trying to mess with you three."

"Okay, thanks, Sergio."

Hayley ended the call and stared at her bowl of gingerbread ingredients. She trusted Bruce. She knew in her gut he had to be telling the truth. But something drew her to the door leading down to the basement. She flicked on the light and descended the stairs into the dank, musty room underneath the house. She knew exactly what she was looking for, and after she moved a few boxes to get to a specific corner, she stood there, frozen in place, stunned and dismayed. Because right in front of her, dusty and untouched, in the exact spot where Bruce had stored it last spring with the winter season over, was his ice-fishing equipment.

Bruce had lied.

He didn't go ice fishing.

So, why would Sal cover for him and say he did?

Or was Sal lying, too?

Chapter Ten

Mona stood in the doorway to her house, eyes blinking, mouth agape. "I don't believe it."

"It's true, I swear," Hayley heaved, panting for air, panic rising. "Can I come in?"

Mona swept the door all the way open and ushered her inside. Hayley expected the usual pandemonium with kids running around in diapers, the older ones upstairs blasting music, food stains on the walls and unidentifiable smears on the tables and countertops. But today it was relatively calm and quiet at the Barnes house, which surprised her.

"Where is everybody?" Hayley inquired, glancing around.

"Mom's got all the little ones. I swear she's a glutton for punishment. But every so often, she likes to play grandma. I have no idea where the older ones are, probably tearing through town, causing trouble. I think Chet might be home. I heard him slamming around upstairs a while ago. Dennis is in his man cave down in the basement, on his back, watching a football game. No surprise there. Can I get you some coffee?"

"No!" Hayley gasped. "I'm jacked up enough already."

"Have you called Sal and asked him about any of this?"

Hayley shook her head. "I wanted to talk to you first and get your advice on what I should do!"

"You can't tiptoe around this, Hayley. If Bruce is lying to you, you need to know. Where is he?"

"At the office."

"On a Saturday?"

"Yes, since he went ice fishing, or at least that's what the official story is at this point, he fell behind on his workload and had to work on his next column."

"What about Sal?"

"I assume he's at home with Rosana today."

"Maybe you should talk to him first. If Bruce is lying, then so is Sal. Maybe you can get the truth out of him before you confront Bruce, so you're not going in blind."

"Mona, do you think Bruce might be the one—?"

"Of course not! Bruce *writes* about crime! He's no *criminal*! And Sal is too fat and lazy to lift a finger and strangle anyone! As for Dennis, well, he's definitely in the clear!"

"How do you know for sure?"

At that moment, Mona's seventeen-year-old son, Chet, ambled into the kitchen and threw open the refrigerator door, lazily perusing the contents inside.

Mona jerked her head around toward him. "Chet, tell Hayley what you told me earlier."

Chet, eyes half-mast, totally annoyed to be drawn into a boring adult conversation, sighed and drawled in a thick Maine accent, "Twenty One Pilots is coming to the Bangor Auditorium, and tickets go on sale tomorrow. Mom won't give me the money to buy two for me and my girlfriend, Jess, before they sell out!"

"I'm not talking about *that*!" Mona barked. "Tell her about going Christmas shopping with your father!"

Chet stared blankly at his mother, but then a lightbulb, albeit a very small one, popped on in his head. "Oh yeah! I went with Dad yesterday Christmas shopping in Ellsworth."

Mona made a sweeping gesture toward her reed-thin, long-haired, gawky son. "See? Dennis is in the clear. Chet is his airtight alibi."

"I'm so happy for you," Hayley mumbled, not feeling any better. "I guess that just solidifies the case against Bruce."

The loud cheers from a football game playing on the TV nearly drowned Hayley out. Mona momentarily marched out of the kitchen and screamed, "For the love of God, Dennis, turn down the damn TV!" After a few seconds, Hayley heard the volume lowering just a bit and Mona returned to the kitchen. Chet popped open a can of soda and disappeared back upstairs to his room. In the interim, Hayley had come to a decision.

"I'm going over to Sal and Rosana's house."

"Wise move," Mona said.

"I'll call you later," Hayley said as she rushed back out the door, hopped in her car, and sped across town to Sal Moretti's modest two-story house on Snow Street. She parked in front, steeled herself for what she might hear, and then got out of her car. With renewed determination, she marched up the steps of the front porch and rang the bell.

After a few moments, Rosana answered the door.

"Hayley, what a nice surprise! Come in, come in," Rosana chirped, the effects of her hangover obviously having mercifully subsided.

Hayley stepped into the foyer. She smelled some kind of bread baking in the oven and could hear Sal cursing in the living room. "Is this a good time?"

"Oh, yes, Sal's just struggling to put the Christmas lights on the tree. I've been nagging him for a week to get it done, but you know how he procrastinates."

"Would you mind if I go talk to him?"

Worry lines suddenly appeared on Rosana's forehead. "No, of course not. Is it something serious?"

"It might be."

Rosana grabbed a fistful of Hayley's sweater. "What is it? Is it about, you know *what*?"

Hayley nodded.

Rosana began to crumble. "Oh, dear, it's Sal, isn't it? I knew it! I knew it all along!"

"No, it's not Sal," Hayley said, trying to be reassuring. "At least I don't think so. But—"

"But *what*?" Rosana wailed, her bottom lip quivering.

"He may know something."

"Oh, dear," Rosana fretted, wringing her hands.

Hayley gently pushed past Rosana and headed into the living room, where Sal was wrestling with a bulky string of Christmas lights he was desperately trying to untangle. He saw Hayley and bellowed, "I am so over Christmas already! All this ridiculous buildup, and then after opening one brand-new tie and eating a little ham, it's all over and done with, just like that!"

"Here, Sal, let me help you," Hayley said, carefully taking the lights from him and setting to work at unsnarling them.

"What are you doing here?" Sal groused.

"Merry Christmas to you too, Sal," Hayley said.

"I'm sorry, I just get stressed when the wife strong-arms me into decorating the tree. I hate Christmas."

"You hate every holiday."

"Can't argue with that."

Hayley could hear Rosana bustling around in the kitchen, keeping herself occupied, and pretending she wasn't eavesdropping on their conversation.

"Sal, I came by to ask you something."

"You're not getting a raise, Hayley. Your Christmas bonus is going to have to be enough this year."

"I didn't get a Christmas bonus."

"Exactly."

Hayley sighed. "That's not why I came. You finally drilled it into my head that I will never get a raise in this lifetime after the last three times I asked."

"Good. Then my work is done."

"Why are you covering for Bruce?"

She finished untangling the Christmas lights and handed them back to Sal, who stared at her blankly.

"What do you mean?"

"I know Bruce didn't go ice fishing with you yesterday."

"No . . . uh . . . he did . . . In fact, we—"

"I found his ice-fishing equipment in the basement, untouched, from last year. How could he go fishing without his pole and supplies?"

"He borrowed some of my stuff," Sal insisted.

She could tell by his flushed face that he wasn't being honest with her.

"Sal, I've worked for you a long time. I know when you're not telling me the truth."

Sal's shoulders slumped as he realized he was caught.

"Okay, yes, he wasn't with me yesterday."

A baking pan clattered to the floor in the kitchen. This startling revelation had obviously spooked Rosana.

"Where was he?"

"I don't know."

"Sal . . ."

"I don't know, Hayley! And that's the God's honest truth! Bruce said he had to go do something, and he didn't want you to know, so he asked me to say he was ice fishing with me."

"Come on, Sal, he must have told you what he was doing?"

Sal vigorously shook his head. "No, he didn't. All he said was, he didn't want me to know. He was afraid if I did, I might slip and say something to you."

Hayley's stomach started flip-flopping.

Sal stepped forward and placed a beefy hand on Hayley's shoulder. "Are you okay? You don't look good."

"I . . . I . . . I'm f-fine," Hayley stuttered.

But she wasn't.

She wasn't fine at all.

"I'm sure whatever he was doing was innocent enough. I mean, we're talking about Bruce Linney. He's basically a Boy Scout, right?"

Hayley nodded and forced a smile. Outside, she appeared to be agreeing with Sal. But inside was an entirely different feeling. A sickening sense of dread was rapidly building inside her.

And now in the forefront of her mind was the looming decision she knew she was going to have to make.

Should she go to the police with this new information?

And if she did, would it lead to her own husband's arrest for murder?

Island Food & Spirits

By Hayley Powell

One of my favorite Christmas traditions is pulling out my recipe box from the pantry and whipping up some of my favorite seasonal appetizer recipes. I take these to my friends' holiday parties or serve them at my own annual shindig I host every year at my house for close family and friends.

Last night, I came upon an index card in the box with my Aunt Diane's handwritten Christmas Pin Wheel appetizer recipe. I had been gorging on those delicious treats ever since I was a little kid! Well, of course, I couldn't resist and set about searching the kitchen for all the necessary ingredients. My party was in two days' time, so I couldn't help patting myself on the back for being so ahead of the game.

As many of you know, I'm a huge procrastinator. I know, I know, I can hear a few of you now yelling, "And terrible organizer!" My boss, Sal, has alerted me to that fact on several occasions—and I happen to be the office manager at the *Island Times*! Organizing is in my job description. Luckily, I haven't been fired yet. I will tell you what I told him, though. I'm a work in progress. I just haven't made much progress as of yet. But I'm an eternal optimist! Someday I will be meticulously organized!

I have really tried over the years. About nine years ago, I looked around my house to see that the Halloween decorations were still up and it was three days past Thanksgiving! I decided now was the time to get my butt in gear. I grabbed a big garbage bag and threw out the pumpkins on the front doorstep, ripped off the paper decorations of witches, ghosts, and goblins off the windows, and even dumped the papier-mâché Thanksgiving turkey from the dining-room table! Then I spent the next two hours dusting and vacuuming! When I was done, I folded my arms proudly and thought to myself, *Now, who's not an organized person?* A couple of weeks later, the answer came back to me in vivid detail. *Me!*

You see, I was sitting at my desk at work, jotting down an upcoming dentist appointment in my calendar, when I suddenly realized to my horror that I only had one week left before my annual Christmas gathering at the house. I had yet to even send out the invites, plan my menu, and, most important, lose the extra seven pounds I had gained at Halloween, not to mention five more at Thanksgiving from the stuffing alone!

I raced home from work, fed the kids, and ordered them up to their rooms to do their homework so I could get cracking on the party planning. First up, a save-the-date e-mail to all my guests. The following morning, the RSVPs began pouring in, twenty out of twenty-five had already confirmed, along with what side dishes, appetizers, and desserts they would be bringing.

I spent the next week baking and cooking to prepare, and before I knew it, it was Friday, the day before the Christmas party. I took the day off from work to drive the kids to the airport in Bangor to catch an early flight to their father's, where they would be spending their Christmas vacation; then I finished a little shopping at the mall. I arrived home in plenty of time to toss some ingredients in the slow cooker for a make-ahead spaghetti sauce I could serve on Christmas Day.

I was feeling quite proud of myself. This new organized me was such a nice improvement over the usual harried and messy me, and so I decided to pamper myself and take a nice, long, luxurious bubble bath upstairs. I filled the tub with water and a decadent dollop of Herbivore Coconut Milk Bath Soak, and sank down into it with a heavy sigh. I popped in my wireless earbuds and listened on my iPod to a string of country hits sung by my favorite crooner, Wade Springer. I drifted off to sleep with lovely thoughts of Wade snuggled in that tiny bathtub with me (this, of course, was before I married my husband, Bruce).

My sweet Wade dream soon gave way to a nightmare. At least I thought it was a nightmare. I was in pitch blackness and all I could hear were feet stomping and people yelling followed by loud pounding on the door.

Suddenly I was jolted awake and sat up with a start. I popped open my eyes and tore the buds out of my ears. I could still hear the yelling and pounding. It wasn't a dream! Before I could react, the door to the bathroom flew open and I found myself staring at a half-dozen heads, all wide-eyed, staring at me lying naked in the tub. Luckily, the last remaining bubbles allowed me a modicum of modesty. Still, I sank back down in the tub as Liddy, Mona, and my brother, Randy, pushed everybody back out into the hallway.

"It's okay," Randy assured them all. "She's alive."

Liddy threw me a towel, which I wrapped around my midsection as I stood up.

"Of course, I'm okay!" I wailed. "Why are you all here?"

"We're here for the party!" Mona bellowed.

"The party is not until tomorrow night!" I explained.

They all stared at me in disbelief.

And that's when I discovered I was not the fastidious organizer I had thought I was. In my haste to get out my save-the-date e-mail, I typed the wrong date. I told everyone the party was on Friday, not Saturday. *Tonight.*

When everyone began arriving, a mystery quickly began brewing as to the whereabouts of the hostess. Things started to get tense when they saw what looked like blood splattered all over the kitchen. Upon closer inspection, it turned out to be spaghetti sauce. My oversized cat, Blueberry, had accidentally knocked the slow cooker off the counter. Although if I was being honest, I would swear he pushed it intentionally in order to crush my Shih Tzu, Leroy, as he innocently passed by underneath. In any event, both pets were found hiding under the kitchen table, licking sauce off themselves. Well, panic quickly set in and the search began for my body, which they all found very much alive upstairs naked in the bathtub.

I was crestfallen that I had mismanaged everything so badly, but I have been blessed with the most wonderful friends and family in the world. Everybody pitched in, mopping the kitchen, turning on the tree lights, putting on

Christmas carols, setting out all the appetizers, and, most important for this crowd, stirring the cocktails.

Within minutes, we were in full party mode, singing and laughing, and as my brother handed me a perfect Eggnog Martini, I realized that this beautiful night with friends and family was the best Christmas gift I could ever ask for.

Well, except maybe for some organizational skills.

Randy's Eggnog Martini

Ingredients:
3 ounces eggnog
1 ounce vanilla vodka
1 ounce Amaretto liqueur
Fresh nutmeg

Fill a shaker with ice and add all your ingredients. Shake until well blended and pour into a chilled martini glass. Grate a little fresh nutmeg over the top.

Christmas Pin Wheel Appetizers

Ingredients:
2 (8-ounce) packages cream cheese, room temperature
1 package ranch dressing mix
1 (4-ounce) jar pimentos, drained and patted dry
1 cup finely shredded sharp cheddar cheese
4 (12-inch) spinach flour tortillas
1 (4-ounce) can green chilies, drained and patted dry
1 (2.25-ounce) can of sliced black olives, drained and patted dry
2 green onions, chopped
½ cup small diced yellow pepper

In a large bowl, mix together the cream cheese and ranch dressing mix and mix until combined.

Add the rest of the ingredients into the cream cheese mixture and continue mixing until combined.

Divide the cream cheese mixture onto the 4 tortillas. Using a spatula, spread evenly over all tortillas.

Tightly roll up the tortilla and wrap in saran wrap and store in the refrigerator for at least 2 hours or even overnight.

Remove tortillas from fridge and using a serrated knife, cut into ½-inch slices and place on plate. You'll be the hit of any holiday party!

Chapter Eleven

If Hayley was sure of one thing, it was that her brother, Randy, was a good actor. There had been a time when Randy had decided he wanted to be the next Daniel Day-Lewis and moved to New York and studied at the American Academy of Dramatic Arts. However, the unrelenting rejection and frustration of life as a struggling actor ultimately became too much to handle, and he had moved back home to Maine. A wise decision in hindsight, because it was there he had started a successful business and met the love of his life.

But Randy had skills, which were on full display in his senior year of high school when the girl who was cast in the high-school production of *Fiddler on the Roof* came down with a case of mono. There was no one to play Fruma-Sarah, the ghost of Lazar Wolf's dead wife, who returns to haunt Tevye. Randy, who had a small role as a Russian dancer, gamely volunteered to fill in at the last minute on opening night. It was unquestionably a triumph of a performance, although some would argue it wasn't due to Randy's strong singing voice and embodiment of the character. Rather, it was more because when he was hoisted up in the air wearing a harness, and had been flung around so wildly by the stage crew on the ground controlling the pulleys, he had unfortunately become dizzy and nauseous and had thrown up on the first row of the audience. Still, Randy had made an indelible impression and it was at that moment he had decided he wanted to become an actor.

So it was somewhat surprising that his performance now, in his own living room, sitting next to his husband, Sergio, was far less impressive. When Hayley had reluctantly shown up at their door with the disturbing news about Bruce, and how he had blatantly lied to her about his whereabouts on the night Carol Waterman had been murdered, both her brother and his husband had not reacted with the utter shock and concern she had expected.

"Huh," Randy had said with a shrug. "Didn't see that coming."

"I will be sure to look into it," Sergio quickly added, before casually offering her a Bailey's Irish Cream. They had been enjoying the drink themselves while decorating their lush green Christmas tree in the corner of the living room, next to the crackling flames in the fireplace.

"Did you not hear what I just said? Bruce is clearly hiding something! There is the disturbing possibility that he was having a secret affair with Carol Waterman, and he may have been the one who *killed* her!" Hayley wailed.

Randy shot Sergio a not-so-subtle furtive look.

"I just saw that!" Hayley snapped.

"What?" Randy said, feigning innocence before shooting Sergio yet another look.

"That! That look! You keep doing that, like you two already know something!"

Randy threw his hands up in the air. "We don't know anything!"

"Sergio, I spent nearly an hour in my car before coming over here. I couldn't bear the thought of going behind my husband's back, exposing him as a liar, but I ultimately decided I had to do what's right. So here I am, standing right here, betraying him, and all you can say is, you'll look into it?"

"Hayley, Bruce is not the killer," Sergio said calmly.

"How do we know that?" Hayley cried. "He lied to me! He didn't smell like fish the way Sal did when he showed up at the party! He said he had gone home and taken a shower! He could have lied about that, too, because he never went fishing! I just don't understand why Sal would cover for him!"

Randy shot Sergio another knowing look.

"Stop doing that!" Hayley howled. "Why are you two being so cagey?"

There was an agonizing silence before Randy finally spoke up. "We should tell her."

"Tell me *what?*" Hayley shouted, becoming more hysterical by the minute.

Sergio sighed. "Come with us."

They both quietly headed for the kitchen.

Hayley paused, confused, and then followed them.

Sergio opened the door that led out to their attached garage and flipped on a light before stepping aside and ushering Hayley past him, where she stopped in her tracks and gasped.

Parked on the far side of the garage was a brand-new lightning-blue Ford Escape sport utility vehicle, with a giant red bow tied around the exterior.

"What? I don't . . . understand . . ."

"It's your Christmas present," Sergio said.

"My *what* . . . ?" Hayley gasped as she stared at the shiny new vehicle.

"From Bruce," Randy gently explained.

Hayley walked over to the SUV and stood in front of it, unable to take her eyes off it. It was a beautiful car, and it had been an achingly long time since Hayley had driven a brand-spanking-new car.

"He lied to you about going ice fishing with Sal. It's because he was up in Ellsworth at the dealership picking it up for you," Sergio said.

"He asked us if he could store it here until Christmas morning. He was going to jog over really early before you got up and drive it back to your place, where it would be waiting for you in the driveway when you came down to open your presents in front of the tree," Randy said with a big smile. Then he turned to Sergio and chided, "Isn't that an incredible present? What did you get me, socks?"

"You will love them. They have little reindeer embryoed on them," Sergio cracked.

"*Embroidered!*" Randy corrected his sometimes-English-challenged husband, whose first language was Portuguese. "Not *embryoed*. An *embryo* is something entirely different!"

"Whatever," Sergio snapped, waving him away with his hand before turning back to Hayley. "Of course, after you and Mona and Rosana Moretti found Carol's body, I had to make sure. I drove up to Ellsworth and talked to everyone at the dealership, and they all confirmed Bruce was there signing papers at the time of the murder."

"Bruce didn't want to spoil the surprise, so he had Sal cover for him and tell you he had been with him ice fishing on Eagle Lake," Randy added.

Hayley heaved a huge sigh of relief.

Her fears were unfounded.

Bruce was in the clear.

Randy stepped forward and grabbed Hayley by the wrist and looked her squarely in the eyes. "But you have to promise us, you won't say anything. You need to pretend to be totally surprised on Christmas morning when Bruce takes you out to the driveway and presents it to you."

Hayley nodded, crossing her heart with her free hand. "I promise."

She could be a good actress, too, if she needed to be.

But at the moment, not even the acting talent of Meryl Streep could hide the enormous relief on her face, now that she had proof her husband wasn't a lying cheat or a marauding killer.

Chapter Twelve

Hayley's mind may have been put at ease regarding her own husband, and according to Rosana's Sal and Mona's Dennis, they, too, were in the clear. So the puzzling question remained: Why did Carol Waterman write that Christmas card, springing the news that she was planning to run off with one of their spouses? It just didn't make any sense. If it was simply a joke, it wasn't a very funny one. At Hayley's suggestion, she and Rosana arrived at Mona's house early the next morning for a cup of coffee and a little girl chat as to what might be going on.

Mona had already been up at six, feeding her wild brood and getting them off to school, at least the few ones left that she hadn't finally pushed out of the nest. So it was unusually quiet in her kitchen, with no rug rats chasing each other around, screaming at the top of their lungs, and smearing the stainless-steel appliances with their dirty, sticky hands.

Mona grabbed the pot from the coffeemaker and filled both their cups before setting down a carton of milk and bowl of sugar on the table with a few teaspoons. She plopped herself down across from Hayley and Rosana and shook her head, baffled. "I have no idea what the hell is going on? What was Carol thinking? Maybe she really was just trying to mess with us, scare us into believing one of our husbands was secretly in love with her?"

Rosana, eyes wide, carefully sipping her steaming coffee, mind racing, said, "I guess we'll never know why she did it."

"Well, at least we can rest easy now, knowing Bruce, Dennis, and Sal are all in the clear for her murder. That's something to be grateful for, right?" Hayley said, always in search of a silver lining.

"What makes you say that?" Rosana squeaked, setting her coffee down because her hands were shaking.

Hayley and Mona both noticed, but chose not to shine a light on her obvious unsteadiness.

"They all have alibis. There were about a dozen employees at the car dealership who saw Bruce signing the papers for my new car, and Mona's son Chet was with Dennis when he went up to Ellsworth for Christmas shopping, and Sal—"

"Sal was ice fishing out on Eagle Lake. Alone. Unless we can question a nearby deer or a trout that may have gotten caught on his fishing line, there is no one to corroborate his story. He could be lying! It still could be him!" Rosana wailed, suddenly panicked again.

"Rosana, calm down!" Mona bellowed. "It wasn't Sal!"

"Mona's right," Hayley said, nodding.

"But how can we be sure?" Rosana asked, her hands still shaking.

"Because he stank of fish when he showed up at the party!" Hayley exclaimed.

"He could have just bought some fish at the Shop 'n Save and rubbed them all over himself as a way to make his story seem more believable!" Rosana cried.

Hayley took Rosana's hands and squeezed them, hoping to comfort her and to help her stop trembling. "You and Sal have been married how many years now?"

"Twenty-six," Rosana whispered.

"Twenty-six years. Have you ever had any reason to believe Sal would be unfaithful, let alone harm anyone?"

Rosana slowly shook her head.

"I've worked for the man eight years, and I can tell you he is a good person. He may yell sometimes and try to act like the tough guy, but we all know that inside he's a mushy sweetheart with not one violent bone in his body!" Hayley confidently declared.

"I suppose you're right," Rosana said. "We had a mouse in the attic once and Sal refused to put one of those sticky traps up there for it to get caught on. You know the ones I'm talking about, where the poor mouse tries to chew his own leg off to escape—"

"Yes, Rosana! We know what you're talking about! There's no need to get so graphic!" Mona barked.

"Sal used a plastic 7UP bottle, a dab of peanut butter, and a few other things to set a humane trap so the mouse wouldn't be hurt and he could set him free in the woods."

"See? That kind of man isn't capable of murdering a woman in cold blood by strangling her with a Christmas garland!" Hayley assured her. "What we need to be asking ourselves is why did Carol send us that card?"

"I'm sure it was to upset me," Rosana said.

Mona raised an eyebrow. "Why?"

Rosana took a deep breath and sighed. "Because we had an unpleasant altercation not too long ago."

"Rosana, why didn't you tell us this before?" Hayley asked.

"Because it wasn't a big deal and I had completely forgotten about it until just now."

"What happened?" Mona asked, leaning in, slurping some coffee from her cup.

"We were both at a potluck dinner back in March, and everybody was supposed to sign up online to let other people know what they were going to bring. Well, I plumb forgot and just brought my homemade turkey chili. Well, guess what? Carol brought turkey chili, too. And she had remembered to register it online. I thought it was just a funny coincidence, but Carol was furious. She accused me of trying to upstage her, since everyone knows I have the best turkey chili recipe in Bar Harbor. She gave me the evil eye all night, especially as people came up to tell me how much they enjoyed my chili. Carol's chili was hardly touched. I felt awful. When I tried to apologize to her after the dinner, she refused to talk to me and just stalked off, furious. I'm sure the Christmas card was her way of getting revenge."

"Maybe," Hayley said to herself. "But hearing your story reminds me of my own run-in with Carol Waterman."

"You too?" Mona barked, slamming her hands down on her kitchen table and knocking over the bowl of sugar. "What did you do to her?"

"Nothing!" Hayley cried. "But there was certainly no love lost between us. Remember that time about a year ago when Carol was complaining about the young couple who lived next door to her? You know, the ones who never mowed their lawn or took care of their house? Carol was apoplectic. She wrote a scathing op-ed about being a responsible neighbor, which they ignored. Then she tried to get the city council to act, and although they promised to address her concerns, they got too distracted by the town budget negotiations and never followed up. Carol was at her wit's end."

"Didn't Carol spray paint something on their garage door late one night?" Rosana asked.

Hayley nodded. " 'Mow Your Damn Lawn.' Everyone who drove by saw it. It was in bright red paint on their white garage door."

"Sergio had to arrest her," Mona remembered.

"Yes, and she had to pay a hefty fine and reimburse the couple for the cost of repairs. About a week after that, Carol suddenly got worried about her reputation around town and didn't want her arrest recorded in the *Island Times* police beat section. She called me at the office and asked me if I would do her a small favor and pull the arrest from the column. I had to tell her it was too late. The paper had already gone to press and it was probably already up on the website. She was livid. She blamed me! She thought I was purposely trying to humiliate her!"

"That's utterly ridiculous!" Rosana gasped.

"There was nothing I could do!" Hayley said.

"Okay, so Carol had reasons to hate the two of you," Mona growled. "But she had no beef with me. Why did she include me in that stupid Christmas card? We'd never had a bad word between us!"

Frustrated, Hayley's shoulders sagged. She was totally stumped.

Mona's house phone rang and she hauled herself up to her feet and shuffled over to answer the call. "Yeah?"

That was Mona's typical phone greeting.

No cheery "hello" or "good morning." Just "yeah?"

Mona listened to whoever was on the other end and then erupted and roared, *"What?"*

More listening.

Hayley and Rosana exchanged curious glances.

Then another loud *"What?"*

Rosana nearly dropped her coffee cup.

Mona shouted a couple more questions. "He did what?" "What day was that?" She followed by shouting, "I'm going to kill that little hoodlum!"

Mona finally slammed down the phone and marched back over to the kitchen table. "That was the principal out at the high school. Apparently, Chet's been in detention the past two weeks and didn't bother to tell me. The principal was just calling to let me know he didn't bother showing up on Saturday."

"What did he do?" Rosana asked.

"A few week ago, he and his delinquent buddy Abel got a bunch of dog carriers and stuffed them with chickens from Abel's family's farm. They let them loose in the school late one Sunday night, so the next morning the whole faculty was running around chasing frantic chickens."

Hayley snorted, unable to stop herself.

"That's not the worst part. On Mondays, the cafeteria always serves chicken chow mein for lunch!"

Hayley and Rosana were now both howling.

"Apparently, the school sent me an e-mail when the bugger got caught, but it mysteriously got deleted from my account before I saw it. The principal gave him two weeks of detention. The last day he bothered to show up was Friday. I swear I'm going to strangle that kid with my bare hands!"

Hayley's laughter subsided as something dawned on her. "Friday?"

"Yeah, so?" Mona grunted.

Hayley suddenly froze. "Mona . . ."

"What? What's wrong?"

"If that's true, if Chet was serving detention at the high school with a teacher supervising him on the day of our Christmas party . . ."

Mona stumbled back like she had just been punched in

the gut. "Then it would have been impossible for him to be up in Ellsworth with his father doing Christmas shopping."

Father and son.

One of them was lying.

Chapter Thirteen

His mother's icy stare chilled him to the bone. Almost to the point where Hayley could see his whole body shaking.

"What?" Chet managed to squeak out, lacking any other more articulate response.

"I asked you *why* you lied to me," Mona growled.

Chet, somewhere in the middle of her large brood age-wise, stood frozen in place like a squirrel in the middle of the road sensing the approach of an oncoming car.

"I . . . I don't know what you—"

"You were in detention when you told me you had gone to Ellsworth with your father for Christmas shopping!" Mona bellowed.

"Oh, right, that," Chet mumbled, his mind racing, desperate to come up with some logical explanation that would appease his angry mother. "I can't really—"

"You can't really *what*?" Mona snapped.

"I can't tell you," Chet whispered, bowing his head, preparing himself for the inevitable onslaught.

"You can't tell me?" Mona shrieked.

Chet, head still down, nodded slightly.

Mona stepped forward menacingly. "Why not?"

There was a long silence. Hayley and Rosana were both

sitting at the kitchen table when an unsuspecting Chet had ambled in to get himself another soda from the fridge, only to be confronted by his furious mother. Both women now sat motionless at the table, watching the intense drama rapidly unfolding in front of them.

The pressure was getting too much for the poor kid.

He glanced over at Hayley and Rosana, hoping to get some support, but both women quickly averted their eyes.

He was on his own.

"Because . . . Dad asked me not to say anything," he stammered, already aware he was inevitably going to lose this battle.

"Oh, really?" Mona scoffed, one eyebrow raised. "Let me ask you something, Chet. Who are you more afraid of?"

"Um . . . I don't . . ."

"It's a simple question. Who makes the hair on your neck stand up more? Who do you fear the most, me or your father?"

This was not a trick question.

The answer was pretty straightforward.

"You," Chet acknowledged.

"Exactly. So do you honestly think it's a good idea to stand there and lie to me when we both know I can be your worst nightmare?" Mona challenged.

"He promised me a motorcycle!" Chet blurted out.

Mona's cheeks were a deep, livid red. "Excuse me?"

She had broken him. He was eager to confess everything in order to avoid corporal punishment. "He said if I lied and said I'd been with him in Ellsworth that day, he'd buy me a Harley-Davidson Street Rod for Christmas, the one I've been wanting all year!"

Mona stared at him, perplexed. "But why?"

"I don't know. I just wanted that bike, like really bad."

Mona considered this startling revelation for a few more moments, then stared back at her son, eyes narrowing. "Go to your room. You're grounded."

"For how long?" Chet whined.

"I don't know! A while! Until you're thirty-seven!"

"But—"

"Go!"

Chet realized arguing his sentence was futile, at least for now, so he spun around and hightailed it out of the kitchen.

Without another word, Mona marched out the back door to the driveway. After another quick look between them, Hayley and Rosana jumped out of their chairs and chased after her.

Outside, Mona was already rummaging through her husband Dennis's pickup truck.

Both Mona and Dennis owned matching Fords.

"What are you doing?" Rosana asked Mona, who was yanking papers out of the glove box.

"Searching for evidence!" Mona howled.

Hayley gingerly took a step forward so she was directly behind Mona. "You don't need to do that, Mona."

"I'm going to prove my deadbeat husband is a lying cheat!"

"The evidence is right here," Hayley said.

Mona stopped and cranked her head around. "What are you talking about?"

"Just take a whiff."

Mona sniffed the air, finally taking in the same lingering smell Hayley had instantly noticed wafting out from inside Dennis's truck.

It was distinct and undeniable.

It was the strong scent of Carol Waterman's favorite perfume.

White Diamonds by Elizabeth Taylor.

The color drained from Mona's face.

"She was in this truck," Mona gasped. Then she flung herself back toward the house, Hayley and Rosana struggling to keep up.

Inside, Mona spotted Chet hovering near the top of the staircase, craning his neck to see what was going on.

"I said go to your room!" Mona barked, startling the kid so he dashed into his bedroom to hide.

Mona yanked open the door leading to the basement and barreled down the stairs, where Dennis was lounging in his man cave. He was sprawled out on the couch, tipping a bottle of beer and watching an old episode of *Knight Rider,* from his DVD boxed set, on the giant sixty-five-inch flat-screen TV hammered to the wall.

"Oh, good, you're home," Dennis said casually, ignorant to his wife's fiery mood. "Is there any of that crab dip left in the fridge?"

Mona stared at the large image of David Hasselhoff on the screen, a stinging reminder of Carol Waterman's thank-you gift to her husband. She snatched the remote off the wooden coffee table and shut off the TV.

Dennis finally took notice of the seething rage on his wife's face. "Something wrong?"

"It was *you*! You killed Carol Waterman!" Mona cried.

Dennis shot up from the couch.

Frankly, it was the fastest Hayley had ever seen him move since she had met him way back in grade school.

"Wh-what did you say?"

"You heard me, Dennis! I know what you did! I have to admit, I have underestimated you all these years! I didn't even know you had the energy to fill a gas tank, let alone strangle a poor, unsuspecting woman!"

"I have no idea what you're prattling on about! What do you mean, I strangled someone?"

"Carol Waterman!"

Dennis's face slowly went pale. "You think I killed Carol?"

"She's obviously been in your truck! We nearly gagged on the smell of her perfume!" Mona wailed.

"It wasn't me. I didn't harm Carol in any way. You have to believe me!" Dennis pleaded.

"Then what the hell is going on, Dennis?" Mona demanded to know.

With a hangdog look, Dennis raised his eyes to his wife. With a deep sigh, he murmured, "Carol and I have gotten close these past few months."

Mona poked an accusing finger at him. "You were having an affair!"

Dennis slowly nodded.

"Dennis, no!" Hayley heard herself saying.

Dennis pressed on, guilt-ridden as he watched his wife's expression slowly fade from shocked to crestfallen. "It started last summer when I did her landscaping. It was the first time a woman had paid attention to me in a long time. You're always so busy working, Mona."

"Yeah, so I can keep a roof over your head!" Mona cracked, close to tears.

Hayley was struck to see Mona on the verge of crying, since her BFF had always been so strong and with a steely reserve, never one to waste time on tears or over-the-top emotion.

"I'd sneak out when you thought I was down here watching TV and getting drunk and I'd drive over to

Carol's house. Then I'd sneak back, in the wee hours of the morning, before you got up to go haul your lobster traps. I had fallen asleep down here and not made it up to bed so many nights over the years, you never even knew I was gone."

"Was she telling the truth in that Christmas card that she sent us? Were the two of you planning to run away together?"

After a long silence, Dennis whispered, "Yes."

Mona's lip quivered.

"We had talked about it for months, and finally decided to pull the trigger that night when you'd be busy helping Hayley with her office Christmas party. I picked her up in my truck and we were halfway to the Trenton Bridge when I suddenly had a change of heart. I just couldn't go through with it. I turned around and took Carol home. She wasn't too happy about it. She called me a coward."

"Why, Dennis? Why did you change your mind?" Mona sniffed.

"Because despite everything, how most of the time you treat me like an old dog ready to be put down, we have a good thing going here, Mona, and I wasn't ready to give that up."

"No, Dennis, *you've* got a good thing going. Not me. I work my fingers to the bone running my lobster business so you have the luxury to get sauced down here, watch old TV shows from the 1980s, and be a lazy cuss most of the year!"

Dennis had no viable answer to this, since what Mona was saying was pretty much on the mark.

Mona shook her head, disgusted. "And the one time a year when you actually go outside and mow a few lawns, you cheat on me!"

"I swear, Mona, I'm going to do whatever it takes to win back your trust! I promise!"

"Good luck with that," Mona spit out as she turned around and marched back up the stairs to the kitchen.

Dennis turned to Hayley and Rosana, hoping they might help him convince Mona in some way. They simply looked at him with revulsion, though, before following Mona back upstairs and leaving a distraught Dennis alone in the basement to wallow in his misery.

Chapter Fourteen

Hayley and Rosana very quickly left Mona to deal with her desperate husband. Dennis had rushed up after her and was presently on his knees, hands clasped in front of him, begging for her forgiveness.

After dropping Rosana off at her house, Hayley drove her Kia toward home, happy in the thought that the clicking noise in her engine would not be a concern for much longer. Soon she would be driving the new Ford Escape that Bruce had bought her for Christmas.

Her mind wandered back to Dennis, who had so adamantly denied strangling Carol Waterman, even after shamefully admitting to an illicit affair. If Dennis, Bruce, and Sal were indeed all innocent of Carol's murder, then who could have done it? There was only one person who explicitly announced her desire to see Carol dead.

Andrea Cho.

Andrea had been at the *Island Times* office earlier on the evening of Carol's murder while Hayley, Mona, and Rosana were setting up for the Christmas party. However, she had left to buy more rum for the eggnog. Hayley had not noticed when Andrea had returned, or if she had brought a bottle of rum with her, but one thing was for sure. She would have had plenty of time to go to Carol

Waterman's house, strangle her, and return to the office in time for the party. The motive was simple. She was convinced Carol was trying to steal her husband, Leonard, away from her.

But was Andrea Cho capable of murder?

Hayley, of course, had to find out.

She called Andrea and Leonard's house throughout the day, but got no answer. Finally, as darkness fell, Hayley decided to just go over and pop in unannounced. She hopped into her car and drove straight to Roberts Avenue, where Andrea and Leonard owned an old rambling Victorian house. She parked on the opposite side of the street, and had just gotten out of her Kia when another car, a Nissan Rogue, pulled into the driveway of the Cho house, which was lit up outside with an array of bright Christmas lights. The driver's-side door flew open and Leonard, bundled up in a long winter coat and gloves, jumped out and slammed the door behind him. He immediately noticed Hayley, who had stopped at the bottom of their front walk.

Leonard smiled. "Good evening, Hayley. What brings you out on this cold night?"

"I was hoping to speak with Andrea."

"Well, she should be home. Come on in. Is something going on at work?"

"Oh, no, this is personal. I just wanted to—" She stopped midsentence.

Leonard studied her face curiously. "Is something wrong?"

Hayley opened her mouth to answer, but didn't know what to say. Her eyes were fixed on what she was watching through the large living-room window of the house. In front of the Christmas tree, Andrea, her blouse open exposing her bra, was reaching up to kiss David Pine, Carol Waterman's much younger boyfriend. David's hands were in the air, as if he was either surrendering to her advances or in a complete state of shock. He backed into the tree, almost knocking it over, and a few Christmas bulbs fell off.

Leonard started to turn around. "What is it?"

Hayley grabbed his arm to stop him. "Leonard, no!"

But it was too late.

He managed to crank his head around in time to see Andrea now working to unbuckle David's belt.

Leonard shook free of Hayley's grip. "I'll kill the creep!"

And then he stormed into the house.

Hayley followed close on his heels.

As he rounded the corner into the living room to see Andrea and David clutching each other, lipstick now smeared all over David's cheeks, Leonard screamed at the top of his lungs, "Get away from my wife!"

David pushed Andrea away from him. She threw her head back defiantly and wiped her mouth with her hand.

David cried, "Leonard, you don't understand! This is not what you think!"

Andrea gave her husband an icy stare. "It's *exactly* what you think, Leonard."

"No!" David cried. "She invited me here for a cocktail party! I thought there would be other people here, but when I showed up, it was just her, and then she pounced on me!"

"Oh, David, just admit it. You love me. You just told me so, and you asked me to leave Leonard so we can be together," Andrea said calmly with a sly smile.

David's eyes popped open. "No! That's a lie! She's just trying to make you jealous!"

Mission accomplished.

Leonard roared like an animal, and dove across the room, tackling David as Andrea casually stepped out of the way. The two men rolled around on the floor, Leonard swinging his fists wildly at David as he tried covering his face to protect himself from the blows.

Hayley turned to Andrea. "Andrea, do something before he kills him!"

But Andrea seemed to be enjoying this duel to the death, especially since she was, in her mind, the ultimate prize.

Hayley couldn't just stand by and allow them to hurt each other, so she raced over and grabbed the back of David's turtleneck in order to yank him away from Leonard. She pulled with all her might and the shirt ripped apart. David stumbled back and landed flat on his back. Leonard was up on his feet now, fists clenched, ready to box. Hayley stepped between the two men, keeping them apart with her outstretched arms.

"Stop this right now or I'll call the police! Do you hear me?"

Leonard ignored her and focused on his wife. "Do you *love* him?"

After keeping him in suspense a few moments longer, Andrea finally sighed. "No, Leonard, you big lug. I love *you.*"

Leonard's rage slowly began to dissipate and he stared numbly at Andrea, utterly confused as to what was going on.

"I just needed to give you a taste of your own medicine," Andrea cooed.

"Because of what happened with Carol Waterman at the basketball game? *She* came on to *me*! I was just sitting there eating my hot dog! I practically had to fight her off!"

"You should have fought harder," Andrea said, pouting.

Hayley couldn't believe she was witnessing this.

Neither could David Pine.

She could tell he felt used and was livid. He pointed a finger at Leonard. "I could have you arrested for assault!"

"Man up. I barely touched you," Leonard scoffed.

Andrea suddenly appeared nervous. "Leonard, he's right. Look at those scratches on his neck."

Hayley quickly eyed some red marks that were clearly visible on David's neck after she had accidentally torn his turtleneck open. She then turned her attention back to Leonard and his hands.

And that's when she knew who killed Carol Waterman.

Andrea, meanwhile, was starting to panic. "David, I'm sorry. This is all my fault. I was jealous and I thought it would be poetic justice if Leonard came home to find me with another man, notably Carol's boyfriend. It was a stupid, childish thing for me to do and—"

Turning toward David, Hayley said solemnly, "It was you."

David looked at her, confused. "What are you talking about?"

Andrea and Leonard appeared confused as well.

Hayley took a cautious step closer toward David. "You killed Carol."

David's eyes widened, feigning astonishment. "What . . . what did you just say?"

"I should have known when you came back to the Christmas party and told us that story about some kids bumping into you, causing you to spill soda all over yourself at the grocery store, so you had to go home and change."

"You're accusing me of murder because I changed out of a stained shirt to go to a party?" David asked incredulously.

"No, I think you made the whole thing up. You didn't have to change your shirt because it got dirty, you had to change your shirt to cover up those scratches! That's why when you returned to the office you were wearing a turtleneck!"

"This . . . this is absurd," David sputtered.

"It all makes sense now. You loved Carol. But that night, when you went to pick up napkins at the store for Mona, you must have stopped by Carol's house to pick her up for the party earlier than planned. She was not supposed to even be there. She had been secretly plotting to run away with Mona's husband, Dennis Barnes. She was just going to leave town and ghost you, avoid the whole confrontation with you, and never be heard from again. But Dennis had had a change of heart. They never got off the island. He broke it off and drove her back home, where she was when you showed up. She was probably distraught over being dumped. You could see she was upset and you probably pressed her until she told you what was wrong."

Hayley could see David cracking.

Her words were hitting far too close to home.

"I'm right, aren't I, David?" Hayley whispered.

David gave her a slight nod. He sniffed and then wiped his nose with his forearm. "I found her crying. She was an emotional mess. I tried comforting her, but she just swatted me away, like some housefly, and told me to leave her alone. I couldn't believe how she was treating me. We had been so close. I thought we were in love, only to find out—"

"She loved someone else and you were just a distraction."

"It made me so angry," David growled.

"And that's when you went crazy."

"I . . . I never meant to kill her . . . I was so in love with her . . . but she was so callous, so unfeeling, she made me feel so small . . . and I guess I kind of blacked out. I didn't know what I was doing."

"You strangled her with the garland and she fought for her life, clawing at your neck, but you were too strong for her and you finally got the best of her. When you snapped out of it, you knew you had to cover up those scratches on your neck and get back to the office with an alibi. Before you left the house, you must have used Carol's phone to send yourself a text from her, breaking your date because she wasn't feeling well, so as not to arouse suspicion why you weren't both at the Christmas party. And you came up with the excuse that some kids caused you to spill soda on your shirt to explain your change in clothing."

David bowed his head.

Leonard put a protective arm around Andrea.

Hayley reached for her phone to call 911.

Suddenly David, like a cornered stray dog with rabies, lashed out, shoving Hayley into the Christmas tree, sending her and the tree crashing to the floor. Then he made a break for the door before Leonard or Andrea had a chance to stop him. As he flung open the door, he stopped in his tracks at the sight of Police Chief Alvares, gun drawn, but down at his side.

"I think you better step back inside, David, we need to talk," Sergio said calmly.

Hayley, tinsel hanging from her hair, crawled out from underneath the ornaments and lights on the branches of the Cho Christmas tree. "Sergio, what are you doing here?"

"Got a noise complaint from next door. They heard a lot of shouting and got worried," Sergio said, one hand gripping David's arm while still holding his weapon at the ready in the other. "Funny thing is, I was already on the lookout for Mr. Pine here. Seems back when he was in high school, he got arrested for shoplifting cigarettes and beer."

"That was a long time ago," David whimpered.

"True, but you were fingerprinted when you were booked, so imagine my surprise when those prints matched the one we found on Carol Waterman's phone, the one you put there when you sent that phony text."

David's shoulders slumped.

"I'm going to read you your rights now, if that's okay with you, David," Sergio said with a smug smile before winking at Hayley.

As she pulled the stringy tinsel from the Christmas tree out of her hair, Hayley couldn't help but notice Andrea and Leonard staring lovingly into each other's eyes. They were hardly able to stop themselves from pawing each other right in front of Bar Harbor's police chief.

Hayley sighed.

At least one marriage had been saved tonight.

Mona's, however, was still hanging in the balance.

Chapter Fifteen

Dennis was noticeably absent when Hayley and Bruce showed up for Mona's Christmas Eve feast, a potluck extravaganza Mona proudly hosted for friends and family every year. Randy and Sergio were in attendance, unsurprisingly, since Randy always provided free booze from his bar. Liddy, unfortunately, had an obligation to spend Christmas Eve with her mother, Celeste, a three-time divorcee who tended to get rather needy around the holidays. Sal and Rosana were also at Mona's house, where Sal spent some of his time in the kitchen, stirring a pot of his homemade oyster stew, a holiday tradition in his family. Mona's kids, six or seven of them—who could really keep track at this point?—were relatively well-behaved. Most of them had mellowed and were watching the seventh or eighth showing of *A Christmas Story* on TV in the family den. Hayley assumed they had all been threatened with bodily harm from their mother if they dared to act up in front of her guests.

Hayley smelled a ham baking in the oven when she and Bruce first toddled through the front door. Hayley had been carrying one of her Gingerbread-Spiced Pumpkin Pies wrapped in tinfoil, while Bruce carefully balanced her

Mile-High Cranberry Meringue Pie in his hands. She could also see into the kitchen, where two giant pots with steam drifting out of them were on the stovetop burners, undoubtedly boiling with water and ready for Mona's fresh lobsters.

Mona, in one of her trademark jokey sweatshirts, this one bright red with *Santa's Favorite Ho* emblazoned on the front, greeted them and snatched the pie from Bruce. "Merry Christmas! Please tell me you brought that delicious Cinnamon-Sugar Apple Pie you made last Christmas!"

Hayley, dismayed, said quietly, "Sorry, I went in a different direction this year."

Mona, attempting to hide her disappointment, but failing miserably, forced a smile. "I'm sure whatever is underneath this foil will taste just as good. Now help yourselves to a drink."

"You don't have to tell me twice," Bruce said before turning to Hayley. "Rum and eggnog?"

Hayley nodded and Bruce dashed off toward the bar next to the fireplace in the living room. As Hayley followed Mona toward the kitchen, she rubbed her brother's back sweetly as they passed him and Sergio, who were both engrossed in a deep conversation with Rosana and Sal. Randy blew her an air-kiss and resumed listening to Rosana, who was prattling on and on, her voice a whisper. Hayley heard Carol Waterman's name mentioned under Rosana's breath, so the topic of their conversation was obvious.

In the kitchen, Mona opened the fridge and set the pie down on the top rack. She turned and took the pumpkin pie from Hayley and slid it in next to the other one.

"Dennis isn't tending bar this year?" Hayley asked.

"Uh, no. Dennis has been banished to his man cave.

He's probably down there sulking, downing a six-pack, and cursing me."

"Have you two at least talked?"

Mona slammed the refrigerator door shut and shuffled over to the oven to check on her ham. "We were up all last night talking. Well, it was mostly me yelling at the top of my lungs, but he did manage to get in a few 'I'm sorry' admissions when I had to stop to catch my breath."

After inspecting her ham, Mona closed the oven. "Needs about twenty more minutes."

"Can you ever see yourself forgiving him?"

Mona wiped her hands with a dish towel and then discarded it on the counter as she stared at Hayley, thinking. After a few moments, she nodded. "I think I already have."

Hayley sighed. "Well, that's a relief. I honestly can't see you and Dennis apart."

Mona gave Hayley a curious look. "Why not?"

"I don't know. You've been together for such a long time, gone through so much, raised an army of kids."

"Sit down, Hayley," Mona instructed.

Suddenly wary, Hayley plopped down in a chair. Mona sat down next to her. "I said I forgive Dennis. That doesn't mean we're going to stay together."

"*What?*" Hayley croaked.

Mona took a deep breath and exhaled. "I've been thinking about things for a while now. Ever since you, me, and Liddy went to Salmon Cove not too long ago and I ran into my old childhood friend—"

"Corey," Hayley said softly.

Mona teared up at the mention of his name, but managed to stay strong and not break down. "Yup."

Hayley knew Mona had fallen hard for the handsome

lobsterman, with his bedroom eyes and intoxicating smile, who had taught her everything she knew. He had a big pickup truck and a sweet dog named Sadie. What wasn't for Mona to like when reuniting with him in Salmon Cove after not having seen each other since they were teenagers?

As if on cue, Corey's lovable, lumbering golden retriever trotted into the room and made a beeline for Mona, who gently stroked Sadie's head. She had adopted the dog after Corey's untimely passing.

"The time I spent with Corey was awfully special," Mona said, eyes fixed on the floor. "It made me realize . . ." Mona stopped as if afraid to say it out loud.

Hayley leaned forward. "What, Mona?"

"I deserve better," she muttered.

They sat there in silence as they listened to Randy launch into a rousing rendition of "Jingle Bells" before he was joined by Sergio and Rosana. They also heard one of Mona's kids, one of the boys, yell from the den, "Keep it down! We're trying to watch a movie!"

Hayley returned her attention to Mona, who now had her elbows on the table, her hands on her face, staring into space as she spoke. "I deserve someone who will always be there for me. I'm not talking distance. Dennis is never more than a few feet away down in the basement."

"I know what you mean, Mona."

"I've always tried to be a good wife, always be there if he needed me, but this whole Carol Waterman train wreck really opened my eyes. It's all one-sided. Dennis has never really been there for me, at least not in a very long time."

Hayley reached out and took Mona's hand. She was a little surprised when the typically emotionally reticent Mona didn't immediately yank it back and bark at Hayley to stop being silly. In fact, Mona squeezed Hayley's comforting hand.

Mona shrugged. "I guess I was afraid of losing him and so I hung on, worried that once all the kids were gone, I'd be alone if Dennis wasn't around. But I'm not afraid anymore, Hayley."

"You work so hard, Mona, you're a good mother, nobody deserves to live their best life more than you."

Mona couldn't fight it any longer. Her eyes welled up with tears and it ticked her off. "Stop being so mushy, Hayley!"

Hayley threw her hands up in surrender. "Sorry!"

Mona wiped the tears away with the sleeve of her sweatshirt and cleared her throat, anxious to wrap up, in her mind, this overwrought conversation. "I've given him until New Year's Day to get packed up and be gone."

Hayley sat back, stunned. She hadn't expected such an accelerated timeline. "Wow!"

"Why drag it out? We both need to move on. He's already got a lead on a new place. He'll still be around to see the kids. I can keep raising them and running the business. I've been pretty much doing it solo, up to this point anyway. Not much is going to change, to be honest. It'll be good to be on my own for a while."

Hayley cracked a smile. "Or at least until you meet *the one*—"

"Now don't go squawking about dumb things like that. I am way too old to start dating. Besides, after putting up with Dennis for so long, I'm done with men! You hear me? *Finito!*"

"Whatever you say, Mona," Hayley said.

"I'm serious, Hayley. Wipe that stupid grin off your face right now. I don't want you fixing me up with anyone, least of all some local yokel. And if you sign me up for one of those dating apps like Splinter—"

"Tinder," Hayley corrected her.

"Whatever! Well, I won't have it, you hear me?" Mona wailed. "Not for me!"

Bruce wandered into the kitchen carrying three drinks in his hands. Hayley popped up from her chair.

"Let me help you," Hayley said, taking her rum and eggnog.

Bruce handed a rose-colored drink to Mona. "Vodka cranberry, I presume."

"Now there's a man who knows what I want," Mona barked.

"What are we talking about?" Bruce asked, left with his own cocktail, a gin on the rocks.

"Nothing!" Mona snapped.

Bruce held up his glass. "Merry Christmas, and here's to a happy new year!"

Hayley and Mona both raised their glasses to their lips, but stopped short of taking a sip, because Bruce wasn't quite done with his toast.

"In the words of Benjamin Franklin, 'Be at war with your vices, at peace with your neighbors, and let every new year find you a better man.'"

"I couldn't agree more," Hayley said, winking conspiratorially at Mona, who was not having it.

"You're acting ridiculous, Hayley!" Mona cried before turning toward Bruce. "And what kind of idiotic quote is that? What are you trying to say? I'm not looking for a better man!"

"It's just a toast, Mona," Bruce said, thoroughly confused.

"And what the hell does Benjamin Franklin know anyway? Didn't he go out and fly a kite in a friggin' thunderstorm? I mean, come on, who does that?"

The more Mona protested, the more Hayley's excitement grew for all the exciting possibilities on the horizon for her best friend in the brand-new year.

Island Food & Spirits

By Hayley Powell

Since the past few weeks have been so hectic, I decided this past weekend I needed to relax a little bit and do some restorative baking therapy to calm the mind. I settled upon a cheesecake recipe, which just happened to be the favorite of Mona, one of my BFFs. I figured it would go a long way in cheering her up after a rather traumatic holiday season. Who wouldn't feel better after a slice of yummy cheesecake, am I right?

For her part, Mona brought over some of her delicious hot buttered rum to enjoy with the cheesecake. After thoroughly stuffing ourselves, we came to the conclusion that instead of wallowing on the couch watching a Lifetime movie, we should get some fresh air and walk off all those calories. Mona's younger kids had earlier left their house to go snow sledding at Little Bunker Hill, located at the Kebo Valley Golf Club, so we headed in that direction.

The golf course has two sledding hills, Little Bunker, a small slope, perfect for younger kids, and the much steeper Big Bunker, a faster, more rigorous, narrower stretch downhill. It has been a long-standing tradition in the winter, for as far back as anyone can remember, at least a century or more, for local kids to drag their sleds to Kebo for some winter fun down one or both of the inclines.

Another tradition was for the older teens, and maybe a few irresponsible adults, to pile up mounds of snow near the bottom of the imposing Big Bunker to make a jump so that the braver souls could aim their toboggans and sleds directly at it. This way, they could see if they could ride their sleds right off the ground, become airborne without flying off and breaking an arm, or worse, crashing into one of the tall, imposing trees that lined the hill.

I was around twelve when I started begging my mom to allow me to ride down Big Bunker because all my friends were going. I didn't want to be the only one regulated to "the baby hill." After much pleading and whining and promising not to be reckless, my mother finally relented. I had a green light to go down Big Bunker with "the big kids."

Finally, when Saturday arrived, I was up early, ready to go, impatiently waiting for my mother to give me a lift to Kebo, where I was to meet Liddy and Mona for our first ride down Big Bunker. That's when my mother dropped a bomb on me and informed me that she had to go into work for a few hours and needed me to keep an eye on my little brother, Randy. There was no way I was going to be stuck with him all day, but before I could open my mouth to protest, my mother said I had to take Randy with me or stay home. So I took him with me.

Randy wasn't happy about the arrangement, either. He would have preferred staying home and watching his favorite Saturday-morning cartoons, like *ThunderCats* and *Teenage Mutant Ninja Turtles*. He grumbled and complained while Mom bundled him up in his snow pants, jacket, hat, and gloves.

Mona and Liddy were already waiting when we pulled into the driveway of the golf course, and I jumped out, angrily dragging my sled and my pouting little brother behind me. That's when I heard my mother call to me from the car, "Hayley, don't forget, you have your little brother with you, so no going down Big Bunker today!"

What?

I whipped around, cheeks red with fury, and was about to argue, but I took one look at my mother's stern face, and I knew I had lost before I had even begun. I just nodded glumly and said, pouting, "Okay."

I stomped over to Mona and Liddy, who were surprised to see Randy in tow, and reported the bad news. No Big Bunker today. It was official. Randy had ruined my life.

After a couple of dull runs down Little Bunker, I could see Mona and Liddy staring longingly over at Big Bunker on the other side of the golf course. We could hear the excited screams and raucous laughter from the older kids who were whizzing down the snow-packed hill. They all seemed to be having the time of their lives. At one point, I spotted my archenemy, Sabrina Merryweather, with a few of her older junior-high cohorts, standing atop Big Bunker, pointing and laughing. I can't be 100 percent sure she was pointing and laughing at us, but I had endured enough humiliation. I grabbed Randy's mitten and told Mona and Liddy to follow me.

Dragging our sleds behind us, we trudged across the golf course to Big Bunker. Randy tried to protest, threatening to tattle to my mother, but I just ripped his mitten off his free hand and stuffed it in his mouth. I figured he'd have so much fun going down the big mountain the first time, he'd want to do it again and again. Then he would back me up when I lied and told my mother that we had stayed at Little Bunker the whole morning.

All four of us piled onto Mona's wooden toboggan, with Mona in front, then Liddy, Randy, and me bringing up the rear. A high-school boy, whom Liddy was smitten with, offered to push us off, and we took off down the steep incline. It was exhilarating! We were all screaming and laughing, the cold wind freezing our cheeks! Even Randy was giggling uncontrollably as we shot toward the bottom of the hill at lightning speed.

Unfortunately, what we hadn't realized, since it was our first time, was that someone needed to steer the toboggan to the left, otherwise we would directly hit the piled-up snow jump.

Well, as you can imagine, the next thing we all knew, the toboggan hit the jump. We went sailing high into the air, with a clear view straight across the golf course of a spazzed-out woman standing atop the smaller hill, waving her arms and yelling. She looked exactly like my mother did when she was really angry.

Well, you can probably guess by now, it *was* my mother. She had come back to pick us up a little early, just in time to unfortunately see Randy fly off the toboggan and land with a painful thud on the snow-covered frozen ground. When the toboggan crashed down, the remaining three of us tumbled off and rolled over each other, winding up on our backs, as if we were about to make snow angels. Meanwhile, the driverless toboggan continued on its way until it finally slid to a stop halfway across the golf course.

I clambered to my feet and ran to check on my brother, who was holding his arm and crying in pain. I slowly turned to see my mother slipping and sliding across the golf course, frantically trying to reach us.

Later, it turned out Randy's arm had been broken. He was forced to wear a cast for the rest of the winter, which he was actually elated about because now he didn't have to go outside in the cold and could stay home and watch his cartoons. So in my mind, I had done him a favor. Sadly, my mother didn't see it quite that way and I was informed that my days of sledding on any hill, large or small, were over for at least a year.

Hot Buttered Rum

Ingredients:
2 ounces dark rum
1 small slice of butter
Pinch of cinnamon
Pinch of nutmeg
1 teaspoon vanilla
Boiling water

Add your butter, cinnamon, nutmeg, and vanilla to a mug and mix.

Add the rum and boiling water and stir well until all combined.

Serve on a chilly day and enjoy!

Mona's Favorite No Bake Cheesecake

Ingredients:

Crust
2 cups plain graham cracker crumbs
½ cup butter melted

Filling
3 (8-ounce) packages cream cheese, room temperature
1½ cups powdered sugar
1 tablespoon vanilla
1 cup heavy whipping cream

Combine your graham crackers and melted butter in a bowl. Pour into a 9-inch springform pan and press into the bottom of the pan and up the sides about 1 inch.

In a stand mixer, or large bowl with a hand mixer, beat the cream cheese until smooth.

Add the sugar and vanilla and beat until smooth.

Add the cream and beat on low until fully incorporated and smooth.

Pour the cream cheese mixture into the prepared crust, cover, and refrigerate for 6 hours or, even better, overnight.

If desired, serve with whipped cream or your favorite berries over the top.

DEATH OF A CHRISTMAS CARD CRAFTER

Peggy Ehrhart

Acknowledgments

Abundant thanks, again, to my agent Evan Marshall, and to my editor at Kensington Books, John Scognamiglio.

Chapter One

"**A**ll I can say is, she must have very nimble fingers!"
Bettina Fraser held up a tiny sweater, too tiny even
to fit a doll. It was complete with ribbing at cuffs, neck-
line, and waist, and was fashioned in alternating red and
green stripes.

"Very nimble," Pamela Paterson agreed. "And Sorrel's
knitted creations make perfect Christmas tree ornaments—
so colorful, but light enough that they don't weigh down
the branches."

"They'll go fast," Bettina said. "We'd better put some
aside if we want any for our own trees."

Pamela nodded, but she was distracted by making
change for a woman who had just handed over a fifty-
dollar bill for a knitted scarf that Pamela herself had knit.

"You always have such nice things at this booth," the
woman said. "I know I can find all my last-minute gifts
here." She tucked the scarf, indigo blue and featuring a
lacy stitch that Pamela had enjoyed mastering, into a canvas tote and held out a hand for the twenty and the ten
Pamela offered.

It was the first day of the Arborville Holiday Craft Fair,
held in St. Willibrod's church hall, with proceeds going to
the Arborville High School art, drama, and music pro-

grams. Pamela was the founder and mainstay of the town's knitting club, nicknamed Knit and Nibble, and the group had organized a table selling yarn creations. Many of the creations had been made by Knit and Nibble members, among them Bettina, who was also Pamela's neighbor and best friend.

Pamela surveyed the large room, which echoed with conversation, laughter, and Christmas music. Residents of Arborville, as well as people from neighboring towns, browsed from table to table, admiring—and buying—the offerings: fanciful pottery creations, wall plaques with inspiring sayings, handmade aprons and children's clothes in gay prints, jewelry fashioned from exotic and not-so-exotic materials, bowls carved from intricately gnarled wood, dolls with whole wardrobes of fashionable clothes, and much, much more. There was also food: Christmas cookies, of course, and cakes and pies and muffins and brownies and homemade candy.

The tables were ranged around the periphery of the room, and in the center a giant Christmas tree decorated with ornaments made by the children in the St. Willibrod's grammar school lent its piney aroma to the scene.

Pamela's gaze roamed here and there, but her eyes lingered for a moment on a small dark-haired figure in a violet jacket, a young woman who was just turning away from a table across the room. The table was bare except for a small stack of boxes, the sort of boxes that might contain Christmas cards.

The young woman surveyed the room too, and when her eyes met Pamela's, her already bright expression became even brighter. Bettina exclaimed, "Penny's here!"

Penny was Pamela's daughter, home from her college in Boston for Christmas vacation. She waved and then began making her way through the crowd. She was carrying one of the boxes, and as she got closer, she held it up.

"I hadn't seen Karma's Christmas card yet," Penny said as she got even closer. "It's really good—but I'm kind of sad because it might be the last one."

"Karma" was Karma Karling, one of the art teachers from the high school. She'd been Penny's favorite teacher when Penny was a student there. Every year since Karma had been at the high school, she had designed a Christmas card to benefit the art program. The cards were sold all around town starting in early November.

"The last one?" Bettina raised her carefully shaped brows. "Is she leaving Arborville?"

Penny had reached Pamela and Bettina's table and she displayed the box, which had a clear lid through which the card could be seen.

" 'Twelve drummers drumming,' " Penny said. "She's been at Arborville High for twelve years and she's used up all the days of Christmas."

"Such a cute idea," Pamela murmured. "I remember the first one—'a partridge in a pear tree.' You were only in fourth grade. But she'll think of another theme, I'm sure. Karma is such a creative person."

Penny opened the box and handed a card each to Pamela and Bettina. "I already sent my Christmas cards," she said, "but I'll use some of these for my Christmas thank-you notes. The twelve days of Christmas only start on Christmas Day."

The card design *was* charming. The twelve drummers were old-fashioned drummers in red, white, and blue uniforms that made them resemble toy soldiers, and they were marching in a tight formation, four abreast. Their drums were snare drums, trimmed with silvery chrome, and suspended from straps that crossed smartly from each drummer's right shoulder to his left hip.

As Pamela was studying the card, Penny had been fingering one of the tiny sweater ornaments. "How could anyone do this?" she asked. "So tiny, and these mittens are even tinier. I have to buy some." Penny reached for the small purse dangling from her shoulder.

Besides the sweaters, Sorrel Wollcott had knit mittens and little stockings, all in bright colors and all furnished with yarn loops for hanging.

"We certainly don't need ornaments." Pamela laughed, picturing the boxes of ornaments she'd brought down from her attic only the previous day. She and Penny would be decorating their tree that evening. "But I can't resist them either—and it's for such a good cause."

"My treat." Penny dipped a hand into her purse and came up with her wallet. "I loved my art classes at Arborville High, and Karma was just the best!" She set aside a tiny blue and yellow striped sweater, a red mitten, and a yellow stocking.

"The sweaters are five each and the mitten and stocking are three each," Pamela said as Penny counted out eleven dollars. Meanwhile, Bettina was dispensing change into the outstretched hand of a woman who had just bought a set of hand-knit pot holders.

Shoppers crisscrossed the gleaming floor, some carrying bags containing the treasures they'd selected, others carrying boxes holding baked goods, as a lively version of "Jingle Bells" provided a soundtrack. Some shoppers carried nothing yet, but greeted friends and formed conversational clusters. Near the Christmas tree, two little boys were engaged in a teasing game that involved circling in opposite directions and then shrieking in mock alarm when they came face-to-face.

But the cheerful din suddenly muted, in a wave that

seemed to emanate from the double doors that faced Arborville Avenue. And most motion ceased, except for the circling of the little boys—until a worried-looking young woman grabbed each by an arm.

At the knitting table near the back of the room, Pamela had at first heard nothing out of the ordinary. But as the atmosphere became more muted still, she could make out the droning rise and fall of a siren.

Bettina finished tucking a matching hat and scarf set into a recycled Co-Op bag and extended it toward a woman who started to reach for it, but then turned away.

"Something's happened," she said as she turned back. "Look—over by the entrance."

A police officer was visible through the milling crowd, just pulling back one of the heavy glass doors. The siren had drawn much closer. Then at its high-pitched peak, it cut off abruptly, trailing away in a resentful moan.

As the officer entered, a few men exited. Pamela recognized one of them as Gus Warburton, who worked for the rec department and could be counted on whenever a community event needed extra hands.

Penny, meanwhile, had circled the table and was standing between her mother and Bettina. Pamela lost sight of the officer as part of the crowd coalesced into a tight knot around him. Other people began to retreat from the entrance in pairs or larger groupings, bending toward one another and engaged in conversations whose seriousness was marked by the somber expressions on their faces.

Pamela caught a few words here and there. Something had happened in the Christmas tree lot and the police had been called—thus the sirens. The Christmas tree lot was set up every year not far from St. Willibrod's by the Aardvark Alliance (named for the Arborville High School football team). Proceeds benefited the school's sports programs.

Bettina stepped out from behind the table and into the path of a middle-aged woman who was among those re-treating from the entrance. Before Bettina could open her mouth, the woman spoke.

"There's a dead body," she said in a tone that implied she scarcely believed her own words. She paused and looked back in the direction she'd come from. "The po-lice . . ." Her voice faltered and she swung around to face Bettina again.

Pamela was about to join Bettina, but Penny seized her arm. And anyway, Bettina had begun to edge toward the table, drawing the middle-aged woman along with her. There was no need to ask the woman for further informa-tion, because now all around them voices were rising and echoing as "Jingle Bells" played in the background. Cer-tain words stood out from the indistinct rumble, like "shock-ing" and "murder," and people who knew more about what had happened supplemented versions of the story purveyed by people who knew less.

Eventually a clear picture emerged. Police had been called shortly after the Christmas tree lot opened at ten a.m. because a member of the Aardvark Alliance had dis-covered a body.

Voices were by turns urgent, curious, angry, and sad. Behind the tables ranged around the room, people who had been cheerfully promoting their wares stood with their hands hanging aimlessly at their sides, their eyes scanning the crowd.

Penny continued to cling to Pamela's arm, though nei-ther spoke. Pamela was fighting to banish from her mind the sense of unreality that had invaded the moment she'd heard the words "There's a dead body." She felt remote from the hubbub around her and barely even connected to her daughter, though Penny was holding on as if for dear life.

Meanwhile, Bettina, along with the middle-aged woman, had joined a group of other women who were alternately craning their necks in this direction and that as if seeking guidance and bending their heads inward to confer.

More police officers had entered the church hall. Now two were stationed at the entrance and another, the woman that Pamela recognized as Officer Sanchez, was making her way across the floor as the milling crowd parted respectfully and then groups regrouped in her wake. She seemed to be heading for a corner near the edge of the stage, where a door led into an inner sanctum.

"Jingle Bells" had just segued into "Good King Wenceslas" when a rasp of static interrupted the music. A voice that Pamela recognized as that of the fair's organizer, Loretta Litton, came on to announce that the craft fair was being suspended for the day. Police had asked that people not linger outside but go on about their business.

Nonetheless, after Pamela and Bettina had packed up the hats and scarves and the pot holders and tea cozies and little knitted ornaments and the rest, and had stowed them away under the Knit and Nibble table, they stepped outside to discover that the milling, murmuring crowd had merely transferred itself from one venue to another.

When they reached the sidewalk, Penny stopped and looked up at her mother, and Pamela felt a twinge in her throat, as if a busy needle had just taken a stitch. She pulled her daughter into a hug and rested her chin on Penny's curly head. Penny hadn't inherited Pamela's height, and though Penny was already a junior in college, Pamela had to constantly remind herself that lack of stature didn't equal lack of maturity.

The Christmas tree lot had already been encircled by yellow crime-scene tape, looped from post to post along the chicken wire fence that the members of the Aardvark Alliance erected every year. A police officer was stationed at the gate, which had been closed. Behind the fence, the trees—deep green and bristly—stood in rows as if denizens of a very orderly forest. The spicy pine scent carried all the way to the sidewalk, and its evocation of a season that should be happy seemed an incongruous contradiction to the crime-scene tape and the uniformed officer.

The people who had vacated the church hall now occupied the sidewalk and spilled over onto the grass that ringed the tree lot's fence—despite the admonitions of the police officer at the gate to stay back. But Pamela continued on her way with Penny in tow, heading toward where she and Bettina had parked when they arrived that morning with their boxes of knitted wares.

Bettina lagged behind, gazing toward the tree lot, and Pamela suspected her friend was loath to depart without a more complete picture of what had happened. Bettina would eventually be covering the story for Arborville's weekly, the *Advocate,* and she took her reportorial duties seriously.

When Pamela was well clear of the crowd, she paused and Penny paused with her. Bettina dodged through the last knot of people and was within a few yards of where Pamela and Penny stood when a second woman broke through the crowd in hot pursuit.

"Bettina! Wait!" the woman called.

It was Marlene Pepper, one of Bettina's friends, a plump middle-aged woman who was normally the soul of good cheer. At the moment, however, her expression reflected not only distress that Arborville's Christmas rituals had been disrupted by this alarming discovery but something deeper. Her mouth was agape, as if frozen in a silent moan and her brows were drawn together with a deep furrow between them.

She caught up with Bettina, seized her hand, and reached out to seize Pamela's hand as well.

"Did you hear who it is?" she asked breathlessly. "So shocking . . . I can't believe . . ." She stopped to pant.

Bettina's mobile features now mirrored Marlene Pepper's, and with her own free hand she grasped the hand that was grasping hers.

"Karma Karling!" Marlene wailed. "Can you believe it? Someone has killed Karma Karling!"

From behind Pamela came another wail, but wordless. Pamela turned to see Penny gazing at her, looking stunned, her eyes glistening with the beginnings of tears. Once again Pamela herself felt a jolt that seemed to disconnect her from the scene playing out before her.

Tucked in a canvas tote for safekeeping was the box of Christmas cards Penny had just bought, Karma Karling's latest Christmas design.

"Oh, dear! Oh, dear!" Bettina freed her hand from Marlene's and leaned toward Penny. In a moment Pamela, Penny, and Bettina were entwined in a three-way hug.

Chapter Two

As soon as Bettina's faithful Toyota had come to a stop in the Frasers' driveway, the front door of her house opened. Onto the porch stepped a pleasant-looking man, somewhat portly, with thick white hair and dressed in a flannel shirt and bib overalls.

"Dear, dear wife!" he cried. "What has happened?"

Bettina was the wife in question. She swung her feet out onto the asphalt as a few long strides carried Wilfred Fraser along the walk that connected porch and driveway.

"I didn't expect you until nearly dinnertime," he said, his genial face puckering with concern. He reached for her hand to draw her out of the car.

"Oh, Wilfred!" Bettina moaned, and she nestled her head against his chest. Her vivid hair, which she herself described as a color not found in nature, was bright against the denim of his overalls, the uniform he'd adopted in retirement.

Pamela and Penny circled the car to join them. When Bettina's gulps and sniffles threatened to cut short her narrative of what had brought them home so early, Pamela took over as Penny sniffled quietly at her side, enveloped in a half hug.

"We must all come inside before we freeze," Wilfred announced—though only he was unprovided with a coat, and the day was not as cold as a day so near Christmas might be.

Woofus the shelter dog raised his head from his nap on Bettina's comfy sofa to watch as people shed their coats and then proceeded on toward the kitchen. Once they were gone, he went back to sleep.

"I'm thinking grilled cheese sandwiches," Wilfred said. And he reached for his apron as the others arranged themselves around the well-scrubbed pine table in the eating area of Bettina's spacious kitchen.

Grilled cheese sandwiches and the comforting presence of Wilfred had eased the shock of the morning's events, but Pamela and Penny were still far from cheerful as they crossed the street to their own house. Yet Pamela turned her key in the lock and stepped into her entry as if into a welcoming haven.

Her house was large, too large for one person, but when Penny was away at college Pamela lived there alone, with only two cats for company. Long ago, before Penny was born, Pamela and her husband had fallen in love with the house, a hundred-year-old house on a tree-lined street in a town that reminded them of the college town where they had met. Michael Paterson's skills as an architect had helped them restore it to its former glory.

Then, when Penny was still in grammar school, he had been killed in a tragic accident on a construction site. Pamela had stayed on in the house, feeling her husband's presence all around her and wanting to keep Penny's life as unchanged as possible—though so much had changed. Now, with Penny almost grown up, perhaps it was Pamela's own life she wanted to keep as unchanged as possible.

Pamela and Penny were greeted by those cats, and by

the spicy fragrance of the Christmas tree they'd anchored in its stand the previous night. Catrina, the black cat who Pamela had adopted as a forlorn stray, was now plump and sleek. Once she'd satisfied herself that her mistress was indeed home, she made her way, with an elegant strut, back to the sofa from which she'd come. Ginger, Catrina's daughter, named for her ginger coat, showed her welcome by weaving about Penny's ankles. Penny stooped to pick her up and the cat rested her paws on Penny's shoulder and nuzzled her neck.

"What shall we do?" Pamela asked after they'd hung their jackets in the closet. She tipped her head to study her daughter's face. Penny's eyes were dry, but previous tears had left their trails on Penny's perfect skin. Penny shrugged. It was barely one p.m. The plan—Pamela's plan anyway—had been to spend the day working at the Knit and Nibble table, then come home to make a pot roast. After she and Penny ate, she had envisioned putting one of her old vinyl Christmas LPs on the stereo and engaging in some mother-daughter bonding as she and Penny decorated the tree together.

"I think I'll just go upstairs," Penny said after a bit.

Pamela pulled her daughter into a hug. "Karla was a wonderful teacher," she said. "You were so lucky to have had her."

"She's *gone*, Mom." Penny pulled back from the hug. "And I hadn't even gotten to see her yet." She sighed. "Now all I have is the box of cards."

Catrina and Ginger were justifiably annoyed the next morning. Pamela's habit most mornings—even before she set water boiling for her own coffee—was to spoon generous servings of cat food into a fresh dish and set it in the corner of the kitchen where meals were accustomed to appear. Only then would she fill her kettle and put it on the stove, after which she would hurry out in her fleecy robe and slippers to retrieve the *Register*.

But on this Sunday morning, she'd brought the paper in first. And now, as Catrina and Ginger prowled around her feet mewing, she stood at the kitchen table scanning the front-page article on what the *Register* was calling "the Arborville Christmas tree lot murder."

"They think she was killed right there," said a small voice behind her.

Pamela turned to see Penny standing in the kitchen doorway, her curls untamed and her face soft with sleep—though faint purplish shadows beneath her eyes suggested that her sleep hadn't been completely restorative.

"It's all online," Penny added. "Lorie Hopkins texted me besides. And Lorie heard there's just going to be a private funeral now, and then a memorial event for her students and everybody in the spring."

Pamela acknowledged Penny with a sad nod and lowered the paper to the table. "I'll get the coffee going," she said, and stepped toward the counter as the cats veered off in Penny's direction. "And toast."

"They haven't eaten." Penny stooped to greet them and then fetched a can of cat food from the cupboard.

Once the cats' breakfast had been served, a small can of chicken-fish blend scooped into a fresh bowl and broken up into tempting morsels with a spoon, Penny took up her role in the humans' breakfast ritual. She arranged Pamela's cut-glass cream pitcher and sugar bowl on the table, poured a dollop of cream into the pitcher, and set out the butter dish. Then she added two cups and saucers and two small plates from the cupboard where Pamela kept her wedding china. Pamela used her china every day, even when she was the only diner—because what was the point in having nice things if you didn't use them?

Meanwhile, Pamela had measured water into her kettle and lit the burner under it, arranged a paper filter in the plastic filter cone over her carafe, and slipped two slices of whole-grain bread from the Co-Op Grocery into the toaster. The next step was to grind the coffee beans. As the clatter of beans in the grinder's chamber became a whir and then subsided into a wheeze, she heard the newspaper rustle.

Penny was sitting at the table studying the *Register.* "The article continues on an inner page," she said. "This is more than I saw online, and I guess Lorie Hopkins hadn't seen the *Register.*"

Pamela turned away from the counter. Only the top of Penny's head was visible as she bent over the newspaper.

"The person who killed her used a piece of Christmas tree trunk." The wondering quality in Penny's voice suggested amazement that something associated with such a joyful season could be used as a lethal weapon.

"How did . . . ?" Pamela tried to picture the scene. Someone with a saw? Thinking, *I just need a piece about a foot long?*

Penny began to answer the question, but she was interrupted by the hoot of the kettle. And as Pamela was pouring the ground beans and then the water into the filter cone, the toast popped up with a *ka-chunk.*

"Sometimes they saw the bottoms off trees to make them fit into the tree stands," Penny explained, looking up. "It says there was a pile of sawn-off pieces at the back of the lot. And that's where they found her body."

She closed the paper, folded it so the headline was no longer visible, and put it aside. The story was still very present in their minds, however, despite the comforts of steaming coffee and buttered toast.

The Christmas tree lot was still a crime scene, with the yellow tape still looped from post to post and a police officer posted at the locked gate. A handwritten sign announced (unnecessarily) that the lot was closed, but it promised extra hours during the week as soon as the police were finished.

Once inside the church hall, however, a person wouldn't have known anything untoward had happened. The tables boasted the same wares that had been on offer the previous day—wall plaques, carved bowls, exotic jewelry, and the rest. Pamela and Bettina had unpacked the knitted creations from the boxes where they had spent the night and arranged them in attractive profusion over the surface of the Knit and Nibble table. Not too many of the little knitted sweater, mitten, and stocking ornaments were left, and Pamela was glad Penny had made her choices the previous day. From the PA system came the cheerful strains of "God Rest You Merry, Gentlemen."

Browsers moved from table to table, pausing to finger and buy, or veer aside to engage in a chat with a neighbor. Children hopped around the floor in the clear space that surrounded the decorated tree, their high-pitched voices punctuating the chatter of their elders.

Bettina had excused herself for a stroll around the room as Pamela was showing an assortment of scarves to an elderly gentleman in a plaid wool jacket that would have suited a woodsman. As he was handing over a twenty and a ten for a lovely pale blue scarf that Pamela recognized as Roland's handiwork, Bettina returned bearing a large flat box.

Pamela thanked her customer and bade him Merry

Christmas. After he left, Bettina opened the box to reveal
twelve cupcakes, six with green icing and six with red, and
all garnished with sparkly colored sugar.

"I was afraid the baked goods people wouldn't be able
to sell everything," she explained, "since the fair had to
close so early yesterday. And it's for such a good cause."

She picked up a green cupcake, delicately peeled away
its fluted paper wrapping, and lifted it to her mouth. But
before taking a bite, she gestured toward the open box and
said, "Help yourself, Pamela. I didn't buy these all for me
and Wilfred."

"Not quite yet." Pamela laughed and made a gesture as
if to push away the idea. "I just had breakfast."

"Breakfast!" Bettina laughed too. "I know you—black
coffee and one piece of whole-grain toast. No wonder
you're so skinny."

Bettina was not skinny, nor was she tall. But she loved
clothes, and her outfits reflected a keen interest in fashion.
Today she was wearing a fit and flare dress in a dramatic
green and crimson print—the crimson nearly the same
color as her hair. The dress was accessorized with several
strands of large golden beads and earrings consisting of
one dangling bead each. On her feet were high-heeled
booties made of forest-green suede. She frequently lamented the fact that her tall and thin friend lacked any interest in the clothes that her body could have displayed to
such advantage.

She took a bite of the cupcake, closing her eyes and
smiling as she savored its flavor. But she opened them
again as Pamela said, "Oh, dear! Now what?"

Lucas Clayborn, Arborville's sole police detective, was
making his way toward the Knit and Nibble table. At his
side was Officer Sanchez, with her dark hair corralled into
a knot and her sweet heart-shaped face somber.

Bettina swallowed the bite of cupcake with a large gulp. The spot of green icing on her cheek didn't detract from her serious mien as she watched him approach. Bettina met frequently with Detective Clayborn as part of her job with the *Advocate* and she greeted him now with a businesslike "Good morning, sir," after which she tucked the cupcake she'd bitten into back in the box.

Though his dress was similar to that of many of the men browsing the craft fair's offerings with their wives—a nondescript winter jacket over a nondescript sports coat—he stood out nonetheless. A certain tightness around the eyes gave his homely face the look of a person with a mission.

He acknowledged Bettina's greeting with a wordless nod and focused his attention on the colorful yarn creations laid out on the table. After a bit he picked up a tiny sweater ornament with red and green stripes.

"Did a member of your Knit and Nibble group make this?" he inquired in an offhand way as he held it out in one large hand.

Could he possibly just be browsing, Pamela asked herself, *despite the purposeful expression? Doing his part for the high-school art, drama, and music programs?*

"No, sir," Bettina said. "We invited all Arborville knitters to contribute their work to our table."

He set the sweater down and picked up a tiny blue mitten, into which he thrust the tip of his index finger. "Must be hard to make something so little," he murmured. "Do you recall the name of the person who's responsible for these?"

His hand, with the mitten still on the finger, swept over the few knitted ornaments that remained.

"Of course." Bettina smiled—there was never any harm in staying on Detective Clayborn's good side. "It was Sorrel Wollcott."

"I'm going to need to take them," Detective Clayborn said, showing no trace of an answering smile.

Pamela heard herself say, "Why?"

"Evidence." Officer Sanchez held out an official-looking plastic bag, and Detective Clayborn dropped the tiny sweaters, mittens, and stockings into it, one by one. "You can call around to the police station tomorrow for a receipt," he added.

"Well," Bettina commented after she had retrieved the cupcake she'd barely had a chance to nibble. "What could that mean?"

They watched him retreat across the floor, with Officer Sanchez at his side. As the two neared the entrance, one of the double doors swung open and Penny stepped into the hall, again wearing the violet jacket that, with its vintage air, was one of her thrift-store finds. Pamela was happy to see that Penny looked more like her lively self than she'd appeared over breakfast. And she was even happy to see that Penny had helped herself to one of her mother's scarves, a hand-knit mohair creation that happened to exactly match the jacket.

Pamela was so focused on the approach of her daughter that she didn't notice another familiar young woman standing right at the Knit and Nibble table—until Bettina tapped her on the arm.

"Holly's having a cupcake," she said. "Are you sure you don't want one now?"

Indeed, Holly Perkins, a fellow member of Knit and Nibble, was in the process of consuming one of the green-icing cupcakes. She took a break to acknowledge Pamela with a smile that displayed her perfect teeth and activated her dimple, and then, lest Bettina feel ignored, she nodded in her direction and proclaimed that the cupcake was "awesome."

"And it looks like you sold a few of my hats," she said, scanning the table. The hats were cheery creations with rainbow stripes that seemed the perfect reflection of Holly's vivid personality. Her smile faded then and she added, "What a shocking thing though—that teacher murdered. I was at the salon all day"—Holly and her husband owned a hair salon—"and was too busy to even check the news till Desmond and I got home."

Pamela was distracted then by a browser who was a knitter herself and seemed more inclined to chat than to buy. As Pamela mustered her social smile and tried to listen enthusiastically to the woman's description of her in-progress cable-knit sweater, she could hear Bettina and Holly greeting Penny, and Penny accepting a cupcake.

When the chatty knitter finally went on her way, Pamela slipped around the table to give her daughter a hug.

"Are you okay?" she asked, stepping back to get a better look at Penny's face.

Penny nodded. "It's better to get out and see people, not just sit at home feeling sad. Laine and Sybil are at their dad's place for the holidays and I'm going to do something with them later, but I'll browse around the craft fair for a bit."

Pamela tried to maintain her pleasant expression, but the reference to her handsome, single neighbor had awakened feelings she thought she had vanquished. Nonetheless, she responded with a cheerful "Good! It will be fun for you to see them."

The Knit and Nibble table was getting busier. A young woman had edged past Penny and was fingering a lacy shawl, and Penny stepped out of the way.

"Isn't that an amazing piece of knitting!" Holly exclaimed, tilting her head in the direction of the newcomer, who looked to be a twentysomething like Holly. Also like

Holly, the newcomer's grooming suggested an artistic bent. Holly's dark tresses sported a bright red streak today, and dangling from her earlobes were large disks enameled in a dizzying op-art pattern. The young woman with whom she had struck up a conversation had bright blue hair cut in an asymmetrical style that dipped to her shoulder on one side, but merely grazed the top of her ear on the other.

"Interesting," was the response, but uttered in a tone that implied being interesting was not a particular accomplishment.

Holly, however, was undeterred. "A shawl like that takes hours and hours to make," she said cheerfully, "but knitting is so relaxing—and so creative at the same time."

"I can think of things that are more creative," the young woman said, letting the shawl drop back onto the table. "*Much* more creative."

"Ohhh!" Holly clapped and offered one of her smiles. "Are you an artist?"

A slight tip of the head and a self-satisfied smile indicated that the answer was yes.

"Is any of your work on display here?" Holly turned, and her graceful wave took in nearly the entire room.

"*Here?*" The young woman's rather pretty features twisted into an unbecoming scowl. "At a holiday craft fair in *Arborville?*"

"There are some awesome things here," Holly exclaimed, "and this is an awesome town!"

"I'm a sculptor," the young woman said, and her pride in making that announcement banished the scowl. "I only exhibit at shows where they are a little more selective," she went on. "*Juried* shows."

Though Penny had stepped aside to let the young woman

get closer to the table, she'd been listening. And she now directed an admiring glance at the young woman—Penny herself had been drawing and painting since she was quite young.

"Have you submitted to the Timberley Arts group?" she asked. "They do a show every other year, like the Venice Biennale, and they display outdoor sculpture all the time."

"I've heard of the group," the young woman said vaguely.

"My teacher—my art teacher at Arborville High—was one of . . . was on . . . the board." Penny gulped, closed her eyes, and swallowed hard. "She was . . . the woman who was just killed . . ." Her voice trailed off.

The young woman seemed not to have absorbed the second half of Penny's statement, or at least not to care about Karma Karling's death and Penny's obvious distress. Pamela had been engaged with a shopper, but Bettina had been watching the exchange and popped out from behind the table to give Penny a hug.

"Karma Karling was Penny's favorite teacher." Bettina's tone was more scolding than explaining.

"Very sad," the young woman said, not sounding very sad. "But maybe I'll submit something. Do they have a website?"

Bettina didn't know if Timberley Arts had a website, and Penny was still struggling with her emotions. But it didn't matter because at that moment the group, which still included Holly, was joined by a tall young man whose dark good looks were accented by skinny jeans in black denim and a dashing black leather jacket.

"Heeey!" he sang out, focusing his gaze on the young woman. "We meet again!"

The addition of a handsome young man to the group altered the dynamic considerably. The young woman's manner shifted from blasé to engaged—at least with the young man. Penny wiped an eye with the back of her hand and ventured the beginnings of a smile. Holly smiled too, though not wide enough to evoke her dimple. And even Bettina's quick up-and-down survey seemed approving.

"So, did you find a good tree Friday night?" the young man asked, tipping his head toward the object of his interest. "Or did the lot close before you had a chance to look around? It was getting pretty late."

"Nothing caught my eye," the young woman said, raising her gaze to meet his and smoothing her hair back with a gesture that showed off a pretty arm and hand, as well as calling attention to the eye-catching color and style of her coiffure. "I made a tour of the lot, but I couldn't find the kind of tree I was looking for."

"The Arborville lot isn't the only lot around," the young man said.

The young woman edged backward, as if she'd engaged long enough with the Knit and Nibble table. The young man edged backward too. They turned toward each other.

"Some interesting things here," the young man said. "Shall we look around?"

And suddenly the young woman seemed to find the craft fair much more appealing as the two walked off together.

"I'll take a turn here for a while," Holly said after they were gone, "if you two want a break."

"I'm fine." Pamela opened the cash box to tuck away a few bills she'd just received in exchange for a delicate white baby blanket that Nell had contributed.

"Well, I've barely had a chance to talk to Penny since she's been home." Bettina had released Penny from the hug, but now she reached out an arm to circle Penny's waist. Addressing Penny, she added, "Let's take a walk around the fair and see what we can see. I still have a few people to check off my Christmas list."

"White Christmas" segued into "Frosty the Snowman," and "Frosty the Snowman" segued into "We Three Kings," as Pamela and Holly chatted with holiday shoppers, complimented people on their choices, made change, and slipped bills into the cash box. Some people strolled along nibbling on cookies, while others relaxed in strategically placed chairs, sipping cups of coffee.

The large Christmas tree in the middle of the floor hid many of the tables on the opposite side of the room, so Pamela hadn't tracked Bettina and Penny as they browsed. She was totally focused on counting the money that had accumulated in the cash box when a jubilant voice cut into her whispered tally.

She glanced up to see Bettina standing before her with a triumphant grin. She must have looked momentarily puzzled because Bettina repeated the statement she had just made, which was "You'll never guess what we just found out."

"About Phoebe Ruskin," Penny added.

"It was all an act." Bettina gave a scornful laugh, then she affected a blasé manner, nothing like her usual self, to say, *"Heard of the group!"* She became Bettina again to exclaim, "My foot! She knows all about them. Because—"

Penny interrupted her. "They rejected her."

"Wait, wait, wait!" Pamela raised her hands, palms outward. She gave Penny a fond smile. "First of all"—she laughed—"who on earth is Phoebe Ruskin?"

Bettina's voice overlapped with Penny's. "The blue-haired woman." Penny continued speaking. "She knows all about them—"

"The Timberley Arts group," Bettina supplied. "She submitted several pieces for this year's Biennale and they rejected them all, and besides that, they asked her to remove a piece of hers that had been on display in the town park because it was vetoed by a new committee member."

Penny took over. "And that new committee member was Karma Karling."

Pamela leaned across the table. "How on earth . . . ?"

"Marlene Pepper knows Phoebe's mother," Bettina said. "I got to chatting with Marlene over by the table where they're selling those adorable dolls. *She* brought the subject up—the blue hair and all, but Phoebe doesn't live in Arborville anymore, and one thing led to another . . ."

This was a lot to digest. Phoebe Ruskin had a good reason to resent Karma Karling, and—as had emerged during her conversation with the tall young man—she had been at the Christmas tree lot late Friday night but had left without buying a tree.

But Pamela put the task of digesting aside for the moment in order to commiserate with Bettina about the fact that her son and daughter-in-law in Boston had forbade her to buy girly things—and those dolls were so *adorable*—for her first and only granddaughter, Morgan.

Chapter Three

Bettina began talking the minute Pamela's front door swung back. "You already know, of course, and I was going to run across the street the minute I saw it in the *Register,* but Clayborn scheduled me for eight a.m. and I barely had time to dress before I had to run out to the police station."

She swept into the entry on a gust of chilly wind and Pamela hurried to close the door behind her.

Pamela *did* already know. A front-page article in that morning's *Register* had announced an arrest in the Karma Karling murder case. In fact, the *Register* was still spread out on Pamela's kitchen table and she'd been sipping her second cup of coffee when the doorbell chimed. She was still in her robe and slippers, and Penny hadn't even emerged from her bedroom yet.

Bettina, on the other hand, was already dressed for the day. She removed the jaunty turquoise beret that hid all but her bangs—and that matched the shadow accenting her hazel eyes—and then the pumpkin-colored down coat that was her winter staple. Beneath the coat was a slacks-and-sweater ensemble in the same turquoise as the beret, accented by a cashmere scarf with a swirling paisley pattern, and silver earrings set with large turquoise stones.

"Sorrel Wollcott." Pamela supplied the name before Bettina spoke again. "I have no idea why the police could possibly think that she was guilty. Except—"

"Exactly!" Bettina's raised index finger acknowledged Pamela's unspoken point. "The tiny sweater, mitten, and stocking ornaments."

"A clue?" Pamela's lips twisted in puzzlement.

"I've been with Clayborn." Bettina paused and glanced past Pamela toward the doorway to the kitchen. "Is there any more coffee?"

"There's more in the carafe. I'll heat it up." Pamela turned and led the way.

In the kitchen she lit the burner under the carafe and watched closely for the tiny bubbles that would indicate the coffee was ready to serve. Bettina didn't take her customary place at the table, however, even after she had helped herself to a cup and saucer from the wedding-china cupboard and splashed a dollop of cream into the cut-glass pitcher. Standing in the middle of the floor, she scanned the counters.

"There's probably toast," she ventured, "but I don't suppose . . ." She hesitated and then interjected, "I could have brought the rest of the cupcakes from yesterday."

"I've started my Christmas baking." Pamela looked up from the stove with a teasing half smile.

"Is there—?"

"Unwrap that foil." Pamela nodded toward a wooden cutting board that held a silvery loaf-shaped object.

A few minutes later, they were seated at the table with fresh cups of coffee and small plates before them. Each plate held a slice of poppy-seed cake, richly golden brown, and dense with the tiny dark pinpoints that were poppy seeds. Pamela baked multiple loaves of the cake every year for Christmas, to give as gifts and to serve at home.

"That's why Clayborn wanted the sweater and mitten and stocking ornaments from the Knit and Nibble table," Bettina explained after she'd sampled the poppy-seed cake, sighed happily, and declared it as good as ever. "And why he wanted to know who made them. A tiny knitted sweater ornament was found at the Christmas tree lot near Karma's body. And a twist of yarn was snagged on the chicken wire fence."

Pamela heard a sharp intake of breath that she knew was her own. "That does seem very suspicious," she said. "But I just can't believe Sorrel would kill someone. She's a fellow *knitter*."

Bettina was engaged in coaxing her coffee to the pale mocha hue she preferred, adding sugar and then cream and stirring. But she had more information to impart.

"Sorrel and Karma went to the Christmas tree lot together Friday night, at about nine, to get a tree for their apartment lobby," she said. "Clayborn talked to their neighbors. They both live—*lived* in the case of Karma—in that big apartment building up at the corner of Arborville Avenue and they were on the decorations committee."

"Just because Sorrel went to the Christmas tree lot with Karma, that doesn't mean Sorrel killed her." Pamela set her coffee cup back on her saucer with a *clunk*. "Lots and lots of people were probably milling around the Christmas tree lot—and maybe the murder didn't even happen there, or that night."

"It *did* happen there," Bettina said. Pamela nodded. Bettina was right—that detail had been in the *Register* the previous day. "There were signs of a scuffle in the dirt, but no signs of a body being dragged in from elsewhere. And besides, that chicken wire fence isn't all that secure, but it *is* a fence."

Pamela nodded again. "There's only the one gate and

it's locked when the lot is closed. When the tree lot was open, the killer couldn't have dragged a body in that way because people would have noticed."

"And it *did* happen that night, according to the ME, most likely before ten p.m., when the tree lot closed." Bettina gave her coffee one last stir and took a sample sip. "It's likely no one heard anything amiss with that loud Christmas music they broadcast. There weren't many customers that late and only two attendants were on duty. Nobody inspects the lot at the end of the evening, especially not way in the back there where they pile the pieces of trunk they cut off. The attendants just take the cash box, turn the lights and music off, and lock the gate behind them with a padlock."

They were quiet then for a bit as Bettina nibbled at her poppy-seed cake and Pamela took a few bites of hers to be companionable, though she'd barely finished her breakfast toast when Bettina arrived.

"Sorrel must be so frightened," Pamela announced suddenly. "We'll have to go see her."

"We will," Bettina said. "We won't have to go to Haversack though"—Haversack was the county seat and the jail was there—"because she'll be out on bail by tomorrow."

"Phoebe Ruskin," said a voice from the doorway. Pamela and Bettina swiveled their heads in that direction to see Penny, in her fleecy robe with her hair still tousled from sleep. "Did you tell Detective Clayborn about Phoebe Ruskin?" She directed the question at Bettina.

"Ohhh!" Bettina's head sagged forward and she tapped her forehead with a clenched fist. "I could have . . . I should have. He *does* listen to me sometimes, and she had a reason to resent Karma, and she was in the tree lot late Friday night."

"We could try to find out a little more about her," Pamela said. "If you're going to suggest that she could be the killer, then the more evidence, the better."

"*Mo-om!*" Penny folded her arms across her chest and affected a stern look that was more amusing than fearsome, given her gentle features. "I didn't mean that you and Bettina should try to solve this crime. I'm sad enough about what happened to Karma without having to worry about my mom and my favorite neighbor getting on the bad side of someone who's willing to murder."

Instead of responding to Penny's statement, Pamela jumped to her feet. "You need some breakfast," she said, "and Bettina drank your coffee, so I'll just get busy here . . ." And the rush of water into the kettle, the clatter of beans into the coffee grinder's chamber, and the growling whir as the beans were ground provided enough distraction that Penny didn't raise the point again.

Soon Penny was settled on an extra chair brought in from the dining room and with toast and coffee before her. Bettina was always curious about her doings at school, and soon Penny was describing the class in Web design she was looking forward to when the spring semester started up again.

Pamela was happy to listen and observe, relieved that Penny seemed to be rebounding from the shock of Karma's murder, and enjoying the way enthusiasm about her future brightened Penny's blue eyes and rosied her complexion. When Penny finished her toast and coffee, she excused herself to get dressed for a mall outing with her friend Lorie Hopkins.

As soon as she disappeared through the doorway, and they heard her feet on the stairs, Bettina darted from the room and returned with her smartphone. Pamela was surprised. Bettina didn't usually interrupt an in-person encounter to commune with someone reaching out to her from cyberspace.

But perhaps she was expecting a call, or a text, or an email, Pamela reflected, and busied herself clearing away the breakfast dishes, putting away what was left of the cream, and returning the extra chair to the dining room.

Meanwhile, Bettina was staring at her device as her fingers tickled and stroked its screen. "Hire a dog-walker," she said suddenly.

Pamela was at the counter now, sponging up toast crumbs. " 'Hire a dog-walker'?" she murmured in response.

Bettina was murmuring too, as if working out an idea before making it public. Pamela caught the word "Woofus," but not much else.

"Doesn't Wilfred enjoy his walks with Woofus?" she asked when Bettina finally raised her head.

"Phoebe Ruskin," Bettina said with a slightly exasperated tone to her voice, as if Pamela hadn't been paying attention. Pamela tried to look pleasantly receptive. "Phoebe Ruskin has a dog-walking business," Bettina went on to explain. "Based in Haversack, but she 'serves surrounding communities,' as her website puts it. I guess sculpting doesn't pay the bills, even though rents in Haversack are nothing like they'd be here in Arborville—or in most of the 'surrounding communities.' "

"So you're thinking"—Pamela smiled now—"we hire her to walk Woofus. And that gives us a chance to—"

Bettina cut in. "—to get to know her better . . . and we'll see what we can see."

Bettina's fingers got busy again and in a moment Pamela was overhearing half a conversation, the upshot of which was that Phoebe liked to interview her four-footed clients before signing them up for the dog-walking service. She would come to Orchard Street the following afternoon at three o'clock to meet Woofus.

"I have to get going." Bettina rose to her feet. "I want to write up my interview with Clayborn while it's still fresh in my mind—though by the time the *Advocate* comes out at the end of the week, everything he told me will have already been in the *Register.*"

"People enjoy the *Advocate,*" Pamela said comfortingly. It was true, however, that Arborvillians jokingly described their weekly newspaper as containing "all the news that fits," and some people allowed issues of the *Advocate* to accumulate on their driveways, slowly turning to papier-mâché in wet weather, despite their plastic wrappers.

A few minutes after Pamela returned to the kitchen after seeing Bettina on her way, Penny appeared in the doorway again. She was dressed to go out, in jeans, boots, and the violet jacket, with Pamela's violet scarf in a fetching twist at the neck. But in her hand she carried a Christmas card. Pamela recognized it as one from the box Penny had bought at the craft fair, Karma Karling's design, with the twelve drummers drumming.

"I was just looking at the cards again," Penny said. "I don't think I'll send any of them. I'll just keep them as a souvenir of Karma. But there's something weird about them."

She held the card out. Pamela took it and laid it on the kitchen table.

"There are thirteen of them"—Penny's finger hovered over the drummers in their smart red, white, and blue uniforms and tight formation—"not just twelve. It's scary," she added with a shudder. "Thirteen drummers, and then . . . she's killed."

The doorbell chimed and Penny sang out, "Coming." She darted from the room, leaving the Christmas card on the table.

It was unusual for Pamela to still be in robe and slippers this late in the morning. Though her job as associate editor of *Fiber Craft* magazine allowed her to work at home most days, she exchanged robe and pajamas for real clothes every morning before sitting down to work.

But before she climbed the stairs to dress, she sat down and studied the ranks of drummers once again. Yes, there were thirteen of them, one in the back row like a stow-away just peeking out from behind another. And unlike the soldierly faces of the others, with their stolid expressions, this drummer—whose drum was not actually visible—had quite distinctive features. His brows were dark, his nose assertive, and his lips had a sardonic twist.

When she was up in her bedroom, Pamela replaced robe and pajamas with the jeans she'd worn the previous day and added a comfy turtleneck in a rich brown with an interesting cable detail up the front. Her wardrobe was simple—jeans and a casual blouse in warm weather, and jeans and a sweater, usually hand-knit, in cold weather. Stepping into the bathroom, she smoothed her dark hair, straight and shoulder-length, with a comb and declared herself ready for the workday.

This workday, however, would be an easy workday. On the previous Friday she'd returned to her boss five articles she'd copyedited, and her Christmas week assignment was merely to read and review *Foraging for Herbal Dyestuffs: Revisiting a Lost Art*. Writing book reviews had recently been added to her job description.

The next stop was her office, just across the hall, where she checked to make sure no important email had arrived since earlier that morning. *Foraging for Herbal Dyestuffs:*

Revisiting a Lost Art was already sitting on the coffee table downstairs. She had dipped into it when it arrived the previous Thursday and was looking forward to more of the author's anecdotes about her own foraging, as well as more of the photographs that showed both the foraged plants and the interesting color effects one could achieve with them.

Downstairs in the entry, Catrina was luxuriating in the small pool of sunlight that reliably set the colors of the thrift-store carpet aglow on bright mornings. She gave Pamela a lazy glance, then closed her amber eyes once again. But Ginger had strolled in from the kitchen and padded after Pamela as she made her way to the sofa and settled into her habitual spot.

It was unusual for Pamela to be sitting on the sofa during the day. Ginger pondered for a moment, as if wondering whether there was any point in joining her or whether she would spring up again in a moment. But after Pamela picked up the book, Ginger hopped up next to her and stretched out. Soon Pamela was engrossed in a description of wild rose madder, and Ginger was purring so intensely, Pamela could feel the vibrations against her thigh.

Chapter Four

B ettina was due at eleven Tuesday morning for the visit to Sorrel that she and Pamela had planned. So when the doorbell chimed a bit before that hour, summoning Pamela away from a discussion of how strains of indigo differed from continent to continent (some of the author's foraging had involved quite adventurous travel), she expected to greet her friend.

The figure visible behind the lace that curtained the door's oval window did not, however, resemble Bettina. Instead of a bulky form garbed in bright pumpkin, topped with an accent of even brighter hair, a slender figure in dark clothing appeared against the faded green of lawn and shrubbery. The only bright spot was an object in the figure's hands. And rather than launching into conversation and stepping toward the threshold the moment the door swung back, the figure remained on the porch.

At first, Pamela barely recognized her, and the confusion must have been obvious, because the first words the figure uttered were, "It's me, Rick's friend Jocelyn Bidwell."

"Oh!" Pamela took a step backward. "Rick" was Richard Larkin, Pamela's next-door neighbor and the father of Penny's friends Laine and Sybil. When he'd moved in, newly divorced, he'd made his interest in Pamela quite plain. But Pamela had hesitated and hesitated, and at last he had turned his attentions elsewhere.

Jocelyn Bidwell, with her lovely olive skin, thick black hair, and elegant features, was the *elsewhere*. For this errand, which seemed to involve the delivery of a poinsettia, she was wrapped in a dark blue (the word *indigo* flashed into Pamela's mind) wool coat with a wide shawl collar and a tie belt looped with just the right casual flair.

Jocelyn smiled, a bit hesitantly. "I don't mean to interrupt," she said, searching Pamela's face as if for some explanation of the startled *Oh!* "But Rick and I just wanted to say 'Merry Christmas' "—she held the poinsettia out with both hands—"and . . . and . . . I hope you like poinsettias."

"I . . . yes, I do." Pamela struggled to muster her social smile. She backed up and pulled the door farther open. "Come in."

Jocelyn raised a foot shod in a sleek boot and stepped over the threshold.

"I . . . have something for you," Pamela said. "For the two of you." She hurried to the kitchen and lifted a foil-wrapped poppy-seed cake from the counter. "It's something I make," she said when she returned, and she thrust it toward Jocelyn. Then she noticed that Jocelyn's hands were still occupied with the poinsettia.

But Jocelyn was resourceful. She slipped gracefully past Pamela and deposited the poinsettia, which was in an attractive clay pot, on the small table where Pamela collected her mail. Then she turned and held out a hand to receive Pamela's offering.

"Is this"—she gazed down at it, then raised her head—"your Christmas poppy-seed cake?" Pamela nodded. "Thank you!" Jocelyn went on. "Rick just loves it. He said you gave him one last year."

Wilfred would have observed, "The way to a man's heart is through his stomach." But no—she hadn't been seeking a path to Richard Larkin's heart. She had just been . . . Well, it had been Bettina's idea to give him a poppy-seed cake, and she hadn't really meant anything by it at all . . .

"Yes," Pamela said, "I gave him one last year. After all we're neighbors, and now you and he have given me this nice . . . this nice . . ." She fluttered a hand in the direction of the poinsettia.

And then the door, which Pamela hadn't shut securely when Jocelyn entered, opened, and suddenly Bettina was there. Pamela sighed with relief and abandoned the attempt at speech.

"Merry Christmas, neighbor!" Bettina greeted Jocelyn with a quick hug. "And to Rick too!"

"The same to you!" Jocelyn seemed to relax in Bettina's presence, but Bettina had that effect on people. After a short back-and-forth with Bettina about the joys of the season, and a repeated thank-you for Pamela, Jocelyn was on her way.

"What was that in her hand?" Bettina asked as soon as the door closed behind her.

"I gave her my other poppy-seed cake," Pamela said. "She brought me this poinsettia, from both of them." She gestured at the poinsettia. It was quite spectacular, with deep red petals—they were really its leaves, Pamela knew—streaked with white.

Bettina raised her carefully shaped brows and nodded toward the poinsettia. "I wonder whose idea it was," she observed, as if to herself. Pamela ignored the comment and stepped to the closet for her jacket. She would have to make another poppy-seed cake now—she'd given away the one that Penny was going to take back to school.

"Wear your warmest jacket," Bettina advised. "It's bitter out there, but I came prepared to walk." She held up a foot to show off a sturdy boot with a rim of fur at the ankle.

Their destination was only half a block away, but Pamela's preference for walking and Bettina's aversion to it was the topic of much teasing between them.

Sorrel's living room, in the stately brick apartment building at the corner of Orchard Street and Arborville Avenue, was a cozy refuge after their exposure—brief as it was—to the stiff wind that froze their faces and made their eyes water. She greeted them with a grateful "hello," took Bettina's coat and Pamela's jacket, and insisted on serving coffee and slices of stollen despite her woebegone state.

Seated on a blue velvet loveseat, with a silver tray bearing refreshments on a graceful coffee table before them, they waited while Sorrel poured three cups of coffee from an ornate silver pot and then settled herself on a needlepoint hassock. Pamela had never visited Sorrel's apartment before, and she gazed around at the Victorian-era art and knickknacks that gave the room a delightful old-fashioned air. Adding to the old-fashioned air was a tabletop Christmas tree decorated with tiny knitted sweaters, stockings, and mittens.

Sorrel herself had an old-fashioned air, with her graying hair rolled into a large bun at the crown of her head and a lace collar peeking from the neck of the roomy cardigan that clothed her plump torso.

"We know you're not guilty," Bettina said after she'd added sugar and cream to her coffee and taken a sip. "But you went to the Christmas tree lot with Karma quite late Friday night, and you were the last person seen with her.

And the police found one of those tiny sweater ornaments of yours at the crime scene."

"I took a few of them with me when we went out to get the tree," Sorrel said mournfully. "I wanted to make sure they'd look nice on the tree we brought home, and I wanted a nice traditional tree like a balsam fir. But then Karma didn't want to use my ornaments, and she wanted a modern-looking tree, like a blue spruce."

Pamela and Bettina nodded sympathetically.

"So we had an argument." Sorrel's lips tightened, stretched into a grimace, then struggled to remain still. "But I didn't kill her. I got so upset that I told her to get whatever tree she wanted and I left. I stuffed the ornaments back into my purse, but I must have dropped one."

"There's a missing hour though," Bettina said. "And that's part of why Clayborn thinks you're guilty. You left this building at nine, and let's say it took fifteen minutes to get to the tree lot, then you had the argument, so you should have been back home well before ten. But he says Mr. Gilly didn't see you come in till nearly eleven." Mr. Gilly was the building super.

"I was still upset." Sorrel blinked a few times, as if she felt tears coming. "So I took my car—I thought Karma could perfectly well walk home—and I drove to that fancy ice-cream shop in Timberley. I bought a quart of eggnog ice cream and I sat in my car and ate it."

"Wouldn't that be your alibi for the missing hour?" Bettina asked.

"The person who served me left for Peru the next day." Sorrel dabbed at her eyes. "Hiking in the Andes."

Pamela had been so distracted by the encounter with Jocelyn that she'd forgotten she wanted to show Bettina the extra little face on the twelve-drummers-drumming card.

So as they approached Bettina's house on their return from visiting Sorrel, she said, "Come across the street for a minute."

She stopped for a minute on the porch to collect her mail from the box—Christmas cards made for quite a handful this time of year—and then led Bettina through the entry to where the card still lay on the kitchen table.

"There are thirteen drummers." She aimed her index finger at the soldiers in their smart uniforms. "And look closely at number thirteen."

Bettina picked the card up and stared at it. "He's kind of hidden," she said after a bit. "Do you have a magnifying glass?"

Pamela did, in the bureau in the living room. In a moment she had fetched it and Bettina was studying the image on the card, now much enlarged.

"Rather handsome," she commented, "in a kind of bad-boy way."

"Almost like a portrait," Pamela said, "or a sort of caricature—of a real person."

Bettina set the magnifying glass down and handed Pamela the card. "What do you think it means?" she asked.

Pamela shook her head. "I don't know."

"I've got to be getting on home," Bettina said, stepping toward the doorway. "Wilfred will be wondering where I am. He's making some of his five-alarm chili for lunch. Do you want to eat with us?"

"I haven't seen much of Penny yet today," Pamela said, "but I'll be over at three, when Phoebe Ruskin comes to meet Woofus. And then we've got Knit and Nibble at your house tonight."

Back in the kitchen, Pamela studied the contents of her refrigerator. The pot roast from Saturday night had furnished several meals, most recently shredded with barbecue sauce and served on crusty rolls that Penny fetched from the Co-Op bakery. But that had been the end of it. Tonight would be pizza from When in Rome.

Lunch would have to be—she closed the refrigerator and opened a cupboard—tuna salad sandwiches on whole-grain bread. And then she would make a shopping list for the excursion to the Co-Op she planned for the next morning.

Penny emerged from her room and descended the stairs as Pamela was starting to chop celery for the tuna salad. "Do you think," Pamela asked once she'd greeted her daughter, "that the extra drummer on Karma's card looks like he could be based on a real person?"

She watched as Penny sat down at the kitchen table and took up the magnifying glass. Penny was dressed to go out, in jeans and a turtleneck Pamela had knit for her long ago, fashioned from ombré yarn that shaded from green, to indigo, to violet.

Penny bent over the card. "He might be," she pronounced after a bit. "The other drummers all look the same, and their faces aren't very realistic."

"Could he be someone Karma knew?" The celery was going unchopped, but Penny and Karma had been close, though in a teacher-student kind of way.

"I don't know, Mom." Penny set the magnifying glass down and moved the card aside. "She didn't really confide in me . . . about boyfriends and things." Penny paused. "And anyway, it doesn't matter if he's real or not, does it? It's still a great card."

No, it didn't matter. What could be more far-fetched than thinking an image on a Christmas card could be a clue in a murder case? Detective Clayborn would just laugh.

Pamela returned to chopping the celery, and soon

mother and daughter were sharing a companionable meal. Penny left then to meet her Arborville not-really-boyfriend, Aaron, and Pamela settled onto the sofa with *Foraging for Herbal Dyestuffs: Revisiting a Lost Art* and *two* cats this time. The sunny patch on the entry carpet had long since retreated.

Woofus's interview with his potential dog-walker got off to a bad start, even before he set eyes on her. He was napping on the sofa in Bettina's comfy living room as Pamela and Bettina chatted in the kitchen, which still smelled deliciously of Wilfred's five-alarm chili. The door-bell rang promptly at three p.m. Observing that Phoebe was certainly prompt, Bettina climbed to her feet and Pamela did likewise.

Before either of them reached the doorway that led to the dining room and the living room beyond, Woofus hur-tled into the kitchen, looking over his shoulder as if he was being pursued. He collided with Bettina, nearly knocking her down. She steadied herself by grasping the back of a chair, and the huge shaggy creature cowered against her and began to whimper. Bettina had changed into an at-home outfit since their visit to Sorrel that morning, and was wearing bright red leggings and a Christmas sweater featuring a large sequined candy cane. Miniature candy canes fashioned from glass dangled from her ears.

"I'll get it," Pamela said, edging past the two of them and hurrying to the door.

The caller was indeed Phoebe, bundled in a dramatic black and white checkerboard-patterned coat, and with her colorful hair tucked under a black stocking cap. Pam-ela invited her in, and by the time she'd divested herself of coat and hat, and smoothed her bright blue hair, Bettina had joined them.

"You both look very familiar," Phoebe said suddenly. She focused her gaze on Bettina. "You especially."

"Oh!" As if propelled by amazement, Bettina's arms sprang away from her body, her hands, with fingers spread wide, hovering at waist level. A smile that implied good-natured submission to life's unpredictability illuminated her features. "What an incredible coincidence!" she exclaimed. "You were at the craft fair!"

Pamela edged away, biting her tongue to keep from laughing. Bettina's acting always struck her as hopelessly unbelievable, yet her audience seemed not to notice.

"I was, yes." Phoebe nodded, not quite as thrilled by the coincidence, it seemed, but accepting that indeed it was one.

"I googled," Bettina said. "New Year's resolution, you know—make sure our dear Woofus gets enough exercise, now that my husband and I have gotten a bit creaky. I googled *dog-walking*. And your name came right up—you have a terrific website, by the way. So artistic! You must get a lot of business!"

Phoebe nodded, frowning slightly. She glanced around the room.

"You're anxious to meet Woofus, of course. Let's do that, and then we'll chat. I'd love to hear about your career as a sculptress—or *sculptor,* I guess, is what everyone is now, everyone who sculpts, that is. None of this 'poet, poetess' business anymore." Bettina steered Phoebe in the direction of the kitchen, and Pamela followed a few paces behind. They entered the kitchen to see Woofus hunched under the pine table and staring at his visitor in alarm.

"Come out and meet Phoebe," Bettina said in a cajoling voice as she bent down to make eye contact with him. A low sound like a cross between a growl and a whimper emerged from his throat and he backed away, bumping into a chair stationed on the opposite side of the table.

Bettina stood up and mustered a cheerful smile. "He's not usually like this," she said, which Pamela knew was an out-and-out lie. Woofus had been adopted from a shelter. His misadventures before he arrived there had given him a bad case of nerves, and it had taken him forever to even get used to Pamela. But Bettina went on, adding, "My husband went out to buy our Christmas goose and Woofus is upset that he didn't get to go along. He so enjoys car rides."

She bent down again, leaning on the table to steady herself. "Come on out, sweetie," she cooed. "Come out and show Phoebe what a friendly dog you are." Phoebe, meanwhile, was not-too-discreetly checking her watch. Her expression, a blend of suspicion and irritation, had barely changed since she arrived except for a slight wrinkle between the brows that came and went.

With a sound that was more growl than whimper this time, Woofus whirled around and dashed out from under the opposite side of the table, overturning the chair he had bumped into. Skidding slightly on the polished floor, he skirted the table and darted for the doorway, snapping at Phoebe's ankle on his way. His feet thumped on the stairs and then there was silence.

Still steadying herself against the table, Bettina watched him go. "He's not usually like this," she said at last. "He'll calm down. Meanwhile, I'll make some coffee and there are Christmas cookies, and we can—"

"We can *what*?" Phoebe enunciated the word so violently that the air in the vicinity of her lips stirred slightly. The wrinkle between her brows deepened. She turned toward the doorway. "*You* can do whatever you want. *I* am going back to my studio because I have better uses for my time than waiting around for temperamental animals to calm down."

"Maybe we were expecting too much of Woofus," Pamela suggested after the door closed behind Phoebe.

Bettina nodded. "We'll have to figure out another way to see if she has an alibi. She's a very likely suspect though—with a motive and then leaving the tree lot Friday night without buying a tree. And she's probably strong too, lifting heavy things or hammering at stone or however she makes her creations."

"She makes outdoor things," Pamela agreed. "They're probably really large. And metal, or something else that's weatherproof."

Chapter Five

The cats had been fed, the pizza had been ordered and eaten, and Penny had gone to Lorie Hopkins' house to binge-watch something that Pamela hadn't caught the name of. Now she stood in front of her closet.

Tonight was Knit and Nibble, which didn't really require dressing up, but it *was* the Christmas season and she'd been wearing the same brown sweater—which wasn't a very Christmasy color—for a couple of days. A flash of forest green in the stack of sweaters on her closet shelf caught her eye and she pulled out a cowl-necked pullover she had made a few years earlier from an alpaca blend. The color was certainly seasonal, and the airy texture created by the extra-large needles she'd used gave it a dressy look.

Downstairs, she pulled her warmest jacket over the sweater, whose cowl would take the place of a scarf, slipped into her gloves, and picked up her knitting bag. Stepping out onto the porch, she was glad her journey that evening was so short. The morning's bitter wind had increased in force and, howling, grazed her exposed skin to a raw tingle.

She was the first to arrive, grateful for the warmth of Bettina's welcoming living room. Bettina's Christmas tree twinkled from the corner near the stairs, and at the other end of the room, a cheery fire blazed in the fireplace. The cushions normally lined up along the hearth had accordingly been moved to the sofa and armchairs, the bright handwoven fabrics of their covers accenting Bettina's sage-green and tan color scheme.

"Come on back to the kitchen," Bettina said after she'd hung up Pamela's coat and Pamela had parked her knitting bag on one of the comfy armchairs that faced the sofa across the coffee table. "Nell's bringing tonight's goody, but I'm getting things organized for the coffee and tea."

But Pamela lingered near the stairs, her attention drawn to an object that had appeared near the tree in the few hours since she'd last been in Bettina's living room.

"What do you think?" Bettina asked, following the direction of Pamela's gaze. "Wilfred just finished it and so he brought it upstairs, even though Christmas isn't till Friday—not that that would make any difference to a cat anyway."

The object consisted of three wooden posts of different heights, the widest one covered with nubby carpet. Platforms of various sizes connected the posts. The topmost one was the largest and it shared part of its surface with a boxlike structure furnished with a round hole, like a doorway.

Just then the doorbell rang, and since Pamela was nearest to the door, she opened it.

"A cat climber!" Holly exclaimed as she stepped over the threshold. "Wherever did you get such an awesome thing?"

The answer was postponed in the general bustle, as Karen Dowling followed Holly across the threshold, and then Nell Bascomb, in her ancient gray coat. Coats, scarves, and hats had to be removed and greetings exchanged.

Holly went immediately to the cat climber, crouching next to it to examine the finer details: how meticulously the wooden surfaces had been sanded smooth, and how the nubby carpeting covered not only the scratching post, but the various-sized platforms too. She slipped an exploratory hand through the hole in the boxlike structure at the top, then extracted it with a giggle. A moment later, a furry butterscotch-colored face appeared.

"Punkin!" Bettina clapped her hands with delight. "So that's where you've gotten to. Wilfred will be so pleased that you've discovered your Christmas present."

"Did Wilfred *make* this amazing thing?" Holly's enthusiasm enhanced her dramatic looks and her dark eyes widened.

Bettina nodded, smiling a proud smile.

"And he cooks too!" Holly shook her head, as if to imply so many talents couldn't lodge in the same being.

"Not tonight though." Nell had reclaimed the parcel she had set aside while divesting herself of the garments she'd bundled herself in for her walk down the hill to Bettina's. She handed the parcel to Bettina, explaining, "Christmasy quick bread, but not too sweet. We all eat too much sugar, especially at this time of year."

Roland DeCamp was the last to arrive. "Chilly out there, just as the weather report predicted," he observed as he slipped off his well-cut wool coat and handed it to Bettina, along with his sleek leather gloves and a luxurious cashmere scarf. He looked around and said, "You're all here." Then he pushed back his starched shirt cuff to consult his impressive watch and added, "I'm not late though. It's two minutes to seven. Everyone else is early."

With that he turned toward the hearth, seeking his accustomed cushion, as Pamela, Holly, and Karen found spots on the sofa.

"Take a comfortable chair, Roland," Bettina called from where she still stood near the coat closet. "I had to move the cushions because of the fire."

"No, no, no," he said. "You and Nell must have the armchairs, and I don't want to crowd the sofa." He imported a wooden chair from the dining room, and after a few more minutes, everyone was settled.

Many hand-knit Christmas presents were in their final stages on this night. "Just a bit more to do on a sleeve," Holly explained, holding up a swath of navy blue knitting that ended in a few inches of ribbing. It was a merino wool sweater for her husband, Desmond, and it had been her project for the past few months.

Bettina was nearing the end of the project that had occupied her for over a year, a Nordic-style sweater for Wilfred, navy blue with red ribbing and bands of snowflakes in red and white. She too was finishing the last sleeve.

Roland opened the elegant leather briefcase that he used instead of a knitting bag and took out two carefully folded pieces of knitting in a soft camel shade. He laid one across his lap and smoothed it out, laid the other on top, and prepared to thread a yarn needle with a strand of yarn in the same camel color.

"You finished all the pieces!" Holly exclaimed from across the room.

Roland looked up with a frown. "Of course I finished all the pieces. And now I'm sewing them together. Christmas is Friday and I have limited time, so I have to set a schedule and stick to it." Roland was a high-powered corporate lawyer whose doctor had prescribed a relaxing hobby and suggested knitting.

"Melanie is going to love it!" Holly offered Roland one of the smiles that called her dimple into play. "I just know she will."

"I know she will too." Roland's lean face was serious. "She picked out the yarn and the pattern."

Pamela had knit a Christmas gift too, a blue cashmere sweater for her mother. But she had finished it earlier in the month, in time to mail it off to the Midwestern state where her parents lived. For the past few meetings of Knit and Nibble, she had lent her talents to Nell's annual Christmas project—hand-knit stockings to be filled with gifts and goodies and delivered to the children at the women's shelter in Haversack. At the moment Pamela was casting on for a new one, using a skein of cheery red yarn she'd found in the bin where she stored leftovers.

At her side Karen was at work with cheery red yarn as well. "A dress for Lily," she explained. "It's not really her first Christmas, but she was only a few days old last year."

It wasn't until people were well launched on their projects, with needles crisscrossing rhythmically and fingers looping and twisting yarn, that anyone spoke again.

"So shocking about Sorrel," Holly commented suddenly. "Those amazing little ornaments she knitted were so sweet. It's hard to think someone like that could be a killer."

"Do you really think she did it?" Karen swiveled on her sofa cushion so she could see Holly's face.

"*I* don't!" Bettina cut in.

From across the room Pamela tried to catch Bettina's eye. She hoped that a look and a subtle grimace would be sufficient to discourage Bettina from going further. But the damage had been done.

Nell glanced up from the complicated maneuver by which she was beginning to shape her stocking's heel. "Oh, no you don't," she said, her white hair bristling. "The Arborville police are perfectly capable of solving this crime without *you*"—she reached out and touched Bettina on the arm—"and *you*"—she fixed Pamela with a stare that Pamela found hard to evade.

"Killing her in the tree lot right before they closed wasn't a bad idea," Roland observed, "because the killer could trust that the body wouldn't be found until the next morning. And that was exactly what happened."

Holly leaned forward. "That makes it sound like it was premeditated, but the police think it was just an argument that got out of hand. The whole story was in the *Register*—imagine, two women arguing about what kind of Christmas tree to buy!"

"I'm with you, Roland," Bettina said, causing Roland to look up in amazement. He and Bettina seldom saw eye-to-eye. "The killer—who is *not* Sorrel—was probably stalking Karma. He followed her to the tree lot, hoping for a chance to make a move. And he got his chance."

"Why are killers always 'he'?" Karen asked in her mild little voice.

"Clayborn calls them that," Bettina said, "though in this case . . ."

"But if the killer was really stalking her"—Holly's knitting was now resting in her lap, having taken second place to the lively discussion under way—"why use a piece of tree trunk? Why not bring a weapon?"

"Guns are loud." Bettina thumped the arm of her armchair. "A knife might leave clues that could be traced, or might even be left in the victim—with fingerprints!"

"The police said she was killed there," Roland observed, "but they've been wrong before—despite what we pay in property taxes to fund their salaries. If the killer is a stalker and not Sorrel, wouldn't it make more sense—?"

A curious sound emanated from Nell's direction, a cross between a whimper and a growl. It was not unlike the sounds Woofus had made earlier that day in his encounter with Phoebe Ruskin. Then Nell half rose from her armchair, her white hair seeming to bristle as she directed scolding looks all around the room.

"This is neither the time nor the place to be discussing such a topic," she said. "It's bad enough that such a tragic event has visited our little town so close to Christmas—and it would be a tragic event at any time of year—but we don't have to rehearse the grisly details and we *certainly*"—she turned to glare at Bettina and then faced front again to glare at Pamela—"shouldn't imagine we can do better at crime-solving than the Arborville police."

With that, she sat down and leaned over to retrieve the half-finished stocking that had fallen onto the carpet.

Chapter Six

Knitters bent to their knitting once again, and Roland to his task of sewing his sweater parts together. All seemed chastened, even shy little Karen. But after a bit, the silence began to hang heavy, as it often does when provoked by a scolding. Then, as if to show that she, at least, hadn't taken offense, Holly spoke up.

"Everyone looks so festive tonight," she said. "Bettina in your candy cane sweater, and Pamela in such an awesome shade of green . . ." She beamed her smile around the room. Roland had even acknowledged the season with a tie that featured a pattern of tiny Christmas trees. Holly herself still sported a bright red streak in her dark hair, and her earrings were tiny tinsely Santas that evoked old-time ornaments.

When no one took up the conversational thread, Holly went on. "And Pamela," she said, "I hope you'll get out that awesome ruby-red tunic-sweater you knitted last year. You looked amazing at Bettina's Christmas Eve party. I could tell all the men were—"

"Yes!" Bettina joined the conversation. "One man in particular . . ."

Pamela gritted her teeth and glared at Bettina, willing

her to be silent. She thought the topic of Richard Larkin as a missed romantic opportunity had been laid to rest, but Bettina was incorrigible. Bettina got Pamela's unspoken message, however.

"Plenty of other men out there," she said brightly. "No need to focus on just the one."

"You should date, Pamela. Really." Holly leaned across Karen, who was seated between them, to speak. Her expression was earnest, and Pamela knew she meant no harm.

"Yes, she should," Bettina agreed. "Do you have any suggestions?"

"Well . . ." Holly leaned back and looked up at the ceiling, as if inspiration might be lurking there. She lowered her head again and snapped her fingers. "Desmond's uncle!" She paused and added hurriedly, "He's not old, not old at all. Much younger than Desmond's father and he—" She paused again. "What do you think, Nell? You have Harold, and Bettina has Wilfred. Pamela needs someone special in her life."

Pamela's fingers stilled. She closed her eyes and imagined herself somewhere else, praying also that her cheeks weren't as red as they felt.

The next voice she heard, however, was not Nell's, but rather Roland's.

"It's Pamela's business whether or not she wants to *date*." He uttered the word as if it was an unsavory term alien to his vocabulary. "I suggest we stick to our knitting, or . . ."

Pamela opened her eyes to see him pushing back his immaculate shirt cuff to consult his impressive watch.

Before he could speak—Roland's announcement at precisely eight o'clock that break time had arrived was a Knit and Nibble ritual—Bettina was on her feet. And a moment later, footsteps on the stairs heralded the arrival of Wilfred, emerging from his den.

Holly leapt up to compliment him on the cat climber, Karen volunteered to help with coffee and tea, and Nell followed her to the kitchen. Pamela was left alone on the sofa, patting her cheeks with her fingers, which felt blessedly cool in contrast to her flushed face. Roland was carefully folding the sweater pieces he'd been working on and laying them neatly in his briefcase.

From the direction of the kitchen came the tantalizing aroma of brewing coffee, rich and spicy. The kitchen was crowded enough, Pamela thought. Besides, she wasn't sure she forgave Bettina yet for bringing up Richard Larkin—again—and launching Holly on her well-meant but embarrassing intrusion into what Roland had so properly identified as Pamela's own business.

"Not too sweet," Nell sang out as she delivered her quick bread, sliced and arranged on a sage-green pottery platter that was part of Bettina's favorite dish set. The quick bread was an appealing golden-brown color and each slice was patterned with the pale and dark shapes of nuts and dried fruit. Nell deposited the platter on the coffee table, along with the pile of small sage-green plates she carried in her other hand.

Following right after her was Holly, bearing a wooden tray that held a sugar bowl and cream pitcher, forks and spoons, and dark green napkins in a rustic weave. She settled it next to the platter of quick bread. Karen was next, with two sage-green mugs. Judging by the dangling tags, the contents were tea.

"One for you, Nell," she announced, setting a mug at the edge of the coffee table near where Nell had resumed her seat in the armchair. "And one for me." She leaned across the coffee table to set the other mug near her own spot on the sofa. "And everyone else is coffee."

Seeing Holly and Karen standing together, Pamela was struck again by how curious friendships could be. It would be hard to imagine two more different young women— Holly with her outgoing chattiness and brunette good looks, and shy little blond Karen. But they were both young marrieds, new to Arborville, and both the proud owners of old houses in much need of renovation, so they had bonded. And they were both knitters too, of course.

She supposed people looking at her and Bettina might also be struck by how curious friendships could be, but she and Bettina had shared so much over the years that Pamela might simmer a bit when the topic of Richard Larkin came up, but she was always willing to forgive.

While she'd been pondering, more trips to and from the kitchen had taken place, and she looked down to see a steaming mug of coffee sitting before her. Across the table, Nell was placing slices of quick bread on the small plates and passing them around, along with forks and napkins. Roland had pulled his wooden chair close to the end of the coffee table, and Wilfred had fetched another chair from the dining room and joined him. With Wilfred sitting right at her elbow, Pamela had a chance to compliment him on the *amazing* (Holly's vocabulary could be catching) cat climber.

Bettina was the first to comment on the quick bread. "Hmmm," she said after the first bite. "Hmmm. It's good, yes. As you say, it's not too sweet."

"I think it's awesome." Holly's fork hovered partway to her mouth as she spoke. "It tastes exactly like something our dear Nell would bake."

It did taste like something from a grandmother's kitchen—sensible, perhaps dating from a frugal era when raisins would be considered quite enough of a treat in themselves, without needing to add much sugar. And it contained other fruit too, dried cranberries maybe, and currants, and the pale golden bits were probably dried apricots.

Pamela sipped her coffee, which was bitter in a pleasant way that complemented the austerity of the quick bread. And, as conversation buzzed around her, she surveyed the cozy room, made especially cozy by the tree, with its shimmering ornaments and twinkling lights, at one end of the room and the fire crackling at the other.

"Stay for a minute," Bettina said, leaning across the coffee table as Pamela bundled up her partly finished stocking and tucked it into her knitting bag, along with the skein of cheery red yarn. Coffee and tea had been drunk and Nell's quick bread nibbled, and then knitting had resumed. But now it was just nine, and even before Roland reminded everyone of that fact, people had begun to pack up for their journeys home.

Holly leaned across the coffee table too and addressed Nell. "You'll take a ride home, I hope," she said. "I can't believe you walked down here, and now it's even colder." Nell's habit of walking most places, for reasons of health as well as concern for the environment, was responsible for the vigor that she had maintained well into her eighties. But she agreed. And soon Pamela and Bettina were bidding a cheery "Good night" and "Merry Christmas" as Holly, Karen, and Nell headed down the driveway toward Holly's orange VW Beetle and Roland followed them en route to his Porsche.

Wilfred had cleaned up the kitchen before retreating once more to his den, but Bettina led Pamela back to the kitchen anyway. Once they arrived, she opened the refrigerator and lifted out a large two-handled pot, which she put on the counter.

"You have to take some of Wilfred's five-alarm chili," she said. "I know Penny likes it."

Pamela smiled, but she held up her hands as if to push the idea away. "Penny and I will be fine. I'm doing a big shopping at the Co-Op tomorrow, and you've invited us for Christmas, and I know we'll be feasting on Wilfred's creations then . . ."

Bettina removed the cover from the two-handled pot. Then she stooped and rummaged in a cupboard until she pulled out a large plastic container and a matching lid. From a drawer she took a ladle and began ladling chili into the container. There was silence while she worked.

When the container was full, she snapped the lid on and presented it to Pamela. "Roland is right," she said. "It *is* your business whether or not you want to date. I'll never say anything about it again."

"Oh, Bettina!" Pamela laughed, though she felt a little catch in her throat. Clutching the container of chili with one hand, she managed a clumsy half hug.

"He bought the goose today." Bettina opened the refrigerator again and pointed to a bulky object shrouded in a plastic bag. "He drove all the way out to Long Hill Farm. And there's to be roast potatoes and roast parsnips and Brussels sprouts and lingonberry relish and some kind of wintry salad."

"I'll make a dessert," Pamela said.

"Something sweet?" Bettina asked hopefully.

"Something delicious," Pamela said. "Something really delicious."

All up and down Orchard Street, houses and yards were bright with lights, and there were no clouds, so a few stars showed as chilly pinpricks against the dark sky.

Penny was still at Lorie Hopkins' house, but Pamela had cats to greet her. Soon she, and they, had settled onto the sofa. The tree had gotten decorated Saturday night after all, and the lights provided a bit of seasonal magic. As the cats purred and a British mystery unfolded on the screen before her, she resumed work on the stocking, to be delivered to Nell in time for Nell's pre-Christmas visit to the Haversack shelter.

Chapter Seven

Chocolate.

Pamela's sleeping mind had completed the conversation she'd had the previous night with Bettina about what form her Christmas dessert would take. An image had arisen of something chocolate, like a cake but not like a cake. Something denser . . . and richer . . . with contrasting textures and flavors. Sweet, yes, but with a little bitterness to add complexity.

So even before she fed the cats, she'd taken a cherished cookbook from her cookbook shelf and leafed through the dessert section until she came to the recipe for Chocolate Mousse Cake.

Now she was on her way to the Co-Op, well bundled against the cold and carrying a few of the canvas totes she used for her shopping. Just as she reached the stately brick apartment building at the corner, the door in the back of the building opened and Mr. Gilly stepped out onto the asphalt of the parking lot. He'd added a quilted utility jacket, a muffler, and a knit cap to his usual work clothes, and he was carrying a large cardboard box.

Mr. Gilly was a conscientious super, she had heard, but he liked to talk. When she was pressed for time and he was working outside, Pamela sometimes pretended not to see him and hurried by. But sometimes she was willing to chat—and there was another reason to linger too. A length of wooden fencing hid the building's trash cans, as well as discarded objects like tables, chairs, bookshelves—all kinds of household goods that people no longer thought they had use for. Pamela had once even adopted a very nice jade plant in a unique clay pot.

Mr. Gilly was heading for the opening at the end of the wooden fence, but when he caught sight of Pamela, he stopped and called out, "Hi there!"

Taking her "How are you?" as a sign that she was in the mood for a chat, he veered toward the sidewalk and lowered the box onto the winter-ravaged grass.

"Sad doings here," he said, tipping his head toward the building and fishing a pack of cigarettes and a lighter from his jacket pocket. "Karma Karling was a nice lady. Who'd have thought Sorrel Wollcott could do such a thing?" He nodded toward the box. "This stuff here was Karma's. Last Friday morning she asked me to carry it down for the trash and I just now got around to doing it." He extracted a cigarette from the pack and lit it. "There's still no tree in the lobby," he added. "The decorations committee disbanded and nobody else wants to take over."

Pamela was starting to get cold, but a box of Karma's discards seemed a tantalizing prospect. Mr. Gilly noticed her staring at it. "Nothing you'd be interested in," he said. "Not like an antique somebody threw away. It's really just trash—papers and such."

But she lingered, chatting with him about his plans for the holidays and his daughter, whose big house in Timberley was a great source of pride for him. When he'd finished his cigarette, he bade Pamela good-bye, stooped for the box, and disappeared through the opening in the fence. Pamela walked on toward the corner, but slowly, then turned and cautiously made her way back to the building's parking lot. She approached the fence and peeked into the opening to make sure Mr. Gilly was gone, then crouched by the box and pried open the flaps, which had been taped down.

Mostly, yes, it was just trash—course outlines for several previous years, handouts with definitions of art terms, lists of materials required for various classes. But near the bottom Pamela came upon something more interesting, a framed photo of a man sitting behind a drum kit. The photo was signed: *To my beloved Karma—All my love, Mack.*

Pamela held the photo in her gloved hands and stared at it hard. The man looked somehow familiar. But who might she know with such piercing eyes beneath dark brows and such a sardonic twist to his mouth? *Oh, my!* she murmured, and a wisp of breath curled into the chilly air. The man in the photo looked like the model for the extra drummer on the card that Karma had designed.

Pamela tucked the photo into one of her canvas bags and then began to return all the papers she had piled on the asphalt to the box. She lifted a loose sheaf of handouts headed *Karma Karling—Mixed Media—Fall 2012* and out floated a newspaper clipping. Pamela recognized it as coming from the "What to Do This Weekend" feature in the *Register*. The heading was LIVE MUSIC IN NORTH JERSEY and one item was circled. It announced that a band called the Mackinations would be playing Saturday and Sunday night in the lounge at the Skycrest Motel on Route 46.

Pamela slipped the newspaper clipping into the tote with the framed photo and returned the rest of the papers to the cardboard box. Bettina would be very interested in the photo and the clipping, Pamela was sure. But there was grocery shopping to do, and something else while she was uptown too, something that had been nagging at her mind since the previous night's Knit and Nibble meeting. So she continued on her way, turning left onto Arborville Avenue and heading north, and when she reached the Co-Op Grocery, she walked right past it.

Arborville's commercial district was charming, with its narrow storefronts, awnings, and attractive signage. And this time of year the charm was enhanced by the holiday decorations on the shops and on the lampposts—garlands of greenery and twinkling lights, illuminated even during the day.

She passed the bank and the hair salon and Hyler's Luncheonette, and another bank, and soon she reached the block where the St. Willibrod's church and hall were located. But St. Willibrod's wasn't her destination today. She veered instead toward the Christmas tree lot. The crime-scene tape was gone now. As the Aardvark Alliance had promised, extra hours had been added to the lot's schedule, so the gate in the chicken wire fence was open.

The tree lot attendants were busy—one was encasing a tree in the netted sheath that would streamline it for transport home, and the other was processing a credit card payment. But Pamela didn't want to talk to them anyway. She just wanted to see for herself the spot where Karma's body had been found. So she made her way through the rows of bristly trees, enjoying the sharp piney fragrance and the sensation of wandering alone in a small forest.

At the back of the lot, she stepped into a cleared place. A saw and a pile of short logs indicated that this was the spot that the *Register* had described as the murder scene. Through the chicken wire fence Pamela could see the St. Willibrod's parking lot and, beyond it, a few houses. The chicken wire showed no signs of having been tampered with, but—she looked closely—a few fibers of something were caught on a nail that fastened the chicken wire to one of the fence posts.

Presumably, the fibers were left from the twist of yarn the police had reported as a clue. Had they imagined Karma hurling Sorrel's hand-knit ornaments against the fence in disgust? The fibers were black though—and none of Sorrel's creations had featured black yarn. Black was definitely not a Christmas color.

At the Co-Op, Pamela pushed her cart up and down the narrow aisles, collecting tomatoes and cucumbers for salad, cat food, butter and eggs for more poppy-seed cakes, and heavy cream and chocolate in various forms for the special Christmas cake. Tonight's dinner would be Wilfred's five-alarm chili, but she paused at the fish counter.

Pamela and Penny would be spending Christmas Eve alone because the Frasers were spending the evening with Wilfred's cousin John and his family. Fish was the traditional Christmas Eve dish, so maybe she'd make bouillabaisse just for the two of them. She'd consult a cookbook at home and buy the fish fresh the next day.

The cheese counter was next, where she pondered the offerings—the buttery wheels of Gouda, the oozing wedges of Brie, the blue-veined Stilton, the Swiss cratered with holes—and finally requested a pound of the Co-Op's special Vermont Cheddar. Her tour of the Co-Op finished up at the bakery counter. She waited while a loaf of her favorite whole-grain bread was sliced and bagged and then pushed her cart toward the checkout.

Woofus, who had recovered from his pique at being left behind when Wilfred fetched the Christmas goose, greeted Pamela enthusiastically as soon as she stepped across the threshold—or perhaps it was the tempting aroma of cheese emanating from one of the canvas totes she carried.

In the kitchen Pamela set her grocery-filled totes on the pine table, well out of Woofus's reach. From the third tote she pulled, first, the framed photo of the dashing drummer.

" 'To my beloved Karma . . .' " Bettina's eyes grew wide as she whispered the words, staring at the photo. She shifted her gaze to Pamela. "Oh, my goodness," she said. "Where did you find this?"

Pamela described her fortuitous meeting with Mr. Gilly and the cardboard box.

"Then she put him on the Christmas card," Bettina said. "*This year's* Christmas card, so he's recent. I wonder if Clayborn knows about him."

"Why would he care?" Pamela's lips formed a skeptical twist. "He thinks he's got his killer."

"But now *we* know about him." Bettina's excitement set her earrings, miniature Christmas tree balls, to swaying. "Karma threw his photo away, so that suggests a love affair gone wrong. And what's a better motive for murder than . . . anger at being rejected?"

But then Bettina's excitement faded.

"How can we find him?" she asked plaintively. "All we know is his first name, Mack."

"We could google *Mack the drummer.*" Pamela paused and allowed her smile to tease. "Or we could"—she slowly pulled the clipping from the tote that had held the framed photo—"pay a visit to the Skycrest Motel on Route 46." She laid the clipping on the table. "Even if the Mackinations aren't playing there now, whoever books the entertainment would probably know how to find him."

Excited again, Bettina darted from the room, startling Woofus, who had been lounging in his favorite corner. She was back in a minute with her smartphone, her fingers already busy on its small screen.

"Here we go, here we go," she murmured as she lowered herself into her chair. "Skycrest Motel . . . appearing in the Skycrest Lounge this Saturday and Sunday, eight p.m. to midnight, the Mackinations."

"That's good news," Pamela said, "and bad. There's no way to follow up till Saturday. Today's only Wednesday."

Bettina nodded. "Don't make any plans for Saturday night though. I'm in the mood for some live music."

"Agreed!" Pamela stood up and gathered her tote bags. "I found something else too," she said as she paused at Bettina's front door. In the excitement of identifying a recent love interest for Karma, and then tracking him to an upcoming gig, she had forgotten all about the fibers she'd noticed on the chicken wire fence.

Now she described that discovery. "The thing is," she concluded, "they were black. That's not a Christmasy color, so I'm sure the twist of yarn the police found at the crime scene didn't have anything to do with Sorrel's yarn ornaments."

As she crossed the street to her own house, it occurred to Pamela that Phoebe Ruskin, with her avant-garde look and artistic leanings, probably had a lot of black garments in her wardrobe. But how could they arrange another meeting with her after the disaster with Woofus?

* * *

Penny was sitting on the living room floor playing with Ginger when Pamela stepped through her front door. A recent addition to the cats' collection of toys had been a feather at the end of a long, flexible wand, and Ginger was getting a very good workout as she leapt and twisted her lithe body in pursuit of this tantalizing prey.

Pamela took her groceries to the kitchen and put the perishable things in the refrigerator, then she returned to the living room and perched on the edge of the sofa.

"Did Karma ever mention knowing a drummer?" she asked as Ginger pounced on the feather, then watched in dismay as it once more took flight.

"Not really," Penny said. "Why?"

Pamela knew that Penny didn't approve of her and Bettina's forays into crime-solving. Pamela's heart had melted when Penny once pointed out that such activities could be dangerous, and having lost her father, she didn't wish to lose her mother too.

"No special reason . . ." Pamela hesitated, already feeling guilty for the lie. She quickly added, "But the details on the cards are so realistic, and then there's that extra little face besides."

"She was friends with the teacher who led the jazz-rock group, Mr. Wetzel," Penny said as the feather arced dramatically and Ginger sprang into the air with her front paws splayed. "But I don't think he was a drummer."

Later, when Penny had gone next door to meet Laine and Sibyl for an expedition to the Haversack thrift store in quest of vintage clothing, Pamela searched for Mr. Wetzel on her smartphone. The high school's website provided his first name, Archie, but he wouldn't be there today with the school on Christmas break. An Archie Wetzel lived in Meadowside though, and the listing included a phone number.

She succeeded in reaching only his voicemail, and she left a message asking if he'd be willing to talk about Karma for an article in the *Advocate*. Archie Wetzel might not be a drummer, but as a friend of Karma's, he might have been privy to information about her personal life.

Chapter Eight

"There isn't going to be snow." Penny was reading the *Register* as Pamela stood at the counter separating the whites from the yolks of the eggs that would go into her poppy-seed cakes. "Maybe it's going to rain for Christmas, but it won't be cold enough to snow."

"It *is* pretty when it snows," Pamela said. At present, nothing outdoors looked pretty at all. The grass was patchy and the trees were bare and the shrubs that didn't lose their leaves looked sad nonetheless. "Maybe we'll get some snow before you go back to school."

"There's probably snow in Boston now," Penny said. And with that, she folded the paper, got up, and left the room.

Pamela worked on. In her favorite bowl, the caramel-colored one with three white stripes circling the rim, she creamed the butter and sugar, then added the egg yolks and vanilla. The poppy seeds had been heated in a cup of milk earlier that morning and allowed to sit for an hour. Now they were added, and the sifted flour, baking powder, and salt too. Finally the egg whites, beaten to a drift of white, were folded in, and the batter was divided between two greased and floured loaf pans.

As she was sliding the loaf pans into the oven, Penny reappeared. She had dressed, but in a slouchy leggings-and-sweatshirt outfit that suggested she wasn't planning to go out anytime soon. She was carrying a large shopping bag from the fanciest store at the mall.

"I have things to wrap," she said.

"Use all the paper you want." Pamela closed the oven door and nodded toward the doorway that led into the dining room. The dining room table had been functioning as a wrapping station for the past few weeks, and Pamela's wrapping supplies were all close at hand.

"Don't come in though," Penny said. That comment and her secret smile gave away the fact that some of the gifts to be wrapped were destined for Pamela herself.

The phone rang a few minutes later. Once the caller identified himself, Pamela was glad Penny had been eager to get on with her task and was now sitting at the dining room table rummaging among rolls of paper and spools of ribbon.

"Archie Wetzel," the voice had said. "I'll talk to the *Advocate*. Just tell me when and where."

Pamela carried the phone's handset into the entry just to make sure Penny wouldn't overhear, and she quickly arranged for him to meet her and Bettina at Hyler's for lunch. As soon as that call ended, she called Bettina.

"I hope you're free for lunch at Hyler's today," she said, and explained that Karma's colleague, Archie Wetzel, had agreed to be interviewed by the *Advocate* on the subject of Karma's legacy. "The Christmas cards, you know," she added. "Twelve years' worth of Christmas cards and their inspiration."

Bettina laughed. "Like who is the handsome drummer that Karma immortalized in this year's design?"

"That's the plan."

"How on earth did you . . . ?" Bettina sounded puzzled, but delighted.

"I'll tell you later, while we're walking uptown together."

Bettina sighed. "I'll wear comfortable shoes."

Penny had finished her wrapping and retreated to her room by the time Pamela took the poppy-seed cakes out of the oven. But she had added several carefully wrapped boxes to the small collection that had already accumulated under the tree. Pamela recognized the vintage wrapping paper that she'd brought home from a particularly good tag sale the previous summer: a busy print of holly leaves accented with berries.

Pamela stepped out onto the porch to gauge which jacket she would need. Bettina, just leaving her own house, saw her and hurried across the street.

"It's not very cold," she observed, "but it feels damp." She'd traded her pumpkin-colored down coat for a red fleece parka with a drawstring waist, and instead of her fur-trimmed boots, she wore her red sneakers.

"Rain is predicted for Christmas," Pamela said. She went back inside to fetch her medium-weight jacket and call good-bye to Penny, and soon they were on their way. As they walked along, Pamela explained how she'd gotten Penny to volunteer the name of Archie Wetzel without actually revealing that she and Bettina were sleuthing.

As was often the case, the community bulletin board, which was a longtime feature of the Co-Op—dating from before the era when anyone looking to give away a puppy or recruit a babysitter could simply post a note on the town's LISTSERV—had attracted a small crowd. It wasn't that the flyers and notices pinned to the bulletin board were all that compelling. It was just that once one person lingered to see what was new, someone else might linger also, and a chat might ensue, thereby attracting more lingerers.

One of the lingerers called out to them as they passed, and Pamela and Bettina turned to see Marlene Pepper waving. "Merry Christmas!" Marlene added to her greeting. "Are Warren and his wife coming down from Boston?"

Warren and his wife—or as Bettina called them, "the Boston children"—were professors and the parents of Morgan, the granddaughter for whom girly gifts had been proscribed.

Soon Bettina and Marlene were deep in conversation, but in a moment the conversation expanded to include a new arrival, a pleasant-looking woman about the same age as Marlene and Bettina.

"I know what you mean," the woman said. "Children have their own ideas, and once they're grown up, you can't say much if you want to ever see them again." She laughed and shook her head. "I love Phoebe to death—but blue hair! Honestly! In the city maybe, but she doesn't live in the city."

Pamela tapped Bettina on the arm, and when Bettina turned toward her, she mouthed the word *Phoebe?*

Bettina turned back toward the group. "Phoebe the dog-walker?" she inquired.

"Oh, my goodness! I am forgetting my manners!" Marlene clutched Bettina's arm with one hand and the new arrival's with the other. "Bettina and Pamela," she said, "meet Georgia Ruskin."

" 'Dog-walker'? Yes." Georgia Ruskin uttered the phrase as if it designated some sort of illicit activity. "After five years of college, paid for by her parents, she wants to be a sculptor, mind you."

"If she has that artistic impulse . . ." Pamela hesitated. Penny had an artistic impulse, so Pamela empathized. But she wasn't sure how she'd feel if Penny ended up walking dogs for a living.

" 'Artistic impulse'!" Georgia snorted. "Oh, she has that all right. Everything has to be just right. *Artistic*. She's going to do my tree for me, so we end up going to three different lots last Friday night until Phoebe finds one she approves of."

"Phoebe's alibi?" Pamela inquired of Bettina when they'd gotten out of earshot of the others. It was getting on toward noon, the time she'd set to meet Archie Wetzel. She'd had to remind Bettina of that fact, interrupting her lament that she'd crocheted a pink baby blanket for little Morgan, only to have her gift refused.

"Unsolicited too." Bettina nodded. "And we're not the police, so why would Georgia Ruskin say Phoebe spent Friday night searching for the perfect Christmas tree unless it was really true?"

Archie Wetzel was standing on the sidewalk outside of Hyler's. Pamela had suggested that would make him easier to find than if he went inside, especially given the crush of people who descended on Hyler's from Arborville's offices and shops at lunchtime.

He was decidedly not the dashing bad-boy type, like Mack, but rather a gentle-looking soul, slender and not too tall, with thinning blond hair and pale, freckly skin. The long black scarf wrapped twice around his neck seemed more a fashion statement than a necessity, however—given the unseasonable weather.

"And which one of you is . . . ?" he asked pleasantly after he'd affirmed that he was indeed Archie Wetzel.

"I'm Bettina Fraser, from the *Advocate*"—Bettina offered her hand and a flirtatious smile—"and this is Pamela Paterson."

"I called you," Pamela said. "My daughter, Penny, graduated from Arborville High a few years ago. She loved her classes with Karma, and she thought maybe you could help Bettina with her article."

Luckily, one of Hyler's spacious booths had gone unclaimed by the lunchtime crowd. Seated on a bench upholstered in burgundy Naugahyde and facing Archie across the worn wooden table, Bettina got right to the point.

"Let's start with the twelfth day and work backward," she suggested. She'd slipped off the red fleece parka to reveal a mistletoe-green turtleneck, which was complemented by her dangling candy cane earrings and her bright red lipstick and nail polish.

The server arrived then, bearing the oversized menus that were a Hyler's institution. The interruption demanded attention to food rather than conversation. Archie's focus on the menu, which hid his face, suggested that he was happy for a chance to ponder not only his lunch possibilities, but also his response to Bettina's suggestion.

"We haven't ordered hamburgers here for a while, have we?" Her own menu still raised, Bettina turned to Pamela, who was seated on the same side of the booth.

"I don't think so," Pamela said. "A hamburger sounds good."

"How about you, Archie?" Bettina lowered her menu. "My treat, to thank you for the interview."

He spoke from behind the menu. "I'd like the cheese omelet, please. And a cup of coffee."

"Done," Bettina declared, laying her menu down on the paper place mat.

The server, a middle-aged woman who was also a Hyler's institution, had been hovering near the booth—Hyler's liked to turn over tables quickly during the lunchtime rush—and stepped forward with her order pad in hand.

Once the burgers, omelet, and coffee had been requested, along with vanilla shakes for Bettina and Pamela, Bettina focused her gaze on Archie. In her hazel eyes, accented with green shadow that matched her turtleneck, Pamela recognized the determination that usually resulted in Bettina's getting people to talk.

"So," she said pleasantly, "the twelfth day of Christmas." Her manner combined curiosity with admiration, as if nothing at that moment was more important than what Archie had to say.

"Well," he said, looking down at his place mat and realigning the knife, fork, and spoon so they paralleled the place mat's edges. "She'd done the other eleven days, so . . . it was time for the drummers."

"There's an extra drummer on the card though." Bettina struggled to maintain eye contact, given Archie's interest in his silverware. "And he doesn't look like the other drummers. He looks like he might be based on a real person."

"She liked her little jokes." He gave the knife one last adjustment. "Karma was very witty."

"Did she know some real person who was a drummer?" Bettina inquired.

The server returned then, with Archie's coffee. He seemed, like Bettina, to require a careful admixture of sugar and cream, so conversation ceased while he added the contents of several sugar packets to his cup, stirred energetically, and then peeled the top off a tiny plastic tub of cream.

"The *Advocate*'s readers will be fascinated by the back-story," Bettina said encouragingly as Archie dribbled the cream into his coffee. "Karma was so popular with the students, and everyone in town looked forward to her Christmas card designs." She laughed. "Such a beautiful woman too. There must have been admirers."

The server interrupted again, bearing two vanilla milkshakes in tall frosted glasses. "And burgers coming right up," she sang out. "Your cheese omelet too, sweetie." She winked at Archie.

"Do you two have something going on?" Bettina said teasingly after she left, for the moment ignoring the milkshake.

"I . . . of course not." Archie's coffee cup paused halfway to his mouth. "I always order a cheese omelet when I come here. Karma and I . . . Cheese omelets were her favorite too."

Something odd was happening to his voice. He set the coffee cup down, swallowed hard, and blinked a few times. "It's just . . . I really miss her."

Bettina sprang from the bench and hurried to the other side of the booth, where she slid in beside Archie.

"Oh, you poor dear man," she crooned in a voice similar to the one she used to comfort Woofus. "It's hard to lose someone you loved."

"I didn't . . . I didn't love her," he moaned, "at least not in that way. It would have been hopeless . . ."

"Yes," Bettina murmured, "there was someone else, wasn't there . . . ?"

"Mack Drayton," Archie said miserably. He grabbed up

the paper napkin from his place setting and dabbed at his eyes.

An oval platter bearing a hamburger appeared in front of Pamela. The hamburger shared the platter with a small pile of French fries, a fluted paper cup of slaw, and a long spear of pickle. Without comment the server spun Bettina's place mat, with its napkin and silverware, around to face her in her new position and deposited a platter identical to Pamela's on it. Pamela nudged Bettina's shake across the table.

Archie's cheese omelet arrived next, accompanied by a fresh napkin.

Bettina was the first to sample her meal, and her verdict was, "Delicious!" Archie picked up his fork and took a tentative bite of his omelet, which was a rich shade of yellow, glistening with butter, and accompanied by four triangles of golden-brown toast.

The taste of food seemed to cheer him, and soon he was eating quite enthusiastically.

Pamela removed the onion slice from her hamburger, replaced the top bun, and took a bite. The ground beef was meaty, slightly rare, and mouth-filling, with just a hint of char from the grill. The bun was a brioche bun like those at the Co-Op bakery counter, not as yielding to the teeth as a conventional hamburger bun, and it stood up well to the juicy burger. The dilled sharpness of the pickle offered the perfect follow-up.

No one spoke for a bit, and when they did, it was to confirm that all three were enjoying their meal and Hyler's certainly deserved the esteem it was held in by Arborvillians.

Pamela sipped at her milkshake and took bites of her

hamburger, interspersed with forkfuls of slaw, quick nips at the pickle, and fries eaten, one by one, with fingers.

"Mack Drayton was the inspiration for that extra drummer on the card," Archie said suddenly. His plate was empty, as was his coffee cup, which had been refilled twice. Perhaps this announcement was intended as thanks for a satisfying meal.

Bettina could be cagey. Instead of turning to him (she was still sharing his side of the booth), she merely said, "Oh?" in an offhand way and continued methodically finishing the last of her French fries.

Some of Pamela's most revealing chats with Penny had occurred in the car. Somehow the idea that Pamela's concentration was mostly on the road, and not on her daughter, had loosened Penny's tongue, almost as if Penny was simply talking to herself—working through an idea best pondered if spoken aloud.

Bettina had presumably had the same experience while raising her two sons. Now she continued eating her fries as Archie spoke.

"She met him over a decade ago, when they were both living in the city and going to school. They finished school and went their separate ways, but they'd recently reconnected. She decided it wasn't working and she stopped seeing him in October—but it was too late to redo the cards."

"I don't think Archie was telling the truth about not loving her," Bettina commented as she and Pamela walked along Arborville Avenue half an hour later. They were en route to the Co-Op for Pamela's bouillabaisse ingredients.

Karma's inspiration for the other eleven days of Christmas had been dealt with summarily (Did she know any pipers? Ever live on a dairy farm? Crave expensive jew-elry? Know much about birds?) because Bettina was eager to maintain the pretense that her goal was an article on Karma's inspiration for the cards. Ultimately, though, she had thanked Archie for his time and told him that, aside from the personal details that had inspired the image for the twelfth day—which she was sure he wouldn't want to appear in the *Advocate*—she didn't think she had enough material for a story.

"I agree," Pamela said. "It was pretty obvious how he felt about her. But he could see the types she was attracted to—the dashing drummer, and maybe he'd been privy to details about her other romances. He knew *he* wasn't dashing, so he'd just resigned himself to being the faithful friend."

Bettina nodded, a bit sadly. "At least that way he could be close to her in *some* way."

They had reached the Co-Op, but Pamela paused at the door. "It sounded like Karma was definitely the one who broke it off with Mack last October," she said. "Not the other way around."

"It sounded that way to me too," Bettina agreed.

"A possessive man could get very angry if he couldn't have the woman he wanted."

"Very." Bettina gave a vigorous nod, and the candy cane earrings swayed.

An impatient voice asked, "Excuse me, but are you ladies going in or not?"

They hurried through the door. Pamela picked up one of the baskets for shoppers in search of only a few items. "Meeting Mack Drayton on Saturday night is going to be interesting," Pamela said as they headed over the worn wooden floor toward the fish counter.

They emerged from the Co-Op sometime later, Pamela carrying a canvas tote that held fresh mussels, shrimp, and sea bass, and leeks and a bulb of fennel. After a quick stop at the wine store next to the Co-Op, they continued south on Arborville Avenue.

"I miss shopping at the Co-Op sometimes," Bettina commented as they walked along. "I hardly ever go there now."

Bettina had been a willing but uninspired cook through most of her married life, with a repertoire of seven menus that repeated week after week. But when Wilfred retired, he'd enthusiastically taken over most kitchen duties and the Frasers' culinary horizons had widened considerably.

From the stereo came the strains of "I Saw Three Ships," courtesy of a vinyl Christmas LP that had come out every year since Pamela was a child. When her parents downsized, the LP became hers. The gentle glow of the Christmas tree illuminated the living room. It was visible from the dining room, where Pamela and Penny sat at a table laid with a lace tablecloth, white linen napkins, Pamela's wedding china with its garlands of pink roses, and tag sale wineglasses etched with a filigree design.

The cats had had a special Christmas Eve meal, a can of something very fancy that included gravy, and they were napping.

Pamela and Penny were eating the bouillabaisse. They chatted about plans for the next day, and the next week—Penny didn't have to return to Boston until after New Year's. She would be a senior in college by the time Christmas rolled around again, and then she would graduate, and Pamela would really be alone in her big house.

But that was too sad a thought to contemplate on an evening that was a prelude to a day of feasting and presents and friends. Pamela poured a bit more Chablis into each of their glasses as "I Saw Three Ships" yielded to "Good King Wenceslas."

They finished up the evening sitting companionably on the sofa, nibbling on slices of poppy-seed cake from one of the loaves Pamela had baked that morning and watching *A Christmas Carol.*

Chapter Nine

It had been many years since Christmas started before the sun came up, with an eager Penny invading her parents' bed. Lately the day had started instead with eager cats, though no more eager than on any other day, demanding breakfast.

Pulling on her fleecy robe and slipping her feet into fleecy slippers, Pamela followed Catrina into the hall. They were joined there by Ginger, who had abandoned the still-sleeping Penny when she sensed that most of the household was stirring. The three proceeded down the stairs.

In the kitchen, while the cats traced complicated patterns around her bare ankles, Pamela opened another can of the special gravy cat food. It slid into the bowl in a compact can-shaped lump, but when it was broken up with a spoon, gravy magically flowed from a cavity in the center. The cats, however, seemed to like it no better than their usual fare.

Next she measured water into the kettle and set it to boil, then dashed outside for the *Register*. The *Advocate* had appeared since she last checked the driveway, so she brought that in too, both encased in flimsy plastic sleeves.

As Pamela was grinding the coffee beans, Penny came in, looking like a years-younger version of herself, with her sleepy eyes and pillow-tousled hair. She waited until the grinder's noise subsided to a whispery whir before offering a Christmas greeting.

"Shall we have Christmas carols with breakfast?" Pamela asked. Penny nodded. "And put the tree lights on too," Pamela added, "even though we can't see them from in here."

The kettle began to whistle then, and soon the familiar aroma of brewing coffee filled the small kitchen, as the boiling water dripped through the ground beans in the filter cone. Penny returned from her errand to the strains of "Silent Night," slipped two slices of whole-grain bread into the toaster, and arranged cups, saucers, and plates from Pamela's wedding china on the table. Not being a devotee of black coffee like her mother, she added the cut-glass sugar bowl and the cream pitcher, with a dollop of cream, to the table setting.

They ate their toast and drank their coffee while paging through the newspapers. Out of loyalty to Bettina, Pamela read the *Advocate* first, though as Bettina had predicted, since the *Advocate* was a weekly, the *Register* had long since reported everything that there was to know (so far) about Karma's murder.

"Shall we see what's waiting for us under the Christmas tree?" Pamela asked after the newspapers had been folded up and the rose-garlanded coffee cups emptied.

Pamela sat on the sofa and Penny on the carpet near the tree, and Catrina and Ginger prowled around in the space between them. The cats were obviously curious about this variation in the usual morning schedule—though it apparently had something to do with the fact that there had been a tree growing in the living room since the previous week.

"You first," Penny said, handing Pamela a large color-fully wrapped box that she recognized as one of the gifts that had arrived from her parents.

Pamela's suspicions about the contents proved correct. Her mother always sent pajamas, for both Penny and Pamela, knowing that the tastes of a college-age woman were hard to anticipate and that Pamela had little need for or interest in fancy clothes.

Indeed, the similar package bearing the *For Penny* tag also contained pajamas. But a second, smaller box with the same wrapping held gold earrings, which were dangly and tiny and delicate, and set with small rubies. An accompanying note identified them as having belonged to Penny's maternal great-grandmother, whose name had been Penelope.

Pamela's other gift from her parents was a dessert cookbook featuring a characteristic dessert from every state in the Union. And Pamela's mother always included checks for her daughter and granddaughter, to fund a post-Christmas shopping trip or, more likely in Pamela's case, be tucked away for a rainy day.

There were also gifts from Michael Paterson's parents: thoughtfully chosen jewelry for Penny and Pamela, and a generous check for Penny.

The cats had presents too: a catnip mouse for Catrina and a catnip bird for Ginger. They'd been delighted with cast-off ribbons, pouncing on a twist of red grosgrain when the heirloom earrings were unwrapped, and then engaging in a tug-of-war with a longer piece from one of the pajama boxes. But as Penny removed the wrapping she herself had put on, to expose—encased in a thick plastic bag—a mouse cleverly sewn from gray velvet, and then drew the mouse from the plastic that had prevented its ecstasy-inducing scent to tempt prematurely, both cats froze in mid-gesture.

Their heads swiveled toward where Penny sat with her back to the tree. The tips of their tails flicked back and forth. Their pupils dilated.

Penny tossed the mouse onto the carpet, and both cats pounced. Catrina landed first, perhaps knowing that the mouse had been intended for her. From Ginger's throat came a low growl and she crouched as if about to attack her mother.

Penny quickly stripped the wrapping off the catnip bird and lobbed it in Ginger's direction. Ginger whirled to see what had just landed and then seized up the bird and rose onto her haunches, clutching it. Catrina carried the mouse toward the arch that led into the dining room.

Suddenly each cat was transformed, caught up in a fit of ecstasy. Catrina writhed on her back, holding the catnip mouse between her front paws and alternately nipping at it and rubbing it against her cheeks. Ginger allowed the bird to drop to the carpet. Then she seized it up again and began licking it furiously as a low rumble issued from her throat.

It seemed an invasion of their privacy to stare at them, so Pamela pointed to the largest box beneath the tree. It was wrapped in a vintage paper that featured Santas looking as if they had stepped from a Currier and Ives print. "That's for you," she said.

Penny pulled it toward her, but before even touching the ribbon, she picked up another large box, wrapped in a vintage paper featuring holly leaves and berries. "And this is for you." She stood up and presented the box to Pamela.

Boots were in the largest box, rugged brown leather boots that Penny had admired in a newspaper advertisement for a store at the mall the first day she was home.

And for Pamela, Penny had found a glazed pottery bowl, caramel colored, with three white stripes circling it near the rim—but smaller than the one she already owned.

"This is perfect!" Pamela exclaimed. Vintage bowls were one of her collections. "Wherever did you find it?"

"The thrift store near campus," Penny said. "We'll go there the next time you come up."

Another box contained a nice down coat for Pamela from Penny, provoking a grateful thank-you and then a teasing "Bettina's idea, I suppose."

"Well," Penny laughed. "I did ask her what she thought you might like."

"What I needed, more like." Pamela laughed too. "She hasn't approved of my coats for years."

By the time Pamela and Penny had unwrapped all their gifts, the cats lay sprawled on the sofa, exhausted by their debauchery, and Penny had accented her fleecy robe with an antique amber necklace Pamela had found at an estate sale.

"There will be something else too," Pamela said. "We'll go to the fancy yarn shop in Timberley next week and you can pick out some yarn and a pattern for me to knit you something."

A few still-wrapped boxes remained under the tree, however. They'd be carried across the street that evening to be presented to Wilfred and Bettina.

Pamela rose from the sofa. "I'd better get dressed," she said. "I have a Chocolate Mousse Cake to make."

Wilfred's roast goose had been a triumph. Occupying one of Bettina's sage-green pottery platters, it had domi-nated the table, which was spread with a rose-colored cloth and set with plates of the same sage green. Sage-green serv-ing bowls had contained roasted potatoes, roasted parsnips, and roasted Brussels sprouts tossed with bacon. A small crystal bowl had offered lingonberry relish. The tart spiciness of the relish had complemented the rich slices of roast goose to perfection.

Bettina's table had been extended with a leaf to accommodate all the guests. Besides Pamela and Penny, Wilfred Jr. and his wife Maxie were there with their two little boys, and the Frasers' other son, Warren, was there with his wife Greta and their daughter Morgan. The two little boys sat on chairs, but had been elevated to dining level with pillows, and Morgan sat in a high chair that had served Wilfred Jr. and Warren years earlier.

Now the main course had been cleared away, as well as the salad that had followed—radicchio with pecans and blue cheese—and the last of the Pinot Noir had been poured into the Swedish crystal wineglasses.

"I think it's my turn to do something useful," Pamela said as she rose to her feet. She had been chatting across the table with Greta about the virtues of natural fabrics and the do-it-yourself ethos after Greta had admired her sweater. It was the ruby-red tunic-sweater that came out only on festive occasions, given that it featured a—to Pamela—daring and illogical feature: cutouts revealing bare shoulders. Greta herself was in a garment that seemed to be made of hemp, a fashion choice in keeping with her unstyled hair and face untouched by cosmetics.

As she talked to Greta, she'd been half overhearing Penny's conversation with Warren, about Penny's impressions of Boston.

"The cake?" At the end of the table, Bettina rose to her feet as well.

The two friends headed to the kitchen together. Once there, Bettina busied herself with coffee preparation, and

Pamela gently lifted the foil that had protected the cake on its trip across the street.

Bettina paused in the midst of scooping ground coffee into her carafe's filter cone. "Ohhh!" she gasped. "That is magnificent!"

The cake was a simple creation, but the layered effect, with three shades of brown—each evoking a different form of chocolate—gave it glamour suitable for a party. The first layer, the darkest, was a dense flourless cake. The second was a truffle-like mousse, not as dark, but still rich-looking and lustrous with heavy cream. The third was scarcely a layer, just a sprinkling of unsweetened cocoa powder whose dusky reddish color made the surface of the cake seem to glow.

Pamela cut the cake into narrow slices and transferred each one to a dessert plate, the dark triangles making for dramatic geometry against the sage-green. She delivered the plates, amid exclamations of delight, as Bettina delivered coffee.

The cake lived up to its appearance, everyone agreed, and Pamela tried to experience it not as its creator, but simply as a fellow diner. The mousse layer yielded easily in the mouth, and its flavor suggested a chocolate truffle. The cake layer mimicked the texture of a brownie. And the cocoa powder that dusted the top gave each bite an appealing hint of bitterness.

When the plates were empty but for streaks of chocolate and the coffee cups had been tipped for the last drops, Wilfred Jr. and Maxie gathered up their yawning little boys, wished everyone "Merry Christmas," and headed back to their own house. Greta carried Morgan up the stairs, and on her return retreated to the kitchen to help Warren with the cleanup.

Wilfred led the way to the living room then, with Bettina following him and taking Pamela's and Penny's hands to draw them along beside her. Wilfred added a log to the fire as Bettina settled Pamela and Penny in the armchairs and took a seat on the sofa. Wilfred joined her, beaming with pleasure at the success of the meal. He looked handsome in the Nordic-style sweater, finally completed, that had been Bettina's gift to him.

"I think there are some unopened gifts still under the tree," Wilfred said with a smile that hinted at surprises, "and maybe elsewhere as well."

"You do yours first." Penny jumped up. In a moment she was offering a gaily wrapped package to Wilfred and Bettina. "You have to both open it together," she said, "because it's for both of you."

Wilfred obediently untied the ribbon and handed the package to Bettina for the paper removal. Bettina peeled the paper away to reveal the back of a stretched canvas. Then she turned it over and uttered a squeal of joy.

"This is too, too amazing!" she cooed. "However did you do this?"

She held it up for Pamela to see, though Pamela had known all the time what the wrapping paper hid.

The Frasers lived in the oldest house on Orchard Street, a Dutch Colonial that dated from the era before Arborville even became Arborville. Their modern kitchen was a recent addition, but from the front their house still resembled the original structure. Penny had made a painting of their house as it might have looked when it was the only house on the street, surrounded by the apple orchard that had provided a livelihood for its owners and later had given the street its name.

Penny opened her gift from the Frasers next. The small box had implied a gift of jewelry, and she wasn't disappointed. She lifted the lid to find a delicate silver disk dangling from a delicate silver chain. Tiny pearls and a tiny diamond were arranged on the disk to form a curious symbol.

"It's your astrological sign," Bettina explained. "Taurus."

"It's beautiful." Penny undid the clasp and Pamela helped her refasten it at the back of her neck. The disk glowed against the red fabric of her dress, the flirty dress that she'd had since high school and that still complemented her lively beauty.

Then she was on her feet again, delivering a long, skinny package to Wilfred, which turned out to contain a chef's knife, and then a boxy package to Bettina.

"From the craft show *Fiber Craft* cosponsored in the city last fall," Pamela explained as Bettina lifted a glass bowl from a nest of tissue. The bowl was a curious free-form shape, flaring at the top, with the color shading downward from intense turquoise to the red-gold hue of sunset.

"Oh!" Bettina squealed again. "You know how much I love things like this. Thank you so much!"

Wilfred stood up now, leaning on the arms of his chair as he rose. "No more presents under the tree," he observed with a Santa-like twinkle in his eye, "but . . ." He disappeared through the arch that led to the dining room, and the kitchen beyond. They heard his cheery greeting as he saluted Warren and Greta and then there was silence.

"You must close your eyes, Pamela," Bettina said. "And don't open them until I say so."

Pamela waited, eyes obediently closed, listening to the fire crackle, then to the sound of Wilfred's feet coming closer, finally to a thump on the floor near the tree and a satisfied grunt.

"Okay!" Bettina and Wilfred sang in unison.

Pamela opened her eyes—and there under the Christmas tree was a second cat climber, identical to the first except that the carpet covering the largest post and the platforms was dark blue instead of dark green.

Now she was the one to squeal, and Penny squealed too.

"A cat climber of my own!" Pamela exclaimed. "I can't think of a nicer present."

Later, Pamela, Penny, Wilfred, and Bettina stood on the Frasers' porch. The snowless yard detracted not one bit from their holiday spirit.

"Merry Christmas! Merry Christmas!" they all wished one another.

And then Wilfred carried the cat climber across the street and set it next to Pamela's Christmas tree.

Chapter Ten

Penny didn't think live music at the Skycrest Lounge on Route 46 sounded very appealing—and besides, she'd been invited to a party at the house that Aaron shared with some of his Wendelstaff College friends.

Route 46 formed the southern border of Haversack. Besides the Skycrest and other motels, anyone driving along it would pass used-car dealerships, fast-food outlets, and the offices of payday moneylenders, among other enterprises.

From behind the wheel of his ancient but lovingly cared-for Mercedes, Wilfred advised, "Keep a sharp eye out. Traffic's moving fast and I'll need some warning to slow down when we come to it."

"Slow down now!" Bettina exclaimed, leaning forward in the passenger seat. "It's right here."

The Skycrest occupied a large expanse of asphalt, much of it taken up by vehicles that ranged from pickup trucks to sporty two-seaters, all illuminated by bright lights on tall poles. The motel—long wings with doors spaced at intervals—stretched out on either side of the office, labeled in red neon OFFICE, and the lounge, labeled in red neon LOUNGE.

Wilfred had to park some distance from the entrance to

the lounge, and as they approached the entrance, they passed a small cluster of people at the end of the concrete apron that ran across the front of the office-lounge complex. Drifts of smoke rose from their midst, and cigarette butts were scattered at their feet, despite the metal receptacle clearly intended for their disposal.

Wilfred pulled open a heavy glass door and they entered a dim room furnished with a few armchairs and large plastic plants. A carpet patterned with swirling designs in maroon, red, and purple covered the floor. Straight ahead, double doors opened into an even dimmer room from which came the sound of music, but not live music.

As they advanced toward the double doors, they dodged around a few people headed in the other direction. A man in a fringed leather jacket was slipping a cigarette from a pack as he chatted, laughing, with a youngish woman. She paused for a moment to rearrange a dramatic poncho, black mohair, that hung to her knees, where her sleek black boots began. A second woman in a capacious leopard-print coat already had her cigarette between her lips.

The band was on a break, and the music was coming from the PA system. Most of the tables were filled, with people of various ages—likely fans of live music who didn't want to travel to the city to hear it, as well as motel guests looking to fill an evening on the road.

Wilfred spotted a free table near the far wall. They threaded their way toward it and settled onto none-too-comfortable wooden chairs. At the next table a raucous crowd of seven or eight people had squeezed themselves around a table intended for four. The table was crowded with glasses and beer pitchers, some full and some empty.

"Reminds me of my youth," Wilfred said, scanning the crowd and tapping his feet in time to the Rolling Stones song that had just come on. "Beer, ladies?" he inquired as a young woman dressed all in black approached from the bar at one end of the room.

"A small one," Bettina said, and Pamela nodded.

The stage where the band performed was at the other end of the room, unoccupied now but for instruments, huge amplifiers, and an impressive mother-of-pearl drum kit trimmed with gleaming chrome.

Bettina had partially risen from her chair and was scanning the crowd. "That's him!" she said suddenly, nudging Pamela. "Look, right there." She directed a finger toward a table at the edge of the stage. Three faces were visible, and the back of a head covered with dark hair. Then the head turned. A profile was visible.

"He's turning!" Bettina hissed. "Watch!"

The owner of the head halfway rose and swiveled, apparently looking toward the bar.

It was Mack Drayton, no question. The assertive nose and the dark brows gave his face a glamour that was almost sinister. He raised an arm in a commanding gesture and his lips parted in a smile that was the facial equivalent of a swagger. A moment later, a black-clad server neared his table.

Their own beer arrived then. Wilfred raised his glass in a toast: "To the new year!" he said, and took a long swallow. Bettina sipped at her beer for a few minutes, as did Pamela. Then Bettina pushed her chair back from the table and said, "I'll go see what I can find out."

"How?" Pamela was startled. It was true they'd come to the Skycrest Lounge to discover whether Mack Drayton had an alibi for the night Karma was killed. However, they hadn't talked about what their strategy would be.

Bettina was on her feet. "Oh, I'm not going to talk to *him*," she said, and began to work her way toward the stage. She had dressed for the occasion in a bright orange jumpsuit that stood out even in the dim light of the Skycrest Lounge, along with dangly earrings featuring large faceted stones.

The Mackinations seemed a varied lot. The other three people sitting at the band table were a *very* young man with a mop of blond curls, a sturdy man of indeterminate age with a shaved head, and a man who could have been Wilfred's double, complete with well-trimmed white hair.

Pamela watched as Bettina stooped toward the white-haired man. He looked up, and his sudden grin suggested she had offered a compliment. (*How?* Pamela wondered. *We just got here and we don't even know who plays what, aside from Mack.*)

But Bettina had her ways. The white-haired man stood and rearranged a few of the empty chairs jumbled near the table. Bettina was soon sitting at his side, alternately talking and listening, her earrings catching the light as they swayed.

Pamela was focused on the scene playing out near the stage, which had just been joined by additional characters. The smokers had returned and were crowding into the remaining empty chairs near the band table. Meanwhile, the band members were vacating their own chairs.

"I'm having fun," Wilfred commented, "even just sitting here taking in the scene." He was on his second beer. Pamela leaned close, straining to hear. The people at the neighboring table were becoming more and more raucous, the women clustered at one end even more so than the men.

"Amazing she left the room long enough for a smoke, with so many women in here tonight," a female voice crowed.

"Finders keepers . . . losers weepers," another female voice responded, singing the words like a lilting tune. "What goes around comes around, and goes around, and comes around . . ."

Up on the stage, the band members took their places. The young man with the mop of blond curls picked up the red guitar, and the sturdy man with the shaved head picked up the bass. Mack settled in behind the impressive drum kit, and the man who looked like Wilfred took a seat at the keyboard.

The people at the next table quieted down. The PA cut out then and, in the sudden silence, Pamela heard one of them say, "Isn't that what they call *karma*?" The prolonged drumroll that introduced the first song drowned out the burst of laughter.

The Mackinations played songs in a jazz-rock sort of style, all instrumentals. The set lasted about forty minutes. Midway through, Bettina rejoined them, and Pamela studied her face for a sign that she had something to report.

"I'll tell you later," she shouted over the amplified music.

Their ears were ringing as they traversed the carpet with the swirling designs and stepped out onto the concrete apron.

"Well?" Pamela inquired once they were outside.

"Nothing definitive." Bettina shook her head sadly. She smiled then. "Though I thought Danny was a pretty good keyboard player, and he hopes I'll come back again."

"Dear wife"—Wilfred wrapped an arm around Bettina's shoulders—"of course he does. You were the most beautiful woman in the Skycrest Lounge tonight."

"Anything *un*definitive?" Pamela asked. They were on the asphalt now, nearing Wilfred's car.

"The Mackinations only play Saturdays and Sundays," Bettina said. "But Danny said they all play with other bands too, and Mack might have had a gig a week ago yesterday. But then again, he might not have."

Chapter Eleven

It was Sunday morning. The house still smelled pleasantly of coffee and toast, the Christmas tree lights were on, and from the stereo came the robust strains of "We Three Kings." Ginger was enjoying the scratching post component of the cat climber, while Catrina lounged on the topmost platform, her tail dangling over the edge. Pamela sat on the sofa, paging through the cookbook that her mother had sent. She had just learned that the characteristic New Jersey dessert was cannoli with ricotta filling.

It was pleasant to enjoy Christmas things with the hubbub of shopping, wrapping, baking, and decorating in the past. She raised her eyes from the cookbook to the tree— so many memories evoked by the ornaments she had collected over the years. Some, the tag sale finds, had doubtless come to her with memories attached, though she would never know what they had meant to their previous owners.

Others were things she and Michael Paterson had brought home from trips—the sparkly pretzel from Milwaukee, the Mardi Gras mask from New Orleans, the carved wooden fish from a weekend at the Jersey Shore. And some were new, like the tiny sweater, mitten, and stocking that Penny had bought at the Knit and Nibble table, their cheerful colors standing out against the dark green of the tree. But contemplating the hand-knit ornaments shattered her tranquility. Poor Sorrel Wollcott, charged with murder, and Pamela and Bettina had really made no progress at all in discovering who was actually responsible for Karma's death.

She stared at the ornaments, harder. One of Sorrel's tiny sweaters was found at the crime scene, yes, but Sorrel had explained how that happened. Something else was found at the crime scene too, something . . .

Pamela tossed the cookbook aside and jumped up. Without even grabbing a jacket, she dashed across the street to ring Bettina's doorbell, pushing the button again and again in her excitement.

"What on earth?" Bettina exclaimed as the door swung back. The cheer that normally softened her features had fled. "What's wrong? Did something happen to Penny?" She grabbed Pamela's arm and pulled her over the threshold.

"We have to go back to the Skycrest tonight." Pamela felt herself panting, trying to breathe. She'd been holding her breath probably since the moment she stared at Sorrel's ornaments and recalled her own visit to the back of the Christmas tree lot.

She finally succeeded in emptying her lungs and filling them with a fresh breath that enabled her to explain to Bettina what she had figured out.

"Yes, yes!" Bettina's cheer returned. "And this is what we'll do"—words tumbled out—"Wilfred will drop us off, and he'll come back at midnight with Woofus, and you'll wear your red sweater with the bare shoulders . . ."

The plan was hatched then, to commence that evening at ten p.m.

"I'll be over," Pamela assured Bettina as she stepped out onto the porch and headed back to her own house.

* * *

The band hadn't taken their second break yet when Pamela and Bettina entered the Skycrest Lounge. That had been the plan—to get there before the smokers stepped outside. The stage was a bright spot at the end of the dim room, the spotlights reflecting off the drum kit, the guitar, and the bass. Mack flourished his drumsticks, nodding in time to the beat and shifting his gaze from the bass player to the audience and back again. The guitar player was bent over his sleek red guitar, his fingers moving furiously, while the bass player plucked steadily at his heavy strings. The keyboard player seemed to be having the most fun, beaming at his bandmates as a torrent of notes streamed from his instrument.

Bettina lingered near the bar as Pamela slipped out of her jacket and took a deep breath. Feeling self-conscious in the eye-catching red tunic-sweater, she headed directly toward the stage. When she reached the table reserved for the band, she paused and waved at Mack. Then she helped herself to the chair next to a woman she recognized as one of the people heading out to smoke the previous night, the woman in the long black poncho.

Up on the stage, the song was ending in a crescendo of sound, with the guitar rising above the rest in a dramatic flourish that went on and on, until Mack brought both drumsticks down at once with a reverberating crash. The audience applauded, the bass player and guitar player slipped their instruments into stands, Mack and the keyboard player stood up, and they all left the stage.

As Mack approached the band table, Pamela took another deep breath. She rose from her chair, held out her arms, and gestured at the empty chair next to her. "Act like you're an old friend," Bettina had said with a wink, "a very *dear* old friend." Bettina was the actress, but as she herself had pointed out, the casting here required some-one younger.

Mack seemed puzzled, but at that moment the server appeared with two glasses of beer (courtesy of Bettina). He shrugged and the puzzlement that had twisted his lips was replaced by the swaggering smile.

Pamela raised her glass. "To old friends," she said.

Mack joined the toast. "Old friends," he echoed.

She leaned close to him and whispered, "You probably don't remember that night last year . . ." Encouraged by his expectant gaze, she went on. "You must meet a lot of women . . . in your line of work. Sitting up there behind that big drum kit."

It was easy to flirt, actually, if the person you were flirt-ing with didn't make your heart pound. Mack seemed happy to talk, and the only requirement on Pamela's part seemed to be plenty of smiles, and laughter in the right places.

The other band members had taken their seats at the band table as well, and the smokers, except for the woman in the poncho, had pulled out packs of cigarettes and headed for the exit.

After about twenty minutes Mack looked at his watch. The PA cut out midway through "The Wind Cries Mary" and he climbed to his feet. "Back to work," he said, lean-ing down to give Pamela's hand a squeeze, and adding, "You won't go away now, will you?"

Pamela wished she could join Bettina, or vice versa, but that would spoil the plan. So she remained where she was, enjoying the music with its rock-and-roll feel and jazzy embellishments, as song followed song. After several songs she stifled a yawn and stole a look at her watch. It was nearing midnight, much later than she usually stayed up. Luckily, Penny had gone to Lorie Hopkins' house for another night of binge-watching. The last one had kept her out till well after midnight.

Things were winding down with the band. Mack had emerged from behind his drum kit and stepped up to a microphone at the side of the stage. "We're the Mackinations," he announced with a satisfied grin, "and we're here every weekend. I'll introduce the band, then we'll do one more tune."

Pamela waited until Mack rejoined her, then she leaned close to his ear and whispered, "I've got a friend waiting, otherwise . . ." and she squeezed his hand. She hoped that anyone watching—especially the woman in the poncho—would imagine that she was setting up a future assignation.

She walked slowly toward the double doors, past Bettina. As she crossed the room with the armchairs and plastic plants, she pulled on her jacket. Once outside the building, she lingered in the parking lot until she was sure Bettina was following her. She turned to make sure, and yes, Bettina was there and someone else was following as well, the woman in the poncho.

She continued on her way, around the side of the motel toward the darker part of the parking lot. She passed Wilfred's Mercedes, with two figures vigilant in the front seat. Behind her, Bettina veered toward the Mercedes, but Pamela kept walking.

As she neared the far corner of the lot, where a few cars were nosed up against a chain-link fence, she looked over her shoulder. The figure in the poncho, barely visible in the increasing darkness, was coming closer.

Pamela paused as if she'd been heading for one of the cars. She slipped her purse off her shoulder and tipped her head as if she was about to draw out her keys. Then she stood with her back to the pursuer, her heart reminding her of its location in her chest with an insistent thud, and sweat prickling her brow.

"Who are you?" growled a voice, low but female.

Pamela felt a hand on her shoulder. She turned and stared at a face that was indistinct in the darkness.

"This isn't the Christmas tree lot," Pamela said, "so there's no murder weapon at hand. And you didn't have to kill Karma, you know. She wasn't interested in him anymore."

"But you"—the growl modulated into shrillness—"you are, and you can't have him!"

She shoved and Pamela felt herself tipping backward. She landed on her back and her head hit the ground with a thump that echoed in her brain like Mack's final drum crash.

Another voice, a welcome voice, intruded then. "Get her, boy!" Wilfred's voice urged. "Rescue Pamela!" The response was a whining bark, then a whimper.

Pamela pushed herself to a sitting position. Wilfred and Bettina stood several yards away, and Woofus was in retreat, galloping across the asphalt toward busy Route 46.

Then her antagonist was upon her, thrusting her backward until she was again flat on the ground, and straddling her prone body, fumbling toward her throat.

Pamela squirmed and managed to roll over, but she still felt the questing hands, now wound tightly in her hair, tugging until her head bent back at a painful angle.

A siren cut through the chilly air then, a sound more welcome, Pamela thought, than any she had ever heard. The police arrived to hear a desperate voice shouting, "I killed Karma, and I'll kill you too. Mack is mine, and he's going to stay mine!"

Chapter Twelve

What a pleasure it was to be tackling a new project—especially a project that involved deciphering a knitting pattern rather than a complicated set of clues!

Pamela drew a skein of robin-egg-blue wool from her knitting bag. She had bought the yarn the previous day, at Penny's direction, on their visit to the fancy yarn shop in Timberley. They had eaten breakfast, read the *Register*'s account of Bernice Treacle's arrest in the parking lot of the Skycrest Motel and Lounge the night before, and then set off.

At Pamela's side Bettina paged through a knitting magazine. "I just don't know," she murmured. "I do need a new project, but a sweater is such a commitment . . ."

"I'm at loose ends too," Holly said.

"And so am I." Karen looked fondly at her daughter Lily, who was modeling her hand-knit red Christmas dress before being taken up to bed by her father. The backdrop was a tree decorated with twinkling lights and homemade paper chains.

Knit and Nibble was at Karen's house that night. Karen and Dave had been gradually upgrading their décor over the past few years. The streamlined sofa in a pretty shade of blue had been an early purchase and had remained. But the coffee table salvaged from a neighbor's garage had been replaced, and two armchairs upholstered in a stripe that coordinated with the sofa had been added. A rocking chair that Dave had refinished completed the living room's seating arrangements.

Nell looked quite at home in the rocking chair. Her hands were already busy at her knitting, and her white hair glowed like a halo in the light from the brass floor lamp at the chair's side. "Idle hands . . . the devil finds work for them," she commented. A wink suggested the words weren't to be taken literally.

"Roland's hands certainly aren't idle." Holly turned to Roland, who was sitting next to her on the sofa and casting on from a skein of maroon yarn.

"I don't like to waste time," he said without looking up, "and I'm trying to count."

"Sorry!" Holly's apology included one of her dimpled smiles. The entire room fell silent, as if any comment, not just one addressed to Roland, would break his concentration.

". . . seventy-eight, seventy-nine, eighty," he whispered, glanced at the pattern book that lay open across his knees, and then looked up.

"What is it?" Bettina inquired.

"A sweater for me." Roland seemed willing to talk now. "Melanie suggested I make something for myself, since I've already made so many things for her."

During Roland's membership in Knit and Nibble, Melanie had valiantly integrated several of his creations into her very chic wardrobe, and perhaps, Pamela suspected, she needed a little break.

"And what's yours?" Holly looked across the room at Pamela, who was sitting in one of the new armchairs.

Pamela held up a knitting magazine open to the pattern Penny had chosen. The photo showed a smiling young woman in an eye-catching sweater patterned with stripes of various widths in blue, pale green, brown, and three shades of pink. "It's for Penny," she said.

"Oh!" Holly clapped her hands. "That will be fun to do! You are so clever, Pamela. And not only do you knit—"

Pamela knew what was coming next, and apparently so did Nell, because the rocking chair creaked as Nell leaned forward and one of her growl-whimper sounds emerged from her throat.

"Yes," Nell said, "what Pamela did was heroic and we should all be glad that Sorrel Wollcott has been cleared of a crime she should never have been charged with in the first place, but it was also very dangerous—"

"Oh, *please*, Nell"—Holly leaned forward too—"it's not every day we can hear firsthand how someone pieced together the clues to solve a murder."

"Might be instructive," Roland grunted. "I vote in favor of letting Pamela talk."

It *had* been dangerous, and her back was still stiff, and she had a lump on the back of her head. She wasn't all that eager to talk, really. But figuring out that Bernice Treacle was the real murderer had been a satisfying accomplishment . . .

So she explained how she knew the twist of yarn the police found at the crime scene couldn't have anything to do with Sorrel and her knitted ornaments, because that yarn was black. The visit to the Skycrest Lounge had brought Bernice Treacle into the picture, wearing her long black mohair poncho. And an overheard conversation had identified her as Mack's possessive girlfriend. Then a catty acquaintance had quipped, "Isn't that what they call *karma?*"—apparently alluding to a rival for Mack's affections.

"It seemed that Bernice didn't believe they had really broken up in October," Pamela said. (*And why should she?* Pamela reflected. *My flirtation with Mack established that faithfulness to one woman isn't in his nature.*)

"So she decided to get rid of the competition, once and for all," Holly concluded. "And the killer *did* stalk Karma! You were right, Roland, and I was wrong."

Roland allowed himself a small smile.

"I know we've all barely done anything so far"—Karen rose from the sofa—"and it's not eight o'clock yet, but . . ."

"She's been baking," Holly said, "from her new cookbook . . ."

". . . that Holly gave me," Karen said, completing the thought. Karen's dessert repertoire had, up until then, been limited to chocolate chip cookies.

"So why don't we . . . ?" Holly led the way into Karen's dining room. Her table—also a recent upgrade—had been spread with a tablecloth featuring sprigs of mistletoe and set with simple white china. She gestured around the table and they took their places.

They lingered at the table for a long while, after doing justice to the Sticky Toffee Pudding Cake and draining the last drops of coffee or tea from their cups.

"Now," Nell said as contentment set in and conversation lapsed, "not only does the devil find work for idle hands, but an idle mind is the devil's workshop—and tempted to solving crimes better left to the police." She aimed meaningful glances at Pamela and Bettina. "So lest anyone here have idle hands, or an idle mind, I've promised fifty knitted bunnies to the Haversack community daycare center by Easter."

They stepped outside and found the ground covered with snow, and flakes swirling in the cone of light cast by the streetlamp. Pamela put up the hood of her new down coat and agreed with Bettina that it was a perfect addition to her winter wardrobe.

KNIT

Cozy Doll Sweater

Bettina's son and daughter-in-law don't want to impose "girly" expectations on their young daughter, so they request that gifts not be the traditional things often given to young girls. Bettina had looked forward to taking her granddaughter shopping for cute outfits and showering her with dolls and doll clothes, but that is not to be. If such gifts were welcome, however, she would be busily at work knitting this cozy doll sweater.

It's not as tiny as the knitted sweaters, mittens, and stockings that feature as tree ornaments in *Death of a Christmas Card Crafter*, but it's small enough to be a quick, fun project, and it's assembled from basic rectangles, so it requires no fancy knitting. Since it uses only about 60 yards of medium-weight yarn, a typical skein of yarn will make plenty of doll sweaters—or you can use odds and ends left from other projects.

Directions are scaled to fit a doll about 15 inches tall and 10 inches around the torso. There are about 4 stitches to the inch if you use medium-weight yarn and size 6 needles, so if your doll is a different size, you can measure your doll and modify the pattern to fit.

If you've never knitted anything at all, it's easier to learn the basics by watching than by reading. The Internet abounds with tutorials that show the process clearly, including casting on and off. Just search on *How to Knit*. You only need to learn the basic knitting stitch. Don't worry about *purl*. That's used in alternating rows to create the *stockinette stitch*—the stitch you see, for example, in a typical sweater. If you use *knit* on every row, you will end up with the stitch called the *garter stitch*. That's a fine stitch for this sweater.

The sweater is created from five rectangles. For the back, cast on 20 stitches, using the simple slip-knot cast-on process or the more complicated *long tail* process. Knit 26 rows and cast off. For the right and left fronts, cast on 10 stitches, knit 26 rows, and cast off. For the sleeves, cast on 14 stitches, knit 26 rows, and cast off.

Casting off is often included in the Internet *How to Knit* tutorials, or you can search specifically for *Casting off*. In each case leave a yarn tail of at least 2 inches when you clip your yarn after casting off. To hide your tails, use a yarn needle—a large needle with a large eye and a blunt end. Thread the needle with each tail, work the needle in and out of the knitted fabric for ½ inch or so, pull the tail through, and cut off the bit of yarn that's left. Thread your yarn needle with the tails left from when you cast on and hide them too.

To assemble the sweater, first thread your yarn needle with more yarn and sew up the long sides of the sleeves to make tubes. Hide the tails. Then lay the back flat and position each front on top of it. The sweater will be wider than it is long, so the rectangle will be horizontal rather than vertical, and the two fronts will fit side by side. It can be helpful to pin each front in place before you begin to sew. Thread your yarn needle again and sew about halfway up each side seam. You need to leave a space on each side long enough to fit a sleeve in.

Now add the sleeves. Continue sewing, but instead of sewing the front and back together, sew the side of one sleeve to the back. When you get to the top, keep going, but now sew along the shoulder, again sewing the front and back together for about 1 inch. Make a knot by passing the needle through a loop of yarn, pull tight, and hide the tail. Then sew the other side of the sleeve to the front, rethreading the yarn needle if necessary. Hide the tails.

For a picture of the finished Cozy Doll Sweater being modeled by a cloth-body doll from an estate sale, as well as some in-progress photos, visit the Knit & Nibble Mysteries page at PeggyEhrhart.com. Click on the cover for *Christmas Card Murder* and scroll down on the page that opens.

NIBBLE

Chocolate Mousse Cake

This delicious cake is a three-layer creation—if you count the dusting of cocoa powder that gives it its distinctive taste. The other two layers are a dense not-too-sweet flourless chocolate cake and a rich chocolate truffle-like mousse. It's not technically a mousse, since it's composed only of chocolate and heavy cream, but the effect is very mousselike.

The cake layer of this cake comes together quite quickly, but the mousse layer requires an hour of chilling, so start the mousse layer first. The cake can also be made a day ahead and stored in the refrigerator.

Ingredients:

For the mousse layer:
1½ cups heavy cream
6 oz. semisweet chocolate chips (⅔ cup)

For the cake layer:
½ cup butter (4 oz.), cut into ½-inch slices
⅓ cup unsweetened cocoa powder
1½ tbsp. cornstarch
¼ tsp. baking powder
¼ tsp. salt
5 oz. semisweet chocolate chips (a bit less than ⅔ cup)
½ cup sugar
3 eggs

For the topping:
3 tbsp. unsweetened cocoa powder

Start the mousse layer:
Heat the cream in a saucepan until tiny bubbles form around the edges. Turn the heat off and whisk in the chocolate chips until they totally melt into the cream. Pour the mixture into a medium-sized heatproof bowl and refrigerate it for one hour, whisking it briefly halfway through.

While the mixture is chilling, make the cake layer:
Butter a 9-inch cake pan, line it with parchment paper, and butter the parchment paper.

Sift the cocoa powder, cornstarch, baking powder, and salt into a small bowl.

Melt the butter and chocolate chips by placing them in an aluminum or other heatproof bowl and setting it over a pot of simmering water. The bowl should be large enough to eventually contain all the cake ingredients. Melt and stir the butter and chocolate chips until the mixture is smooth. Take the bowl off the pan of water and mix in the sugar. A wire whisk works best for this. Mix in the eggs, one at a time, using the wire whisk and beating energetically. Stir or whisk in the dry ingredients. Use a rubber spatula to scoop the batter into the prepared cake pan. Tap the pan on the counter a few times to get rid of obvious bubbles.

Bake the cake at 325 degrees for about 20 minutes. Test for doneness by sticking a wooden toothpick in the center. If the toothpick comes out clean, the cake is done.

Let the cake cool briefly, then remove it from the cake pan. To do this, cover a dinner plate with plastic wrap, place the dinner plate over the pan, hold the pan and plate together with both hands—one on each side—and turn the whole thing over. Lift the pan off. Carefully peel off the parchment paper. The top of the cake tends to stick to whatever it comes into contact with—thus the plastic wrap, and your cake will be easier to serve if it is bottom-side-down on its serving plate. So now take the plate you plan to serve it on, place it over the cake, and turn the whole thing over again. Carefully peel the plastic wrap off the cake's top.

Let your cake rest and cool while you continue with your mousse layer. Remove the chilled cream and chocolate mixture from the refrigerator and beat it with an electric mixer on high until it becomes very stiff. It will whip just like whipping cream.

Make sure your cake is cool, then scoop the mousse onto the top using your rubber spatula and spread it evenly to the edges using the rubber spatula or a table knife. Put the 2 tbsp. of cocoa powder in a small mesh strainer and shake it over the cake.

Your cake is now ready to serve, or it can be refrigerated until serving time. It will slice more neatly if you use a long, slender knife and wipe the blade clean between slices. Store leftovers in the refrigerator.

For a picture of the completed Chocolate Mousse Cake, visit the Knit & Nibble Mysteries page at PeggyEhrhart.com. Click on the cover for *Christmas Card Murder* and scroll down on the page that opens.

BONUS NIBBLE

Nell's "Not Too Sweet" Quick Bread

Quick bread is so named because it doesn't require yeast; thus, there's no waiting for the dough to rise. Quick breads have a cakelike texture, and in fact many contain sugar and are more like desserts than bread. They are perfect to serve sliced with coffee or tea as a midmorning or afternoon snack.

This recipe hints at the holiday season because it's dense with dried fruit and nuts, suggesting fruitcake or stollen, but it's not nearly as rich or sweet. It can be made at the last minute with cupboard staples, like evaporated milk instead of fresh—and you can use the evaporated milk right out of the can without diluting it.

Add any combination of dried fruits you like, including raisins, currants, cranberries, apricots, dates, figs, pineapple, or cherries. If you only have one kind of dried fruit handy, say raisins, you can just use raisins.

Ingredients:
2 cups flour—no need to sift
½ cup sugar
1½ tsp. baking powder
1½ tsp. baking soda
½ tsp. salt
¾ cup milk
1 egg beaten lightly with a fork
2 tbsp. butter, melted
1 cup dried fruit, chopped if the pieces are large
1 cup walnuts or pecans, chopped

If your fruit is *very* dry, put it in a small bowl an hour or so before you plan to make your quick bread and add 3 tbsp. of boiling water. Stir the moistened fruit from time to time in order to make sure it all comes in contact with the liquid and plumps up.

You don't need a beater for this recipe, just a large spoon.

Mix the dry ingredients in a large bowl. Add the milk, and then the beaten egg and the melted butter. Stir until the batter is smooth with no dry bits. Then stir in the fruit and the nuts.

Scoop the batter into a greased 5-inch x 9-inch loaf pan and bake at 350 degrees for 45 minutes to an hour. To test for doneness, stick a wooden toothpick into the middle of the top. If the toothpick comes out clean, your quick bread is finished.

This is good sliced and served warm with butter, even for breakfast. You can warm slices in the microwave for subsequent servings.

For pictures of Nell's "Not Too Sweet" Quick Bread, visit the Knit & Nibble Mysteries page at PeggyEhrhart.com. Click on the cover for *Christmas Card Murder* and scroll down on the page that opens.

Note: The recipe for Pamela's poppy-seed cake appears at the end of *Silent Knit, Deadly Knit* and photos are on the website page for that book.